Wings of the Falcon
Barbara Michaels

"This author never fails to entertain."
— *Cleveland Plain Dealer*

"With Barbara Michaels, you always get a great story."

— *Ocala Star-Banner*

"Barbara Michaels' thrillers are always a highly satisfying blend of unearthly terrors and supernatural suppositions."

— *Publishers Weekly*

"A master!"

— *Library Journal*

"Michaels has a fine downright way with the supernatural. Good firm style and many picturesque twists."
— *San Francisco Chronicle*

"Miss Michaels is a specialist. When the seances get going and the ghosts walk (and talk), even nonbelievers take notice."

— *New York Times*

"We are not normally disposed to read Gothic novels . . . but when Michaels turns her talents to the genre, we admit to being hooked!"

— *Denver Post*

BARBARA MICHAELS
WINGS OF THE FALCON

BERKLEY BOOKS, NEW YORK

This Berkley book contains the complete
text of the original hardcover edition.
It has been completely reset in a typeface
designed for easy reading and was printed
from new film.

WINGS OF THE FALCON

A Berkley Book / published by arrangement with
Dodd, Mead & Company

PRINTING HISTORY
Dodd, Mead edition / published 1977
Berkley edition / September 1988

ISBN: 0-425-11045-1

A BERKLEY BOOK ® TM 757,375
Berkley Books are published by The Berkley Publishing Group,
200 Madison Avenue, New York, New York 10016.
The name "BERKLEY" and the "B" logo
are trademarks belonging to Berkley Publishing Corporation.

PRINTED IN THE UNITED STATES OF AMERICA

10 9 8 7 6 5 4 3 2 1

To Joan and Fred
Caroline, Mary Ann, and Nancy
and the four-footed Hartsocks
whose number is, at this time,
indeterminate.

AUTHOR'S NOTE

Though all of the characters in this book are completely fictitious, some of the more improbable events are based on actual fact. The history of the Risorgimento in Italy is filled with incidents as dramatic as any writer could invent. The Falcon, of course, is an invention; but Emilio and Attilio Bandiera are not. The town of Parezzo is imaginary, but Perugia's insurrection and the retaliation of the papal troops are factual. Captain De Merode is a fictitious character, but Schmidt of Perugia and other mercenary commanders supplied the data on which I based my fanatical soldier. There is not and never was a family like the Tarcontis. However, their Etruscan cemetery resembles real ones and the tomb of the princess is based on the historical Regolini-Galassi tomb. Several early excavators claim to have seen perfectly preserved bodies crumble as the air entered the tomb. Even the white rabbits come from a factual account by Mrs. Hamilton Gray.

The historical background of Italy in 1860 is as accurate as I could make it. I hope I have succeeded in conveying the courage and dedication of the men who fought to unite Italy and free her of her medieval institutions.

CHAPTER 1

Authors who write in the first person cannot expect their readers to be seriously concerned about the survival of the main character. A heroine who can describe her trials and tribulations in carefully chosen phrases obviously lived through those trials without serious damage. Yet I remember being absolutely breathless with suspense when the madwoman entered Miss Jane Eyre's chamber and rent her wedding veil asunder; and I bit my nails to the quick as I followed the perils of Mrs. Radcliffe's haunted heroines.

Not being Miss Brontë or Mrs. Radcliffe, I have no hope of engaging my reader's attention to *that* extent. Yet some of the experiences that befell me, at a certain period of my life, were as distressing and almost as improbable as any of my favorite heroines' adventures. Perhaps my youth and inexperience made my problems seem worse than they were. But even now, when I am a good many years older (I prefer not to state how many)—even now a reminiscent shiver passes through me as I remember Lord Shelton, and that dreadful moment when he held me helpless in his grasp, with his breath hot on my averted face and his hands tearing at my gown.

I anticipate. It is necessary to explain how I found myself in such a predicament; and that explanation must incorporate some of my family history.

My father was an artist—not a very good one, I fear. It is a pity, in a way, that his father was able to leave him a small sum of money, for without it Father would have had to seek gainful employment instead of pursuing the elusive genius of art. His small inheritance was enough to keep him in relative comfort for several years, while he traveled on the continent, ending, finally, in that artists' mecca, Rome. To a young man of romantic tastes and ardent spirits, the old capital of the Caesars had many attractions beyond its artistic treasures—the colorful models who waited for employment on the Spanish Steps, the companionship of other struggling young artists, the wine and laughter and song in the soft Italian nights.

Father was a remarkably good-looking man, even when he was dying. Consumption is not a disfiguring disease. Indeed, that is one of its diabolical qualities, that it should give its victims a ghastly illusion of health and beauty just before the end. Father's slenderness and delicacy of features were intensified by the ravages of the disease. The pallor of his complexion was refined by soft dark hair and lustrous black eyes framed by lashes so long and thick that any woman would have envied them.

Knowing him as he was in his decline, I can imagine how handsome he was at twenty, when he met my mother, and I can understand how he won her heart so quickly. Her family did not find it so easy to understand; for she was the daughter of a noble Italian house. In the ordinary course of events my father would never have met her. A romantic accident threw them together. The carriage in which she was traveling to Rome was delayed by bad weather, and in the darkness was set upon by bandits. Her attendants fled or were overcome; and Father happened upon the scene at the most critical moment, just as the miscreants were dragging the lady from the carriage. As his horse came thundering down upon them, the bandits thought him the leader of a troop of defenders, so that there was time for him to lift my mother's fainting form into the saddle and escape before they discovered their error.

By the fitful moonlight he had seen enough to make out the shrinking form of a woman, beset by the men who threatened her person or her property, or both; but it was not until they reached the inn, fortunately not many miles distant, that he saw the face of the girl he had saved.

I resemble her only in my coloring—which some might find surprising, for I am fair-haired and blue-eyed. In fact, not all Italians are dark. Those of the northern regions are often fair, and there was some such strain in my mother's family. My features are more like those of my father, and although he could not be overly modest about his looks without denigrating mine, he would never allow that any woman could equal my mother's beauty.

Of course the circumstances of their first meeting were romantic enough to dazzle any young man. My mother was in a dead faint when he carried her into the inn and placed her on a settle by the hearth. The firelight turned her tumbled ringlets to red-gold; and this gleaming halo framed a countenance of pure perfection. As he knelt beside her, supporting her head upon his arm, her lashes fluttered and lifted. The first thing she saw was his face—young, handsome, glowing with emotion; the first sensation she was conscious of feeling was the strength of his arm, tenderly yet respectfully embracing her.

It is no wonder they fell in love at first sight. What is wonderful is that their love should have won out over all obstacles. That first night they were both too young and too bewitched by one another to think sensibly, or they would have realized that their only hope lay in an immediate elopement. But the practical difficulties were great. For one thing, it was virtually impossible for them to be married in a country where Protestants were not even allowed to hold church services. So the authorities were notified of the attack upon the carriage, and Prince Tarconti was informed that his daughter was safe; but not before the lovers had had time to converse for hours in a language more eloquent than Father's fluent if ungrammatical Italian.

How well I knew each detail of that romantic history! It was my favorite bedtime story in childhood, and if my mother was the saint to whom I addressed my childish prayers, a certain Count Ugo Fosilini was the villain of my youthful nightmares. A remote family connection, he was the suitor destined for Francesca Tarconti by her aristocratic father; she had been on her way to visit his parents in Rome when Fate intervened. It was natural that he should be the emissary sent by Prince Tarconti to recover his daughter. As soon as Count Ugo set eyes on my father he knew he had a rival; and he took care to insult him by offering him money as a reward for the rescue.

Of course Father dashed the gold indignantly to the ground. The gesture was gallant but ill-advised, for it confirmed what the

Count had until then only suspected. My mother was at once removed to the Fosilini palazzo in Rome, where she was kept a virtual prisoner. This was not enough for the Count. He was too arrogant to challenge a man whom he considered his social inferior, so he hired assassins, of whom there were plenty to be found in Rome. My father was saved only through the devotion of his friends, struggling young writers and artists like himself. Some of them were members of a revolutionary secret society, so they were more than willing to frustrate the plans of Count Ugo, whose reputation as a cruel landlord was well known. The members of one such group aided my father when he followed Mother to the family estate in the hills of Umbria, and they were instrumental in assisting in the couple's eventual escape from Italy. That was the most exciting chapter in the story—Mother's flight from the sleeping castle, accompanied by a devoted maidservant, through whom she had maintained communication with Father; their desperate ride through the night, with Mother in men's clothing, astride her plunging steed; the fishing boat in Genoa, and the rough patriots who sailed it, carrying, quite often, other cargo than fish; and the triumphant landing in Marseilles.

They were married in London. My mother's rejection of all she had left was total; she even gave up her religion. At first the young couple lived obscurely, fearing retaliation; but as the months passed they realized that Mother's family had reacted with the cold arrogance typical of their class. Finally they learned, through friends in Italy, that Prince Tarconti had disinherited his daughter and forbidden her name to be pronounced in his hearing. To her family she was as good as dead.

Alas, in only too short a time she was. She died at my birth; and when Father wrote to Italy, to announce the two events, he received no reply. Since he had acted only out of a sense of common decency, he was not sorry that the correspondence ended there.

The succeeding years—seventeen of them—may be passed over quickly. They were not good years for him; but I did not know that until it was too late. With the selfishness of youth I wore the pretty dresses, played with the expensive toys, and accepted the presence of maids and nurses without wondering where the money came from, or why Father was so often absent from home. He continued to paint and, I assumed, to sell his paintings. It was not until one winter night, when he collapsed in a fit of uncontrollable coughing as he bent to kiss me good night, that I realized he was ill.

I was too young to understand the ominous portent of the attack. He was quick to reassure me; and the action of a lady of his acquaintance, in sending him to the south of France, undoubtedly did prolong his life. I remained in England, in boarding school. I did not realize that my school fees were part of Mrs. Barton's payment for my father's services; nor that the term "patroness" was a euphemism for her real role in his life.

She was not the first of his "patrons"—nor the last. I understand that now. I do not judge him. I still believe he did it primarily for me, to give me the comfort and security he could supply in no other way.

After the incident I have mentioned, his health seemed to improve, as it sometimes does with this illness. I saw very little of him, and I was selfish enough to resent his neglect, as I saw it. I cannot completely blame myself for failing to understand why he had to keep me from him. He even managed to delude the innocent ladies who ran the boarding school. It was in Yorkshire, far from the vicious gossip of London, but the dear old Misses Smith would not have believed the gossip if they had heard it. They adored my father, and always hovered over him when he came on his rare visits, accepting him as the gentleman of means he pretended to be.

Yet *I* loved him; and *I* ought to have sensed the increasing desperation under his smiling manner.

He had good reason to be desperate that winter before my eighteenth birthday. The precarious pattern of existence he had built was tottering on its foundation—and I, like a dweller in a house riddled with insects, would have lived on in fancied security until the floor collapsed under my feet. Certainly I would never have guessed from his manner, when he came to fetch me for the Christmas holidays, that anything was amiss. He had never looked more handsome, and the dear old ladies fluttered about him, offering him wine and seed cake. He was wearing a magnificent new watch chain of heavy gold, all hung with beautiful little trinkets—carved cameos and lockets and the like—which I longed to examine.

I sat demurely, though, my hands folded in my lap, as the
Misses Smith had taught me, while my future was discussed.
With beaming pride the ladies told him that my education was
complete. I was the star student, the parlor boarder, accomplished in all forms of needlework, from *broderie anglaise* to
cross-stitch. My sampler, a magnificent picture of a lady and
gentleman in a grove of trees—with apples as large as the lady's
powdered head—was proudly displayed. My skill on pianoforte
and harp was praised, my knowledge of French commended. As
I was soon to learn, my father was an accomplished actor, but he
found it difficult to dissemble that day. The elder Miss Smith
broke off in the midst of her speech to comment with concern on
the gray shade of his cheeks, and to press more Madeira on him.

I think it was only in recent weeks that he had begun to face
the truth about his condition. Now he was being forced to face
another unpalatable truth he had tried to ignore. My schooldays
were almost over. I must leave school for . . . where? That was
the problem now, and it must have seemed to him that
everything was collapsing at once.

He had played a role for many years. He carried off the rest of
the visit in style, and we took our places in the handsome
traveling coach, well wrapped in furs and robes against the chill
of winter. Snow was beginning to fall as we drove away from the
school, but I was too happy to care about the weather. I had not
seen my father for almost a year.

I did most of the talking, babbling on about Mary
Wentworth's shocking flirtation with the curate, and Alice
Johnson's cheating at map drawing, while Father listened with a
smile. As the afternoon drew on, my tongue slowed; finally I fell
asleep.

I woke with a start. The shadows of early evening filled the
interior of the coach. Father was bending over me. In the
dimness his face shone with a pearly pallor, and something in
his expression filled me with alarm.

"What is it?" I cried, struggling against drowsiness.

Instantly he withdrew into the corner of the seat.

"Nothing, my love. I apologize for waking you. I was
studying your face. You are so like . . ."

He turned his face away. I was moved, for I thought I
understood his distress.

"Am I really like Mama? I thought—"

"You resemble her more and more as you grow. Do you know, Francesca, that you are the same age she was when I first saw her?"

"If it distresses you to speak of her," I began, touching his hand.

Roughly he drew it away.

"No! I must speak of her and of other things I have been afraid to face. I was not always such a coward, my darling; but when she died, something died in me too, my manhood, perhaps. . . ."

Then he realized that his mood was alarming me. He took my hand in his and smiled.

"Don't be upset. I feel the chagrin of a father who sees his daughter growing away from him, who foresees the time when another man will win her smiles. You are a young woman now, my love. Is there no man who has touched your heart?"

This was the sort of talk I found pleasurable, if mildly embarrassing—the sort of talk we girls indulged in late at night, after the lights were out. I believe I blushed.

"Mary Ellen's brother is very handsome," I began. "When he came to visit her last year we talked for a while; I found him so pleasant! Mary Ellen said he liked me very much."

"Did she indeed." Father's voice sounded tired. I could not see his features clearly. He went on, as if to himself, "But what opportunity would you have, in that little island of innocence, to meet young men? And which of them would offer, if he knew. . . . What am I to do? What in heaven's name am I to do with you?"

"But, Father," I exclaimed. "I don't want to marry. Why can't I stay with you?"

My father let out a groan and buried his face in his hands. Now genuinely frightened, I tugged at his fingers.

"What is it? Father, are you ill? Are you in pain?"

A long shudder passed through his body. Then he lowered his hands and smiled at me. His voice was calm when he said,

"No. . . . It is only a little pain, my darling. Of course you must stay with me. We will not be parted again, until. . . . Francesca, have I ever spoken to you of your mother's family?"

"Often. What cruel people they must have been."

"I should not have given you that impression," he said slowly. "I was wrong. I, of all people, should have understood their grief at losing her."

"But wicked Count Ugo," I began.

My father muttered something I did not quite catch. I thought I heard the word "fool," but did not know whether it applied to the Count, or to me—or to himself.

"Even he must be excused," he said aloud. "I too would have fought to keep her. And he is an old man now, if he is still alive. I suppose he married and had children of his own. Let us not speak of him. Your grandfather—"

"He was cruel," I said firmly. Yet the word struck me strangely. The stern old man had been one of the villains of the story; yet he was closely related to me, part of my blood; my mother's father, the same to her as my adored parent was to me.

Father shook his head vigorously.

"He did what any father would have done. I can understand him now that I too have a beloved daughter. He was not unkind to her, Francesca. She loved him."

"She loved you more," I said.

"Yes."

He relapsed into silence after that. I thought he was remembering the past. I know now that he was struggling with a cruel decision. That night, after our supper in the inn where we broke our journey, he called for paper and ink and sat writing late. I remember the way the candlelight touched his long, delicate fingers, and the shadows it cast across his face. The hollows of his eye-sockets and sunken cheeks became shapes of darkness, like the stark modeling of a tragic mask.

II

The holidays were sheer delight. We had lodgings in a fine old house in Leicester, maintained by a genteel elderly widow. Like most women, she fell genteelly in love with Father, and we made merry together, decking the house with Christmas boughs and holly. We even had a Christmas tree. Prince Albert had introduced this German custom when he married the queen, and the pretty fir trees, decked with candles and ornaments, were now popular. I had made Father a pair of slippers embroidered with purple pansies and sprays of an eccentric-looking vegetable which was supposed to be rosemary—"for remembrance," as I explained to him. The gifts I received were magnificent, surpassing even his usual extravagance—a new pelisse, trimmed with ermine and silver buttons, a tiny muff of gray squirrel, a coral necklace, books, music for the pianoforte . . . too many to be recalled. I went reluctantly back to school, cheered only by Father's promise that he would come for me soon.

I expected to finish out the term, but to my surprise and delight the moment of our next meeting came sooner than I dared hope. It was early in April, when the buds were beginning to swell with green promise, that Father next appeared. He came without advance warning, and when I saw him I did not need Miss Bertha Smith's hastily checked exclamation to be alerted to the change in his appearance.

He was handsomer than ever, if that was possible, with a fine rosy flush on his cheeks; but he was terribly thin. Father admitted cheerfully that he had been ill, and was still plagued by a slight cough. But fine weather would soon set him up.

I accepted this facile good cheer, because I wanted to believe it. There was nothing I, or anyone else, could have done for him; yet I am still haunted by remorse when I think. . . .

My boxes and parcels, hastily packed, were loaded onto the carriage. The Misses Smith embraced me, weeping. I wept too, and sobbed bitterly as I bade farewell to my friends. When the carriage drove off and I leaned out the window, waving at the other girls, I was sure they were a little jealous of me for having such a young, handsome father. Little did I know that I would never see any of them again, despite our promises of continued correspondence and future meetings; or that they, the daughters of small merchants and prosperous tradesmen, had far more hopeful futures than I.

III

Father had taken a house in Richmond, outside London. It was a tiny box of a place, but it had lovely gardens. We led a very retired life; I played for him on the pianoforte he had hired, and worked at my drawing. I had a small talent for this skill and, with his help, made considerable progress. I suppose that eventually I might have become bored with our lack of social life, for we saw no one except tradesmen and servants, but during those short weeks Father's company was all I desired. He seemed quite gay; but sometimes I would hear him coughing at night.

One afternoon I came back to the house after finishing a sketch of the garden with its beds of daffodils. I was anxious to show it to Father; I felt it was the best thing I had ever done. I was wearing a white muslin gown, with rose-colored ribbons, and ribbons of the same shade trimmed my broad-brimmed hat. The day was unseasonably warm, so I took the hat off as soon as I entered the house. I thought Father was resting, as he usually did in the afternoon.

I came in through the side door, so I did not see the carriage. I had no warning of guests until I approached the parlor door and heard voices. Such was my haste, and my stupid innocence, that it never occurred to me to wait, or even to knock. I merely thought, Good, Father is awake—and opened the door.

I heard one sentence before they were aware of my presence.

"But, my dear, surely you did not think you could elude me forever, after such—"

A cry from my father made the speaker break off. He turned on his heel, in a quick, violent movement.

He did not look like a man who could move so fast. He was tall and heavily built; not fat, but with a flabbiness of face and body that suggested self-indulgence. I was immediately struck by his attire, with its small, peculiar touches of almost feminine elegance—gloves of pearl-gray satin, a stickpin that was a single huge opal, and a cloak lined with sea-green satin.

There was no reason why his appearance should have filled me with such instinctive repugnance that I actually fell back a few steps. He was not young, but his fleshy jowls and wrinkled cheeks were not more unattractive than the faces of other men I had seen. Perhaps it was his eyes, of a gray so pale that they seemed to blend with the unhealthy pallor of his cheeks. A slow smile parted his lips, and I saw that his teeth were stained an ugly yellow. I soon learned that he did not smile often, perhaps for this reason.

My father, who had stood paralyzed during the few seconds of time that elapsed, now moved as if to approach me. The other

man did not turn, but one arm shot out to bar Father's way. His
lips had closed, to hide the ugly teeth, but he was still smiling.

"Why, Allen," he said, in a mocking tone. "I understand
now the incentive for your—er—actions of late. No effort is too
great to keep this pearl snug in its little casket, eh? Will you
introduce me? No? Then . . ." His arm still outstretched, he
made me a courtly bow and addressed me directly. "I am
Shelton, my dear. Allen hasn't mentioned me? How ungrateful!
His oldest and dearest friend—the patron who appreciates his
talents so generously. . . . But I am a man of broad tastes, I
assure you. My interests are not limited to any single field
of . . . art."

I didn't understand what he was hinting. I thought him ugly
and unprepossessing, but courteous. Indeed, if he had bought
Father's paintings—for so I interpreted his remarks—he de-
served a pleasant answer. So I made him a curtsy, and said,

"How do you do, sir. I have been at school; you must excuse
my ignorance of my father's business affairs. I hope in future to
be closer to him."

I thought this a rather neatly turned little speech, and was
chagrined to observe that it struck Mr. Shelton quite dumb for a
moment. His eyes narrowed till they were mere slits in his face.
Then he began to chuckle softly.

"Father," he said, between chuckles. "Why, Allen, I would
never have supposed you had a child of . . . What are you, my
dear—fifteen or sixteen?"

"Almost eighteen," I said.

"Such a great age! (By the by, my dear, I am Lord Shelton;
you must call my 'my lord,' or 'your lordship,' eh? That's a
good girl.) Yes, a lovely age; so tender, so untouched. . . . But,
Allen, I must scold you for concealing this charming young
lady. I would like to be of service to her, as I am of service to
her father. The three of us should get on famously together,
don't you think?"

From my father came a horrible, choking gasp. He fell
forward, clutching at Shelton's outstretched arm.

His lordship was quick to act. Lowering Father's limp body to
the floor, he bellowed for the servants in a stentorian voice quite
unlike his normal lisping whisper. The maid came running,
followed by the cook, and they dragged me forcibly from my

father. He was still choking, and from his parted lips issued a bright crimson stream.

He died three days later. I was with him at the end. So was my Lord Shelton. There was no way of keeping him out of the house; indeed, I had no desire to do so, for during those three dreadful days he managed everything. I would not have eaten or slept if he had not ordered the meals and directed the servants; and they jumped to obey his slightest wish as they had never obeyed my gentle, easygoing father.

If I thought of Lord Shelton at all, it was to regret my first critical thoughts, for he was unfailingly kind, almost paternal, in his manner. The only thing that bothered me was that he would not allow me to be alone with Father. He said it would be too distressing for me; but in fact Father lay unconscious the entire time, breathing with difficulty.

The night Father died I knew the end was near. The doctor had come and gone for the last time; there was nothing he could do. I knelt by the bed holding Father's limp hand, praying for some last word from him. His lordship sat at the foot of the bed, still as a statue, his eyes never leaving my face. He did not speak. The only sounds that broke the dead silence were the yawns of the housemaid, who was present "for the sake of propriety," as his lordship had remarked.

They say that the souls of the dying go out with the tide, or with the turn from night to day. It was at that moment, when a promise of dawn indicated the coming of morning, that my father's eyes opened.

He did not see me. His gaze was fixed on a spot beyond and above me, outside the candle's feeble light—a spot deep in darkness. So intent was his look that involuntarily I turned my head to see what it was he beheld. There was nothing there.

"Francesca," he said. His voice was young and strong. A faint smile played about his lips. "Soon, my darling; soon."

Then, with horrifying abruptness and a strength utterly incommensurate with the ravages of his disease, he sat bolt upright. His eyes turned wildly, passing over me, and focusing finally on the man who sat at the foot of the bed. His lordship rose to his feet. My father tore his hand from my grasp and pointed, his finger quivering. In the same strong voice he cried,

"It is a dead man who speaks to you, Shelton. As you act

toward my defenseless child, may God requite you in kind. Remember!''

A great gush of blood ended the speech. He fell back on the pillow.

I felt as if some invisible artery had broken in me as well; as if the vital fluid had escaped, leaving only a shell. With a steady hand I closed my father's staring eyes. Blind instinct must have told me that collapse was not far away, and that I must move now or be beyond the capability of movement. I rose; like a sleepwalker I passed his lordship, who was still standing, his hands raised as if to ward off a blow. His face, shining with perspiration, looked like a mask of yellowed wax. I was able to reach my own room, and my bed, before unconsciousness claimed me.

IV

I passed the next few days in the same trancelike state. I don't think I would have moved at all if the housemaid had not told me what to do. Her name was Bessie; she was a good-natured, rather stupid girl, and I attributed her care for me to genuine kindness. ''You must eat something, Miss Fran, see the nice soup cook has made for you.'' ''No, Miss Fran, you must not wear that dress, it is not respectful to your poor papa to wear colors. Here is a new black frock his lordship ordered for you.''

His lordship was often mentioned. He had ordered the funeral arrangements and selected the coffin. He paid the bills, too, although I did not think of that; it never occurred to me to wonder how the house was being run. But he did not come near me until the day after the funeral.

There is some purpose to the rituals of death. They allow a vent for grief, so that it does not turn inward. The services were short and simple, the mourners few—besides me, there were only the servants and his lordship. Father was buried in the little cemetery of the nearby church, St. Margaret's. It was a beautiful spring day. I stood in tearless calm by the grave, his lordship beside me, but when the first clods struck hollow on the coffin, I felt an echoing blow in my heart. I wept that night, for the first time, while Bessie comforted me in her clumsy way.

Later that night, after she had tiptoed out under the false

impression that I slept, I lay staring into the darkness. I wished that the comfortable stupor of those early days had not left me, for the thoughts that now pressed in were not pleasant. I was alone. What was to become of me? For the first time I thought about money. Not proper, perhaps, for a newly bereaved daughter; but I was discovering a hard inner core of practicality which I had not had to draw upon until then.

It brings a wry smile to my lips now to recall that I thought of his lordship as my best hope. Had he not promised to be of assistance to me? Had he not carried out the sorrowful duties attendant upon death with tactful care? And was he not, by his own claim, my father's friend? So young, so foolish was I that I even interpreted Father's dying speech as an appeal to a trusted comrade. I was glad, therefore, on the following evening, when his lordship was announced.

I was sitting in the parlor; the last gentle light of sunset was fading in the west. I had asked Bessie to bring my embroidery, but I was not making much progress with it. Painful thoughts would intrude.

I rose to greet him, putting my work down on the table, and despite my feelings of gratitude I did not care for the way his narrow gray eyes moved over me. I was wearing my only black dress, the one he had ordered for me; I was suddenly conscious of the way it clung to the contours of bosom and waist.

"Your lordship." I made him a curtsy. "I am glad you have come; I wanted to thank you—"

"There is no need for that." He advanced a few steps into the room and then turned to Bessie, who was lingering by the door. "The room is abominably dark," he said curtly. "Bring more candles."

When she had obeyed, he seemed to be more at ease.

"There, that is better. You may go now."

Inexperienced as I was, I knew he should not have been giving orders to my servant in my presence. But it would not have been gracious to say so, after all he had done. Yet, when the door had closed after Bessie, I had a panicky feeling of abandonment. I told myself I was behaving foolishly. . . . But his look was so odd! He kept turning his head, searching the shadowy corners. I started to sit down and then, though I could not have said why, I decided to remain standing.

"You have been so kind," I said, while he continued to inspect the room like a tyrant afraid of assassins. "I am glad to have the opportunity to thank—"

"Your father was my friend." He interrupted again. The word "thank" seemed to vex him. "Yes, my dearest friend. I feel his loss."

"So do I," I said softly.

"As his friend . . ." He hesitated for a moment and then seemed to take courage. "After all," he said loudly, "what other choice is there? I am doing the chit a kindness."

I felt as if he were not addressing me, but some invisible third person. It was not a comfortable feeling.

"Your lordship," I said distinctly.

He looked squarely at me, and a light came to his narrow eyes.

"A kindness," he repeated. "Yes; it would be a crime to let such beauty fade, in a factory or on the streets. Someone will enjoy it, she is too young, too naïve. . . . Why not I? I have the best right. I'll protect her. I'll crown that golden hair with rubies, though it is like a crown itself. . . ."

He began advancing toward me. His face was horrible, flushed and swollen; his tongue darted in and out like that of a serpent, moistening his lips. I backed away. He stopped and his eyes narrowed cunningly.

"Wouldn't you like rubies, sweetheart? Emeralds, if you prefer; by God, you are worth it, you'll be a sensation if I choose to display you instead of keeping you all to myself. And pretty clothes, my love; gowns of satin and silk instead of that ugly black, fine lace around those pretty white shoulders. . . ."

With one of those quick, serpentine movements, so unexpected from a man of his bulk, he darted forward and caught me in his arms.

No man had ever held me in that way before. His gross, flabby body against mine sickened me. Although he was not heavily muscled, he was so much bigger than I that my frantic struggles were of no avail. I tried to scream. Only a faint cry came from my straining throat, and he laughed aloud and pressed me closer to him.

"Don't waste your breath calling for Bessie, sweetheart. She's too busy counting the gold I have given her. It is my money that has paid her wages all along—or didn't you know that?"

I stopped struggling for a moment as the sense of his words penetrated my mind. His head struck, as a snake's might; I turned my own head to avoid his lips and felt them hot and wet against my neck. He continued to mumble, between kisses, saying horrible things, things that hurt even more than the pressure of his arms.

"Paid her wages—and everything else, the food that went into your pretty little mouth, my love. . . . How do you think Allen got his money, my darling? I gave him everything, the ungrateful——" I don't remember the word; it was one I had never heard. He went on, gasping, "Ungrateful. Ran away; stole. . . . You owe me for that, little love, you must pay your father's debts. Doing you a favor. Kindness on my part. Haven't had a woman for. . . . Almost a new experience, an interesting change. . . . You're like him, you know. Except for that golden crown of hair. . . ."

The dreadful, mumbling monologue went on and on. Understanding only a small part of what he meant, I felt my senses falter. Coward that I was, I almost welcomed the merciful anesthesia of unconsciousness, but when his clawing hand closed on the collar of my dress and ripped it down over my shoulders, the cool air struck my bare flesh like a dash of ice water. I revived; I struggled again, and tried again to scream. The sound was muffled by his lordship's mouth closing over mine. His touch filled me with such loathing that I summoned up enough strength to bite him. He swore, but he freed my mouth long enough to enable me to give one last despairing cry.

I do not believe that miracles occur in this modern age, at least not to unworthy persons like myself. What happened was not a miracle, it was surprising only in its timing. But there was one strange thing; I cannot account for it even now. The cry that came to my lips, the name I called upon, was not Bessie's, nor that of my father, so recently gone from me.

"Mother!" I screamed.

I had one glimpse of his lordship's face looming over me, filling all my vision like a devil's mask; I closed my eyes, knowing that I was lost, praying for unconsciousness. Then suddenly I felt myself falling. I tried to scream again but there wasn't a scream left in me; I could only gasp for breath, and give an undignified grunt as I landed on the carpet in a sitting position. Momentarily I expected to feel Lord Shelton's arms grasping me again. When nothing happened, I dared to open my eyes.

I will never forget my first sight of *him*. Under the circumstances any man would have looked like an avenging hero to me—Saint George, Apollo, Perseus rolled into one. And he was so handsome! Tall and broad-shouldered, his hair a mass of clustering golden ringlets, his features strong. . . . He appeared larger than life as he towered over me. His face was set in a scowl and his strong brown hands held Lord Shelton by the throat. He shook him as a terrier might shake a rat; and then, with a gesture of magnificent contempt, he flung the limp body away. His lordship struck a chair, which collapsed under his weight and let him roll ignominiously to the floor amid the broken splinters.

Then my rescuer turned to me. He dropped to one knee. His eyes were blue; they blazed like pools of deep water with sunlight in their depths. My hands flew to my breast in an effort to gather the rags of my dress around me. At once the young man turned his eyes away.

"Are you hurt?" he asked, in a deep, reverberant baritone. "If he has harmed you, I will kill him."

I was hurt, certainly; his lordship's fingers had left aching spots that would be bruises in a few hours, and his nails had raked my shoulders. But I knew what my rescuer meant. I had acquired worldly wisdom quickly and painfully.

"No," I croaked. "No, you mustn't kill him, he didn't. . . . You will only get into trouble."

"Bah," said my hero vigorously. "Who cares for that? This *cretino*, this vandal has dared to touch you. . . . Do you allow—may I have the honor to carry you to your room? Then I will return to deal with this creature."

He had the most beautiful hands. Long-fingered and slender, yet utterly masculine in their sinewy strength, they hesitated, giving me time to withdraw, or protest. I did neither. As he gathered me gently into his arms I let my head fall against his broad chest. He rose effortlessly to his feet. Then he turned to his lordship, who was crawling toward the door.

"He glides, like the serpent he is," remarked my hero with satisfaction. "Will you not arise, villain, and let me kick you? I am sorry now that I dirtied my hands on such trash."

His lordship gathered himself together and staggered to his feet. He would have looked pathetic—his clothing disordered, his age very apparent—had it not been for the naked malevolence in his eyes.

"Nor do I use my hands to avenge an injury," he snarled. "There are better ways. You have no right—"

"I have the best right," said the strange young man emphatically. "Old rascal, I would challenge you if you were worthy of the honor. Those of my race do not fight with low persons."

"Your race?" His lordship sneered. "I am Lord Shelton—"

"And I am the Conte Andrea del Baldino Tarconti. My father is Prince Tarconti; and we trace our ancestry back three thousand years to the kings of Etruria. Yes. . . ." he went on, as his lordship turned an ugly purplish shade, "Yes, you see that I do have the right. I am this lady's cousin, and her natural protector; and since you claim to have a few drops of gentle blood, I may trouble myself to kill you after all, my lord."

CHAPTER 2

To call my cousin Andrea impetuous is to do him no more than justice. The circumstances of our first meeting necessitated behavior that might not have been characteristic; as he afterwards said, the sight that met his horrified eyes when, in response to my desperate cry, he burst through the door could only be answered by immediate, vigorous action. I was soon to learn, however, that such action was habitual to him; he was enthusiastic, forthright, direct.

When I opened my eyes the morning after his dramatic appearance, it was his hearty voice outside my door that had awakened me. Without that assurance of his reality I think I should have considered that I had been dreaming. Then I turned over in my bed and received further confirmation; my body ached from head to foot.

From the tones of Andrea's voice I gathered that he was expostulating with someone, but I was unable to hear another voice, he spoke so loudly and so continuously. Finally the door opened and Bessie's head came in—only her head, no more. Seeing me awake, she allowed the rest of her person to follow her head.

"Miss?" she quavered. "Are you ready to get up, miss?"

"Yes," I said shortly. I had not forgiven her for her part in my betrayal, although Andrea had reduced her to tears and howls of repentance the previous night, when he heard what she had done. "Female Judas," was the mildest of the epithets he applied to her. He had proposed flinging her out into the night, but it was obvious that I could not remain in the house without an attendant, so Andrea had allowed her to stay, promising to spend the night himself in order to ensure my safety. Whether he had done so or not I did not know. I had not expected to sleep at all that night, but I fell into oblivion as soon as Bessie had put me to bed. Now, except for my bodily aches, I felt amazingly cheerful. I wondered if my cousin was really as handsome as I remembered.

I did not find out for some time, since Andrea refused to come into my bedchamber, even after Bessie had wrapped me in my dressing gown. It covered me from my chin to my toes, and seemed to me quite a respectable garment; but when I came out of my room Andrea took one look at me, blushed deeply, and looked elsewhere. Even when we were seated at the breakfast table, with Bessie serving us, he found it hard to look directly at me.

It may seem strange that I was able to eat, and heartily, devouring eggs and chops with my usual appetite. Our social system makes hypocrites of women, but I was not old enough to pretend to feelings I did not have. The growing admiration in my cousin's blue eyes assured me that I had nothing more to fear. It is easy to accept miracles when one is seventeen. As the meal progressed, Andrea grew more at ease, and finally he said naïvely, "In England, a young lady may appear in her night-clothes without impropriety, is it so?"

I stopped eating, a forkful of food halfway to my lips, and contemplated the ample folds of my dressing gown in some dismay. It had not occurred to me that that was the cause of his embarrassment; Father and I had always breakfasted so.

"It is not my night attire, really," I said. "I don't think. . . . Surely, since you are a member of the family—a cousin—"

"A half cousin only," said Andrea, with what seemed to me to be unnecessary precision. "Your mother and my father were only half brother and sister."

"I know nothing of the family," I said.

Andrea started to speak and then looked significantly at Bessie, who was standing by the sideboard, her hands folded and her eyes fixed on him with the anxious appeal of a dog.

"Send her away," he said, indicating Bessie with a toss of his head. "She spoils my appetite."

At which Bessie let out a howl and, without waiting for my order, bolted from the room.

I looked at Andrea, whose broad forehead had smoothed out and who was eating with every evidence of pleasure. It was obvious that Bessie's feelings for him included more complex emotions than simple fear. No wonder. With my newborn sophistication, I thought that my cousin's path through life must be strewn with heartbroken females of all ages and social classes. He was even more handsome than I remembered. Despite his northern coloring and beautiful blue eyes, one might have known him to be a foreigner; his fair hair was a little longer than an Englishman might have worn it, although he was clean-shaven.

He looked at me, and it was my turn to blush. I had not meant to stare so rudely. To cover my confusion I said, "What did you mean, we are half cousins?"

"But it is very simple. Our grandfather married twice. My father and your mother were children of different mothers. My grandmother was an English lady; that is why I speak English so well."

"Ah, I see. Your grandmother taught you."

"Not my grandmother; she died before I was born. Her sister, who came to Italy when Grandmother married into the family, was my teacher—if it is teaching to shout a word very loudly, and then strike, very hard, when the young pupil does not understand."

"She sounds horrid," I said indignantly.

"She *is* horrid," said Andrea, smiling broadly. "She is *una tipica*—how do you say it?—a typical English old maid. That is a term she did not teach us, but we learned it, my brother and I, and used it to torment the poor lady. Our parents died of fever, within two weeks of one another, when we were infants, so Aunt Rhoda had the task of bringing us up. However, I do not know that she did such a good job of it. We learned English only because she refused to learn Italian. She despises the language, the country, and all its inhabitants."

"I am so confused! You mention a brother. . . ."

"Did not your mother speak of the family? But no, her resentment—"

"She died when I was born," I said. "But she was not resentful; it was my grandfather who refused to forgive her, or acknowledge my existence."

Andrea flung his head back and laughed heartily, displaying a set of splendid white teeth.

"Yes, he would do that. He is horrid, too—a horrible old man. But he is mellowing; I think he will receive you kindly."

"You think so? Didn't he send you?" I put my hand to my head, which really did feel as if it were whirling around. "I must be more confused than I realized. I didn't even ask how you happened to appear so miraculously. It was like an answer to a prayer."

My cousin's keen blue eyes softened.

"Perhaps it was. Who knows? Although I am not a likely agent of the heavenly powers. But, of course, I forget; you did not know of your father's letter; he said he was writing without your knowledge."

"I didn't know."

"It was a fine letter," Andrea said. "He wrote that he was dying, that you would be left alone, with no money and no protector; and he suggested that you might have need of protection. How he knew this. . . . But I distress you. Forgive me."

I had bowed my head, remembering the night in the inn when Father had sat writing, his face set and tired. It must have hurt him to be forced to appeal to the cruel old man—to admit his failure and face the knowledge of his imminent death. But what an eloquent letter it must have been, to overcome my grandfather's long-cherished resentment.

I said as much to Andrea, and was faintly amused to see my cousin look uncomfortable. As I had already learned, his face reflected every passing emotion; he was not a guileful man.

"Well, to be truthful, he did not—that is, he. . . . How can I say this?" Andrea demanded of the empty air.

"Be candid," I said. "You can't hurt my feelings; I have none for my grandfather, so why should I care what he thinks of me? You don't mean to say that you acted without his knowledge or consent? My dear cousin—"

"That is not quite how it was." Andrea sighed deeply and ran his fingers through his bright curls. "I think I must explain about the family. You should know about them if you are to live with them."

"But I don't know that I shall. If I am not welcome in my grandfather's house—"

"But of course you are welcome! Besides, where else is there for you to go?"

I was silent.

"So," Andrea resumed cheerfully, "I will explain the family. There is Grandfather, of course. He is . . . ah, but it is impossible to describe him. Only stand up to him, don't let him bully you, and you will get along. Then there is Aunt Rhoda. She is our great-aunt, really, but we call her 'aunt.' I have told you about her. She and Grandfather fight constantly."

He smiled reminiscently. It was clear that he found his brawling relations quite entertaining. I was not at all sure I would find them so. Nor was I getting a very clear picture of them. Description was not Andrea's strong point.

"Your brother," I said. "Is he older or younger than you?"

"We are twins. He is the heir, however; he was born first. Though you would not think so; he is not strong, poor Stefano. But he is very clever. He reads a great deal. He has nothing better to do, being so sickly. It is he you must thank for my coming. I would never have had the sense to think of it, or the intelligence to plan things. I have the strength in the family, but Stefano has the brains."

I had already conceived a girlish admiration for my cousin. Now, suddenly, I liked him too, liked him very much. His modesty and good nature were as irresistible as his handsome face.

"I will look forward to meeting your brother and thanking him," I said. "But I can never forget that it was you who actually—"

"No, no, you must not thank me, what else could I do? Only what any gentleman would do. After all," he added, his eyes twinkling, "that is what Aunt Rhoda taught me to be. A poor imitation of an English gentleman, as Stefano says. Now you know about the family—"

"Is that all of them?" I asked, overwhelmed with a premature attack of stage fright.

Andrea laughed again.

"Oh, there are always relatives visiting. Cousins and aunts and other people. You will like them. And they are sure to love you, Cousin. But we have talked enough. Time is passing. We must leave this house as soon as possible."

He flung his napkin down and bounded to his feet. I was beginning to find his energy a little overwhelming.

"But," I began.

"No buts! That is one of Aunt Rhoda's favorite sayings. In this case she would be right." His hands braced on the table, he leaned toward me. His face was serious. "I don't understand your father's way of life; it is not my business to understand. But in his letter he said he had nothing—no property, no money. I do not know who has paid the rent for this house, Cousin. I do not say this to hurt you or make you afraid, but I do not think you should stay here. I have many things to arrange; you will forgive me if I leave you? You shall be packing while I am gone so that we can be away from here by nightfall. Do not worry," he added, kindly, while I gaped like a fish out of water. "Stefano has planned it all, he told me what I must do."

Not being acquainted with the admirable Stefano, I did not find this information as reassuring as he meant it to be. But out of the chaos into which his words had thrown me, one thought came to the fore.

"Wait," I cried, for he was already striding briskly toward the door. "Cousin—I am ashamed to confess it, but I am afraid. What if his lordship should return?"

"His lordship? Ah, the villain of last night." Andrea turned. The sunlight pouring in through the windows of the breakfast room turned his golden curls into a shining halo. His face was as beautiful as an angel's and as benevolent as a saint's. "I have taken care of him, there is nothing to fear. I was out early this morning. And I did it myself," he added, with obvious satisfaction. "Stefano did not instruct me, for of course he did not know of *that* matter."

"Did what?" I gasped. I think I knew the answer before he spoke.

"Killed him," said Andrea calmly. "These meetings always take place at dawn. Hurry with your packing, little Cousin."

II

By the time I had recovered from my shock at this last speech, he was gone. I could hardly pursue him along the street in my dressing gown, so I did the only thing I could do—I began my packing. I cannot say that I did it neatly. Weeks later, when my trunks were unpacked, I was provoked at the jumble of clothing and ornaments, books and fancy work that had been tumbled in anyhow. Yet it was a wonder I was able to do anything at all. I suppose my brain was numbed by the series of stunning surprises I had received in such a short time. Certainly I felt no regret at his lordship's death, nor any horror at Andrea's act. But as the day wore on and he did not return, I began to be frightened for him. There were laws against dueling. He was a stranger, and his lordship was a peer of the realm, with powerful friends.

Late in the afternoon, when the doorbell finally rang, I flew to answer it without waiting for Bessie. My disappointment was extreme when I saw, not my cousin, but a stranger—an elderly woman, stout and gray-haired, who stared severely at me through her gold pince-nez. I was about to tell her that she had the wrong house when she asked if I was not Miss Fairbourn. I admitted that I was. She nodded.

"I am Miss Perkins. Alberta Perkins. I was sent by Count Tarconti. May I come in?"

"I suppose so," I said stupidly. "Where is the Count?"

"I presume his letter will explain." She withdrew an envelope from her large handbag, but withheld it from my eager fingers. "It would be better, would it not, to peruse your letter within?"

I led the way to the parlor. She immediately handed me the letter. Rudely, I left her standing while I ripped it open.

The handwriting was characteristic of my cousin—bold, dashing, and ill-spelt. Apparently Aunt Rhoda's tutelage had not extended to the writing of English. I do not attempt to reproduce the exact words, but the general sense was as follows:

Dear Cousin.

Here is Miss Perkins, your companion, who will bring you to us in Italy. She is highly recommended, and speaks Latin! Forgive me that I do not escort you; but friends have told me that your stupid English law [the word "stupid" had been scored out, but I could still read it] makes it necessary for me to leave without delay or risk prison. I will greet you on the happy day of your arrival.

Your devoted cousin,
Andrea

I looked at Miss Perkins, who was studying me through her pince-nez.

"I don't understand," I said weakly.

"I'm not sure that I do, either," said Miss Perkins. "But perhaps we might sit down and talk about it."

My immediate anxieties about Andrea being relieved, I was able to study Miss Perkins with more attention. She was—well, not to put too fine a face upon it, she was ugly. Short and stout, with square shoulders and a massive bosom, she had features of almost masculine prominence—a jutting nose, a protruding chin, and bushy gray eyebrows. Except for her bosom and her hair, which was worn in an untidy bun, I might have taken her for a man. Her clothing, though feminine in design, was quite severe except for one item—her bonnet. The ribbons that tied it under her chins were bright crimson, and this color matched the feathers that were attached, somewhat insecurely, on the left side.

I liked that bonnet. I could not have explained my reaction then, in so many words. Now I know that I recognized in it a hidden, almost shamefaced romantic streak, a love of soft feminine things that Miss Perkins was unable to indulge in otherwise.

There were other attractive features about her. Her eyes, though narrow and light gray in color, had a mild, benevolent expression. And her voice was beautiful—a soft, deep contralto. I smiled tentatively at her, and she responded with a broad, beaming grin.

"Please sit down," I said. "And forgive my inattention. Would you care for refreshment? A cup of tea, perhaps?"

"I would dearly love a cup of tea," said Miss Perkins.

Within five minutes we were chatting like old friends. One thing we had in common from the start was our amazement at

Andrea. Apparently he had simply walked into the employment bureau where she had come to apply for a new position, and, finding her at liberty, had hired her on the spot. He had given her only the briefest explanation of the problem, and then had pressed a huge roll of bills into her hand. Her protests were waved aside—"I am a judge of character, madame, and I saw at once you are someone to be trusted. Besides, I am entrusting to your care my beloved young cousin; what is mere money compared to that?"

I could not help laughing as she repeated this characteristic speech, with a roll of her eyes and an inimitable imitation of Andrea's delightful accent. Immediately she sobered.

"Pray don't think I mean to mock the Count," she said earnestly. "I, too, fancy myself a judge of character, and I have seldom been so impressed by a young man's kindness and honesty. If he has a fault—forgive me if I appear to criticize—I would judge him to be somewhat impetuous."

"He certainly is that," I admitted. "Miss Perkins, I think it is only fair to you to tell you why Andrea found it necessary to depart with such haste."

"Lack of candor is not one of his failings," Miss Perkins said. "He told me why. And if his version of the story is accurate. . . . It was only the barest outline he gave me; don't think I mean to inquire into a subject which must be exceedingly painful. . . ."

Never would I have supposed myself capable of recounting such embarrassing details to a stranger. But there was something about that woman. . . . I even told her as much as I could decently say about Father's difficulties. Miss Perkins made no comment, but her eyes flashed and her big hands clenched as she listened. If she had expressed sympathy, I might have broken down. As it was, I was able to complete my account fairly calmly. I felt a strange relief when I had done so.

"Your cousin did quite right," said Miss Perkins energetically. "Well, my dear, you have had a difficult time, but that is over and done with. You must start thinking about the future."

Different as they were in every other way, Andrea and Miss Perkins had one characteristic in common. When they acted, they acted with dispatch. Miss Perkins agreed with Andrea that I should not stay in the house. She moved me out that very evening to respectable lodgings, and we remained there for the three days that passed before we found passage on a steamer going to Civitavecchia, the port of Rome.

It was with indescribable emotions that I stood on the deck of the ship and watched the roofs of London fade into a black smudge on the horizon. My old life was over. What would the new one bring? I felt a qualm. Then I looked to my right, where Miss Perkins stood, her big hands clutching the rail and her crimson plume blowing bravely in the breeze; and I had a feeling that things were going to work out after all.

III

I had immediate cause to be grateful for Miss Perkins' presence. As soon as we entered the Channel, I became horribly seasick. She had not a moment's discomfort. In between tending to me she made frequent expeditions onto the deck, from which she would return with a beaming face and animated accounts of the conversations she had had with other travelers, the sailors, and even with the captain. She was insatiably curious, and I felt that by the time we reached Italy she could have commanded the ship herself, and steered it into port. Her example shamed me so that I was finally persuaded to drag my miserable body on deck. There, as she had suggested, the air did me good, and it was not long before I was over my discomfort.

Although my physical ailments were overcome, I became more and more prey to other worries as the voyage went on. I had not had time to brood, in the hurry and confusion of departure; but now, at leisure, I began to wonder what was in store for me. To say that I was going to my mother's family sounded well enough, and yet it was like entrusting myself to utter strangers, in an alien land. As for the country to which I was traveling, I knew nothing of it except for some of the heroic deeds of the ancient Romans. Oh, yes; I could also sing, accompanying myself on the pianoforte, two Italian songs.

Miss Perkins did her best to remedy my ignorance. She had managed to obtain a small grammar and spent several hours a day teaching herself Italian. But as she herself admitted, the Tuscan form of the language was apt to be of limited use. The long Italian peninsula contained many dialects, unintelligible even to natives of neighboring districts. It also contained many kingdoms and states. There was no Italian nation.

Yet, according to Miss Perkins, the dream of unity had animated patriots for half a century. It was from this amazing woman, who seemed to know something about every subject under the sun, that I first heard the names of Mazzini and Cavour, of King Victor Emmanuel and Garibaldi—and of Pius the Ninth, called Pio Nono by his subjects, who was not only the reigning Pope, but the temporal monarch of the country in which my grandfather's estates were situated.

Miss Perkins had a habit of rubbing her nose vigorously with her knuckles when she was agitated. I believe I have implied that her nose was quite large, possibly as the result of this process. When she mentioned Pio Nono, the gesture became almost violent.

"They called him *il papa liberale* when he first assumed the throne of Peter," she said. "He began well; a general amnesty freed hundreds of political prisoners whom his predecessors had punished without trial. He even relaxed the strict press censorship. But if Italy is to be unified, the Pope must give up his temporal powers, and that he refuses to do. He rules now in a most tyrannical manner. Of course we cannot expect other nations to enjoy our English liberties; but there is no such thing as freedom of speech or of the press in Rome—the cradle of the republican form of government! As for freedom of religion—"

She would have gone on, her indignation rising, if I had not interrupted.

"I don't understand what you mean by temporal ruler. Is the Pope a king, then, with his own army?"

"Exactly. Not that his army is much good," said Miss Perkins, with a sniff. "He had to flee from Rome during the rebellion of 1849, and it took a French army to restore him. He would not be there now if the French and the Austrians did not keep troops in Italy to maintain the status quo."

"But what do France and Austria have to do with Italy?" I asked.

"A very good question!" Miss Perkins struck the rail with her fist. "They have no moral right to interfere. But neither Louis Napoleon nor the Emperor wants a strong united Italy challenging them in Europe. By supporting the Pope they keep the country permanently divided, for the Papal States lie directly across the center of the peninsula, between the kingdom of Piedmont in the north and the Kingdom of the Two Sicilies in the south.''

"There are three countries in Italy, then," I said, thinking I had got it straight at last.

"There are more than three. But these are the most important. Victor Emmanuel, king of Piedmont, is the hope of the liberals. He would rule constitutionally, with legal safeguards for the liberties of his subjects. Francis the Second, the king of Naples and Sicily—for that is what is meant by the 'Two Sicilies'—is a tyrant even worse than the Pope. His opponents are flung into prison without trial—"

One of Miss Perkins' few weaknesses was that she was apt to lecture at length, especially when her indignation was aroused. I therefore interrupted her again. I had learned that I could do this with impunity, for under her forbidding exterior she was as mild as a lamb, and never scolded.

"I had no idea you were such a fiery revolutionary, Miss P. You spoke of this man Garibaldi with great enthusiasm yesterday; I think you must be one of his disciples."

"We have mutual friends," said Miss Perkins primly.

I had to laugh; the idea of my friend and the swashbuckling Italian adventurer having any acquaintances in common was ludicrous. But Miss Perkins was quite serious.

"Mrs. Roberts, with whom he stayed in London five years ago, is an acquaintance of mine. I was fortunate enough to meet the General at her house."

"I suppose he is very handsome," I said slyly.

"Yes . . . no." Miss Perkins considered the question. "I suppose he isn't really handsome. He is only of medium height, rather stocky, and his face is pleasant rather than beautiful. But one doesn't think of his looks when one meets him. His charm lies in his simplicity, his humility—and one's knowledge of the lion-hearted courage that animates him. All his life he has fought for freedom, even as an exile in South America. In Rome, he and his volunteers carried on an epic struggle against the French; when finally the city fell, Garibaldi refused to surrender. His devoted wife fled with him; she died in his arms as they hid in a fisherman's hut, with enemy troops hot on their trail. Last year he fought with the Piedmontese against Austria, and they say that he is about to set sail for Sicily, where the oppressed people have risen against their government. If he—"

One of the ship's officers came by at that moment and invited us to come along and see how the ship was steered. I was relieved at the interruption. I was not much interested in the workings of the ship, but I was even less interested in the cause of Italian liberation. Little did I realize that this dull, abstract subject, as I thought of it, was to become one of burning interest to me, and soon.

By the time we landed I knew more about modern Italian politics than I wanted to know. Miss Perkins also lectured me on Roman history and antiquities. If someone had heard us in conversation, they would have thought her the excited young woman on her first voyage abroad, and me the world-weary sophisticate. She fairly bubbled with excitement at the prospect of seeing the land of Michelangelo and Raphael, of Julius Caesar and Brutus—whom she admired much more than she did Caesar. I could not share her raptures. As the moment of confrontation approached, I became increasingly nervous. What if Grandfather refused to receive me? What if Andrea was not there to support me?

When we steamed into the harbor of Civitavecchia on a bright spring morning, Miss Perkins could hardly contain herself. Clutching the rail, she muttered Latin verses interspersed with comments to me.

"Precisely as it was in imperial times; the verses of Rutilius might still apply! *'Molibus aequoreum concluditur amphiteatrum. . . .'* Yes, yes, the amphitheater of water within, and the twin moles stretching out toward the island. . . . Dear me, how fascinating! *'Interior medias sinus invitatus. . . .'*"

And much more.

The town itself dampened even Miss Perkins' enthusiasm. Every traveler who has approached Rome through this, its major port, has spoken of its filthy streets and inns and its thieving inhabitants. Miss Perkins took one look at it and took measures to get us out of there as quickly as possible.

Unfortunately it was necessary for us to spend the night in

Civitavecchia. Modern transportation, like everything else modern, was frowned upon in the Papal States; there was no railroad in the region we must reach. So we sought out an inn, where we might hope to hire a carriage and driver. Such had been Miss Perkins' efficiency throughout that I was not surprised to hear her direct our driver to a particular *albergo*, which turned out to be somewhat less filthy and run-down than the others we had seen from the carriage. We were received by the host without much show of courtesy until Miss Perkins mentioned our destination. The Tarconti name wrought a miraculous change; we were shown to the best chamber the place afforded and, with a deep bow, the host begged our indulgence while he went to see what could be done for us in the way of transportation. In the meantime, if we would honor his inn by partaking of refreshment, however inadequate for persons of our quality. . . .

As soon as we were alone, Miss Perkins dropped into a chair and pursed her lips in a silent whistle—a habit she had ordered me not to emulate, since it was not ladylike. The crimson plume was drooping, but Miss Perkins was still undaunted, as her first comment proved.

"Heavens, how exhausting it is to make one's wants known in a mixture of three languages and a series of frantic gestures! I believe I am beginning to grasp the local dialect, however."

"You are amazing," I said sincerely. "I shudder to think of making this trip without you. I could never have done it."

"You would have managed somehow," said Miss Perkins. "It is surprising how efficient one becomes when one must. As for my abilities, you may thank me when we reach the Castello Tarconti. Congratulations at this point would be premature."

It was not long, however, before the host returned with good news. He had found a coach and a driver who knew the road, and we might set out first thing in the morning. Cheered by this information, we sought our hard and lumpy bed and slept soundly.

We were up early next morning and had to wait for the carriage, which was late. Miss Perkins badgered the host until he threw up his hands and fled, promising to make inquiries. Miss Perkins then turned her attention to some of the other guests who were awaiting breakfast and transportation in the inn parlor. After conversing with one of them, a pleasant-looking gentleman wearing modish checked trousers, she let out a cry of excitement.

"*È vero?*" she demanded eagerly. "Is it true?"

The gentleman nodded and handed her the newspaper he had been reading, as if this would verify the statement she had questioned.

"What is it?" I asked curiously. I thought I had recognized a familiar name amid the torrent of Italian the two had exchanged.

"Garibaldi," exclaimed Miss Perkins, proving me correct. "He has landed in Sicily! He sailed a few days ago, secretly, from Genoa, with a thousand volunteers."

"I'm glad to hear it," I said with a smile. "At least I'm glad if you are."

"More than glad—delighted! He will easily conquer that Bourbon tyrant and free the oppressed people, first of Sicily and then of the Neapolitan kingdom. That region will join the kingdom of Piedmont, as Tuscany has just done, and the Papal States will be next—"

At this point the host returned to tell us our carriage was ready. His timing may not have been entirely fortuitous; Miss Perkins' loud enthusiasm was making people look askance at us, and the kindly gentleman in the checked trousers had moved away. It was not wise to speak with favor of General Garibaldi, or of invasion, in His Holiness's domain.

The carriage was a shabby equipage, but after inspecting it closely, Miss Perkins pronounced it sound. The driver was subjected to an even more piercing scrutiny. What could be seen of his face, between his shock of untidy black hair and a ferocious moustache, looked amiable enough. His name was Giovanni, and he assured us, with expressive gestures, that he was prepared to lay down his life to defend us and get us safely to our destination.

Miss Perkins muttered, "Typical Italian braggadocio; but I think the fellow is trustworthy." We had just taken our places within the carriage when a pair of riders came quietly out of the stables and took up positions behind the coach. They looked like the bandits in the wild tales some of the girls at school had read surreptitiously. They were heavily bearded; wide-brimmed slouch hats and neckerchiefs hid even more of their faces; they wore blouselike shirts and loose trousers which were tucked into their boots. From the belt of one man protruded something that looked, even to my inexperienced eye, like the handle of a pistol.

Miss Perkins put her head out the window and shouted for the host. At first he pretended not to understand her, but her gesticulations were not to be ignored. They exchanged further gestures and shouts; then Miss Perkins withdrew into the coach and looked doubtfully at me.

"He says they have been hired to protect us. The roads are infested with robbers."

"Oh, dear," I exclaimed.

Miss Perkins rubbed her nose thoughtfully.

"The danger of robbers may not be great, but the country is certainly in a disturbed state, and a guard might not be a bad idea."

"But they may be robbers themselves," I protested. The fierce aspects of the two men frightened me.

"There would be no sense in that," Miss Perkins said; and I was relieved to see she had stopped rubbing her nose, which meant that she was satisfied in her own mind. "If the host meant to set thieves on us, he would keep them out of sight until we were in the countryside, with no witnesses about. I think we may proceed, and be grateful for the guards."

Soon we were out of the city and bumping along a rough road through a flat region covered with heath and low bushes. The landscape was uninteresting, with only an occasional ruined tower or broken bridge to break the monotony; but after a time we left the coast and headed inland, toward a range of undulating hills. The scenery grew wilder and more rugged, and as the sun sank lower, we had fine views of hillsides covered with dark foliage, shining in the westering rays.

We stopped for the night at a village called Palo, where the inn had been recommended. It was a simple place, but clean, and the food was fairly good. There were no other travelers, so we had the place to ourselves; and wearied by the activities of the day, we soon fell asleep.

The sun was barely above the horizon when I awoke next morning. Miss Perkins was not in the bed. I had come to rely on her so much that at first I was panic-stricken by her absence; but I forced myself to be calm. After all, I could not have her with me forever. . . . I paused in the middle of dressing, one foot half into my stocking; and I really believe this was the first time since Father's death—the first time in my life, in fact—that I thought about someone else's problems.

Miss Perkins had been hired to accompany me on my journey; no doubt she would be sent home afterwards. Her expenses would be paid, I thought I knew Andrea well enough to be sure of his generosity; but what would become of her after that? I had already observed that her clothing, though once good, was shabby, and her wardrobe was far from extensive. Even the brave red plume showed signs of wear. She had been "available" when Andrea sought a companion for me. Perhaps she had long been available for a paying situation. No longer young, far from prepossessing in appearance, eccentric in her habits. . . . I could see that she might not easily find another position. Not that she had hinted, even indirectly, of being in need. . . .

It was this cheerful courage that endeared her to me, among other qualities. I was very young and not very sensible, but thank heaven I had sense enough to value these qualities. Was it possible that my unknown grandfather might let her stay with me as a sort of governess-companion? Perhaps if we both made ourselves very useful to him. . . . There was another English lady, Andrea's great-aunt, at the castle; she might enjoy Miss Perkins' companionship.

At least it was something to think about. I finished dressing and went out in search of Miss Perkins and breakfast. I could hear the normal cheerful morning sounds of any country house—chickens clucking, the splashing of water, voices calling out, a burst of laughter.

I found Miss Perkins in the courtyard, where the chickens strutted and scratched and a fat black cat sunned itself on a pile of broken stones. Miss Perkins was sitting on a block of wood, her skirts hitched up, talking animatedly to one of our guards. Which one I could not have said; they looked very much alike, with their fierce black whiskers and swaggering, piratical clothing. I stood listening for a moment, unnoticed. The conversation seemed friendly, and I was amused to observe that Miss Perkins was using her hands freely, in quite an Italian manner. Then I caught a word or two that I thought I understood. Interested, I moved forward, and the guard caught sight of me. He gave a start, and Miss Perkins turned.

"Ah, good morning, Francesca. I hope you slept well. A beautiful morning, is it not? I have been chatting with this young man. Antonio is his name."

Antonio's broad-brimmed hat was already in his hand. He swept it toward the ground in a low bow. When he straightened, I saw that the fierce beard was deceptive. His eyes were big and brown and gentle, with long, curling lashes, and his cheeks— what I could see of them—were as soft as a girl's. He was much younger than I had thought; and now that I had time to study it, I rather liked the effect of his casual costume. The loose shirt set off his broad shoulders and the scarlet sash was tied tightly around his slim waist. He smiled shyly at me, said something I did not understand, and began to back away. As he turned I saw something that made me gasp. Miss Perkins pinched my arm; not until Antonio had gone into the inn did she speak.

"He understands a little English. You would not wish to speak tactlessly, I am sure."

"But his hand," I exclaimed. "It was his left hand that held his hat; his right is. . . . Did my eyes deceive me?"

"They did not. He has lost his right hand."

"Poor young man! What an unfortunate accident."

"It was no accident. That is the punishment the Holy Father's troops deal out to rebels. Do you remember my telling you about the risings last year in the Papal States?"

"I have forgotten," I muttered, still staring horrified at the door through which Antonio had gone.

"You should pay closer attention. This is not ancient history, Francesca; it happened last year, in 1859 of the Christian era. Last summer, when Piedmont persuaded Napoleon to join in a war against Austria, the patriots in the central parts of Italy rose against the occupying Austrian troops. They hoped Piedmont and France would aid them against a common enemy; but Louis Napoleon betrayed his allies. He made a separate peace with Austria. The Italian state of Tuscany gained its freedom, and won union with Piedmont. However, the rebellions here in the Papal States were crushed by Pio Nono's mercenaries. The most notorious of these soldiers is Schmidt, the commandant in Perugia. That is where Antonio fought. Most of the captured rebels were executed. Antonio's family has some influence; he was only condemned to lose the hand he had dared raise against his lord. They plunged the stump into hot tar afterwards, to stop the—''

"Don't!" I begged.

"Oh, it would be very convenient if we could live our comfortable lives without hearing of such horrors," Miss Perkins said angrily. "But so long as they happen, it would be cowardly to hide our heads. You are not in England, Francesca. Life has many perils, and it is better to be prepared for them."

The words struck home with a force I am sure she had not intended. If my father had not tried to shield me from the unpleasant facts of life—if he had let me share his difficulties— who knows, he might have been able to break free of the horrible bonds that held him. At least I would have been better prepared to deal with Lord Shelton. I had been saved then by a miracle; I could not count on a second one.

Seeing my stricken face, Miss Perkins became repentant.

"Forgive me for speaking so roughly. Really, I must learn to watch my tongue, there is no excuse—"

"No," I said. "You were right. How does Antonio. . . . I suppose he trained himself to use his left hand.''

"Yes, doesn't he do beautifully? I had quite a good talk with him; such an opportunity to improve my Italian. He speaks the beautiful Tuscan dialect. And he told me about some interesting antiquities which we will see on today's trip. Did you know that your grandfather's estates are situated in the old kingdom of the Etruscans? A fascinating people! They are frequently mentioned by Roman writers, but only in the last thirty years have their ruins come to light. I had no idea. . . ."

I thought she had dragged the Etruscans—whoever they were—into the conversation in order to distract me from my painful thoughts. But I did Miss P. an injustice. The Etruscans were just as interesting to her as the other subjects she had mentioned since we met, and during the course of the day I learned a great deal about them. According to Miss Perkins, the country through which we were passing had once been part of their powerful empire, which had dominated central Italy in the seventh and sixth centuries B.C., and had later ruled Rome. She babbled on about Mr. Dennis and Mrs. Hamilton Gray, who had written books about Etruscan antiquities; and once I thought she was going to fall out the coach window when we passed a rugged cliff in which we could see strangely regular openings, like doors cut into the rock. Miss Perkins explained that they were just that—the doors to ancient Etruscan tombs, which, like many dwellings of the dead, had been built in imitation of real houses.

"Fascinating!" she exclaimed, after I had pulled her back into the coach and, with difficulty, persuaded her to retain her seat. "I do hope there are tombs on your grandfather's land. He may allow me to do some digging, if indeed he has not excavated himself, like Prince Buonaparte and the Duchess of Sermoneta. Only imagine, dear Francesca, the thrill of discovering a princess's tomb, like the one General Galassi found in 1836. You know of it, of course?"

"No," I said, with affectionate resignation. "But I suspect you are going to tell me about it."

She did, and at some length. My initial prejudice soon gave way to interest; for what girl could resist the allurement of buried treasures, rich jewels, and mystery?

Like all pagans, who did not possess the Christian's assurance of a spiritual heaven, the Etruscans placed the vain adornments of life in the tombs of their dead—food and drink, cosmetics, weapons, jewels. Naturally most of the tombs were robbed; and although one must condemn the robbery as morally reprehensible, one must also admit that the thieves had common sense, on their side. They could eat the food and sell the gold, which was more than the dead person could do.

However, the tomb to which Miss Perkins had referred somehow escaped discovery until modern times. There had been two burials in the sepulcher. One had been that of a warrior. His weapons were buried with him, along with many other beautiful and curious objects. In the inner chamber of the tomb there had been another body. It had long since fallen into dust, but the ornaments it had worn to the grave still lay on the ground, where they had fallen when the flesh and bone crumbled. They were all of massive gold—headdress, breastplate, necklaces and chains, earrings and bracelets and brooches. The delicacy of the workmanship was unsurpassed in its skill; indeed, according to Miss Perkins, modern jewelers would not have been able to duplicate some of the work. I could not help being thrilled by the description of the long-dead princess's parure, and for a while afterwards I peered from the window as eagerly as Miss Perkins, looking for Etruscan tombs.

As the day waned, so did my enthusiasm. Even Miss Perkins fell silent; and after we had dined on the contents of a basket prepared for us by the innkeeper, she dozed off. I have to confess that she snored. But this did not prevent me from following her into slumber.

I was awakened with a shock as the carriage gave a violent lurch and stopped, so suddenly that I was thrown from my seat. Dizzy with sleep, I struggled to right myself, hearing a medley of sounds that filled me with alarm. The rapid pound of horses' hooves mingled with shouts and curses and the explosions of firearms. Before I had time to recover my wits or my upright position, the carriage door was wrenched open. I couldn't see who had opened it; Miss Perkins, her bonnet askew but her courage high, blocked my view.

"How dare you?" she demanded indignantly. "What is the meaning of—"

The speech ended in a gasp as she fell forward. A man's hand had seized her and unceremoniously pulled her out of the carriage. Now seriously alarmed, I followed her out with more haste than dignity.

Poor Miss Perkins, blinking and rumpled, was held by the arm by the ruffian who had removed her from the carriage. He was tall and redheaded; his crimson jacket, dirty white breeches, and tall plumed hat matched the costume worn by half a dozen other men who surrounded the carriage. All carried muskets. One of these weapons was leveled at our driver, whose rotund face had lost its healthy pink color.

The fact that the men were soldiers did not reassure me as to their intentions. I had never seen more villainous faces.

I had removed my bonnet earlier; my hair curled damply around my face and neck. I pushed it back, knowing that I did not present a very imposing appearance, but too angry to care.

"Let go of her at once," I cried.

The man did so; but as his eyes swept over me I realized that he had not been responding to my order. He had simply found a new interest.

"Be careful," said Miss Perkins in a low voice. Then, as the man reached out for me, she stepped between us and spoke to him in a sharp voice. She spoke English; to my surprise the man answered in the same language, and in a rich Irish brogue.

"Will you be listenin' to the tongue of the old bitch," he exclaimed. "Don't be interfering now, you lads; I saw the little darlin' first. . . . Only see the golden hair of her!" And, pushing Miss Perkins rudely aside, he caught a strand of my hair in his dirty fingers.

At that interesting moment another of the soldiers called out—not in English, but in French—and the Irishman released me. A man on horseback appeared from beyond the carriage.

The rider was obviously an officer. His uniform, in contrast to those of his men, was a model of military neatness. His cuirass and helmet had been polished till they shone. The waving plume in his helmet was as snowy white as his tightly fitting breeches. The gold epaulets and the gold-hilted sword slung at his side confirmed his rank, and even the dust of the road did not hide the fact that his boots were of the finest leather.

"Thank heaven," said Miss Perkins, with a sigh of relief. At once she cried out to the officer, in French. "Your assistance, sir, if you please! Or does the Holy Father allow his soldiers to molest helpless Englishwomen?"

Leaning forward, one arm on the pommel of his saddle, the officer inspected us with insolent deliberation before replying.

"You travel, madame, through a troubled country at a troubled time. You must expect some slight inconvenience. We are on the track of a dangerous criminal. Have you seen such a man?"

"We have seen no one," Miss Perkins replied.

"Then you will not object if we search your carriage, to make sure no one is hidden there?"

"You doubt my word?" Miss Perkins demanded. "I had always been led to believe that Roman officers were gentlemen."

"They are soldiers first," was the curt reply. "Even now, madame, some of my men pursue two suspicious characters who were following your carriage. They must have been guilty, or they would not have fled at the sight of us."

"Yet I have heard that the sight of papal soldiers is not always welcome," said Miss Perkins. "Even to the innocent."

The officer's lips tightened.

"Stand aside, madame. Corporal, inspect the carriage."

One of the men saluted and moved forward. With a shrug Miss Perkins stepped out of his way.

"A helpless woman must yield to bullies," she said. "Be assured, sir, that the British consul will hear of this."

"The British consul is some distance from here," said the officer. "I advise you not to be so free with your tongue, madame."

I thought this very good advice, and dared to poke Miss Perkins in the ribs, a gesture she ignored. I couldn't imagine why she was being so belligerent. Her speeches were provocative; yet my anxious ear seemed to detect an underlying note of uncertainty, as if she were worried about something other than the perilous situation in which we found ourselves.

The search of the carriage was quite thorough. The soldier even lifted the seats. Finally he descended and saluted again.

"No one, sir."

"I told you so," said Miss Perkins.

The clatter of approaching hoofbeats prevented the young officer's reply. He turned as several other soldiers rode up. It was not necessary for them to report failure; they had no prisoners. I heard Miss Perkins give a soft sigh.

The officer turned back to us.

"It is necessary, madame, for me to ask you the identity of the two men who rode with you."

"I have no idea," said Miss Perkins calmly. "Until you mentioned them, I was unaware that we had any such escort."

The officer was not stupid. When he asked the question, he watched me, not Miss Perkins. As he had hoped, my face betrayed my surprise at her answer.

"Indeed," he said softly, his eyes still on me. "Then I fear, madame, that you must come with us."

"Impossible," said Miss Perkins angrily. "We are already late. I do not wish to be delayed. It is dangerous to be out after dark on these roads."

"More dangerous than you realize. It is no use arguing with me, madame; you have no choice. Get into the carriage, or my men will assist you to do so." As she hesitated, sputtering angrily, he added in a soft voice, "I myself will assist mademoiselle. She has said nothing; perhaps she is less foolish than you, and is amenable to persuasion."

He began to dismount. I looked at Miss Perkins, making no attempt to conceal my alarm. She nodded at me, and said clearly,

"Perhaps, sir, you will send a messenger to Prince Tarconti, telling him that you are holding his granddaughter a prisoner and that she will, therefore, be delayed."

The officer's reaction would have been amusing if I had been in any mood to find humor in the situation. He stood motionless, one foot still in the stirrup. Then he finished dismounting and came toward us. His expression was no longer hostile.

"This young lady is the granddaughter of Prince Tarconti?"

"You may accompany us to the castle and see for yourself, if you doubt," said Miss Perkins.

"But, madame—why did you not say so at once?"

"You gave me no opportunity, sir," said Miss Perkins, now in control of the situation and enjoying it immensely.

"But then—you will accept my apologies, madame? My apologies, and my escort. The roads are dangerous; I would not have any relation of the Prince in danger through my negligence."

"Certainly, sir," said Miss Perkins graciously. "Would you care to join us in the carriage?"

The officer accepted the invitation with alacrity. His name, he informed us, was Captain Raoul De Merode. He was not a bad-looking man, though I thought his features too sharp and his dark eyes too close-set. When he removed his helmet his appearance was improved, for his face was softened by thick brown hair, scarcely darker in color than his tanned countenance. But I was not misled by his smile. He had been ready enough to be rude—perhaps worse than rude—to two unde-

fended women when he thought them unimportant. I knew
Miss Perkins was no more deceived by his present courtesy.
She had some hidden motive behind her actions, but what it
was I could not guess. I could only follow her lead, trusting to
her better understanding.

One thing she certainly wanted was information. Adjusting
her plume to its former cocky position, she leaned forward and
asked, "Who is this dangerous criminal you are pursuing,
Captain? A murderer—a brigand?"

"One might call him a brigand. Or a traitor. He is quite a
famous character in these parts; you would not have heard of
him, being strangers here. . . ."

His voice was as smooth as cream, his face guileless, but
suddenly I had a feeling that he and Miss Perkins were playing
a game of wits, in which I was only a spectator.

"If you would tell me his name I would know whether I had
heard of him," said Miss Perkins, showing all her teeth in a
broad smile.

"They call him Il Falcone," said De Merode. This time he
got no reaction from either of us. I had never heard the name,
and if Miss Perkins had, she was too clever to betray the fact.

"The Falcon," she translated, unnecessarily. "How very
romantic!"

"Childish," De Merode corrected, with a snap of his even
white teeth. "These people are like that—like spoiled children
who don't know what is good for them. But the games they
play are sinister, dangerous games, and one day they will be
punished as they deserve."

"By their fond *papa*," said Miss Perkins gently.

"His Holiness is the spiritual father of us all," the captain
said sternly. "He is also the ruler of these peasants. By
disobeying him they offend God twice over."

"How you must dislike your present service," said Miss
Perkins. "For a daring young officer to pursue ragged
peasants. . . ."

"A soldier does not question his orders. And, to be truthful,
it is not the peasants who give us trouble. Without the anarchists
to stir them up, they would be docile enough. The rebels are
men of the so-called educated classes, who have read too much
and thought too little."

His thin lips curved in a smile, as if he appreciated his own bon mot.

"Is this Falcon person an educated man, then?" Miss Perkins inquired.

"I don't know who he is, or what he is. If I did . . ."

I could contain my curiosity no longer. "Do you mean that this man's identity is unknown? How can that be?"

"He is an elusive creature," De Merode said. "And he commands a certain loyalty—though to use that word of the brigands who make up his guerrilla troops is to do them too much honor. We have caught and—er—questioned several of his men. They died without divulging his name."

Miss Perkins' face grew stern, and despite the warmth of the day I felt a sudden chill.

"They—died?" I repeated.

The captain's eyes turned to me.

"They were executed, mademoiselle. The price of treason is death—even in your country."

Under the concealment of her skirt Miss Perkins' fingers found my hand and pinched it warningly. I subsided; but there was no doubt in my mind that De Merode had tortured the unfortunate men who had fallen into his hands.

"You spoke of guerrilla troops," said Miss Perkins. "Does this man have his own army, then?"

De Merode's thin lips curled.

"They are not soldiers, they are bandits. They hide behind rocks and pick off my men as we ride. They rescue the prisoners we arrest—men who have spoken out against His Holiness or printed derogatory articles in their underground newspapers. They encourage the peasants to resist taxation, they plaster the walls with inflammatory posters. Wherever there is trouble in this province, you may be sure the Falcon is behind it."

"Tell us about him," said Miss Perkins persuasively.

"The man himself? I wish I could. He doesn't always wear a mask, and yet although he has been seen dozens of times, we have no consistent description of him. Sometimes his hair is gray, sometimes it is black; sometimes he is bearded, and then again he will appear with a patch over one eye and flowing moustaches. He is always well mounted. He rides like a centaur, and on at least three occasions he has escaped capture by outriding his pursuers. Like his own person, his horses change appearance." De Merode spoke as if he had forgotten we were present. He must have recapitulated this information again and again, in the hope of discovering some clue to the unknown's identity. "Despite his gray wigs, he must be young; no elderly man could accomplish the physical feats he had performed. A man who has access to horses of such quality, and so many of them, must be a man of wealth. And if the proclamations issued in his name are written by him, he is well educated."

"Young, rich, well educated," Miss Perkins repeated. "Forgive me, Captain, but you paint a portrait which is irresistible to impressionable females. Don't tell me that he is also handsome, or we will lose our hearts to your rebel."

"I don't know what he looks like," said De Merode sharply. "And I would advise you not to say such things; I know you are joking, but in these parts we have lost our sense of humor where Il Falcone is concerned. Anyone who is suspected of assisting him is subject to arrest. That is why—forgive me—I was suspicious of you. One of the men who was following you looked like a certain Antonio Cadorna, who is known to be one of the Falcon's lieutenants."

"But surely you don't suspect us now," said Miss Perkins.

"Hardly. There is no more loyal subject of His Holiness than Prince Tarconti."

"Indeed," said Miss Perkins thoughtfully.

She pinched me again when I started to speak. Thereafter she lapsed into silence, broken by ostentatious yawns. I decided she had learned what she wanted to know.

If the yawns were meant as hints, they had their effect. Soon the captain excused himself and resumed his place on horseback.

"Miss Perkins," I exclaimed, as soon as the carriage started up again. "What on earth has—"

"Sssh." Miss Perkins gestured toward the carriage window. One of the soldiers was riding close by. I didn't see how he could overhear, but Miss Perkins' grave face kept me silent. She said aloud, "Sit next to me, my dear, put your head on my shoulder and try to sleep. We still have some distance to go."

I obeyed. We could then converse in soft tones without being overheard.

"Are these ruffians really soldiers?" I whispered. "One of them was Irish—"

"They come from all the Catholic countries of Europe," Miss Perkins replied. "Pio Nono has enlisted an army of crusaders, as he calls them, so that he won't have to depend on the support of Napoleon, whom he hates. Some of them are honest fanatics, but many are only unemployed scoundrels who enjoy violence for its own sake. This young captain is one of the fanatics. He must be related to the Belgian De Merode who organized this army at the pope's request."

"And the Falcon—I have never heard such a wild tale! Why did you deny knowing Antonio?"

"Because he warned me this morning that he and his friend were wanted by the authorities. They accompanied us in order to protect us from ordinary bandits, of whom there are plenty, but I knew that if we should encounter a troop of soldiers, our guards would have to retreat. They were no match for so many armed men."

"But why should they bother to protect us?"

"I'm not sure," Miss Perkins said. "But the rebels hope for aid from England; they know they have English sympathy for their cause, since they are fighting for freedom. Your grandfather seems to be an important person; they may think you can influence him."

"He sounds like a man whom it would be hard to influence," I whispered. "A hard man."

"We must not judge him. . . . I liked Antonio. I convinced him that I sympathized with his cause, so he was ready to confide in me—up to a point. I do not think he was completely candid with me. He certainly did not tell me he was one of the Falcon's men."

"Then you had heard of this mysterious adventurer?"

"Oh, yes. I have followed the cause of Italian liberation with some interest. Il Falcone is not one of the well-known heroes of the movement; he seems to limit his activities to this province. Yet in his own way he is famous enough."

"He sounds very romantic," I murmured.

"Don't be misled by the romantic trappings," said Miss Perkins dryly. "If what I have heard of that young man is correct, he is a very shrewd person indeed. The mystery and the swashbuckling serve several practical purposes. They conceal the Falcon's identity and they appeal to the peasants. As the Captain said, the poorer classes are apathetic, and yet no revolution can hope to succeed without their support. By playing the role of an Italian Robin Hood, our friend the Falcon hopes to win them over. I don't envy him the job. The poor creatures are so downtrodden, so wretchedly poor, so uneducated that they are afraid to rebel."

"I think it is very exciting," I said.

Miss Perkins was silent for a long time. I began to think she had no more to say on the subject. Then she spoke in a voice I had heard from her once before.

"Exciting? Yes, I suppose it seems so to you. To me it is noble and terrible and pitiful. They are so young, these boys like Antonio, with their brave moustaches and their shining courage. . . . But I have seen so many noble causes fail, Francesca. The race is not always to the swift, and virtue does not always triumph. Not on this plane of existence, at any rate."

This time, when she fell silent, I had no wish to pursue the subject.

I fell asleep finally, but my sleep was troubled. I dreamed of a rider, a man on a big black horse, who fled before me as I tried to follow him. It was important to me that I catch up with him, but although I seemed to be running faster than any mortal could run, I made no progress for a long time. Then slowly I began to shorten the distance between us. I still could not see the rider's face. Finally I was close, so close that I had only to stretch out my hand to touch him. As I did so, the figures of man and horse shifted, and changed outline. It was no longer a rider I followed, it was a bird—a falcon, with a cruel hooked beak, made for killing, whose flight took it straight up into the sky out of my reach.

CHAPTER 3

When I awoke, the interior of the coach was dusky with twilight. It took me a moment to realize where I was. I was stiff and aching with the discomfort of travel, and my dreams had left me in a state of depression. Or perhaps it was not the dreams. I was now close to the climax I had dreaded for days—the meeting with the unknown people who would decide my fate.

The view from the window of the carriage was not one to lighten dismal spirits. The sky was still bright, but I could not see much of the blue heavens; towering hills, shrouded thickly by underbrush, closed in around us. There was no sign of human habitation, only trees and an occasional strange rock formation. The road, which had never been good, had deteriorated even more, and the carriage jolted badly. It was this rough motion that had awakened me, in spite of the fact that Miss Perkins had wedged me into my corner of the seat with a variety of bundles and bags.

"Ah, you are awake," she said, as I stretched my cramped limbs and yawned. "I was about to rouse you; we are almost there."

"Oh, dear," I said involuntarily. "I hope—I do hope Andrea is there to welcome us."

"Well, well, I daresay we will manage somehow even if he is not. What interesting country this is! Quite picturesque in its natural wildness. I noticed several tumuli—mounds, you know —that may be Etruscan tombs."

Her cheerful voice put me to shame. I sat up and tried to straighten my clothing and smooth my hair. It was impossible to see anything out the window now, for trees lined the narrow road so closely that their branches scraped the sides of the coach.

"Where is our escort?" I asked.

"They left us a few miles back—when Captain De Merode was satisfied that we were really going toward the Castello Tarconti. He promised, however, to call on us soon."

"He is a suspicious man, isn't he?"

"Yes, I fear he is not interested in your charming blue eyes."

"I'm glad of that! I have never met a man who gave me such an impression of cold cruelty."

Miss Perkins' reply was an anguished grunt, as the carriage lurched into and out of a deep hole. Then she let out an exclamation.

"Look, Francesca."

Through the window on her side of the coach I saw a view that made me catch my breath. The trees and shrubs had vanished; we were traveling along the edge of a deep ravine, with nothing between the chasm and the wheels of the carriage. The slope was not really sheer, and the rock face was broken by innumerable hardy plants and small trees that clung tenaciously to the rough surface, but it was an alarming sight. How far down the cleft descended I could not tell; the lower slopes were hidden in vegetation. The sun's rays, striking straight down through a break in the western hills, cast a strange and brilliant light on the upper levels of greenery, and I had an impression of uncontrolled, almost savage, exuberance—of vines and creepers and brambles twined in a tangled mass.

Then I realized that Miss Perkins had been looking, not at the ravine, but at what lay beyond, on the crest of the hill.

Only my nervous apprehension made Castello Tarconti appear ominous as it sprawled across the hilltop. With the rich light of evening gilding its stone and plastered walls, it really was quite an attractive sight; the outline of the towers and chimneys and quaint turrets against the evening sky had considerable charm. As I was to learn, it was even larger than it appeared—a jumble of wings and additions from different centuries, as multichambered as a beehive. The Princes of Tarconti had palaces in Rome and Florence, and a villa in the lake country, but this was their ancient family seat, and they

preferred the bucolic pleasures of the country to the pageantry
of cities and courts. So the original fortified tower had grown
into a great château, surrounded by extensive gardens and
provided with every modern comfort.

"A large place," remarked Miss Perkins, rubbing her nose
vigorously.

Neither of us spoke as the carriage strained up the last steep
approach and passed under a sculptured arch into a long avenue
lined with towering cypresses.

"At least the gate was open," I said, as we rolled along a
graveled avenue that was much smoother than the road.

Miss Perkins chuckled. "That's the spirit. We will regard the
open gate as a good omen."

The carriage emerged from the tree-bordered avenue into a
broad park with fountains and flower beds. The facade of the
house, immediately before us, was staggering in its sheer size.
At each end were towers topped by turreted spires. A great
staircase mounted superbly to a terrace whose balustrades were
adorned with flowering plants in pots—roses, orange trees,
gardenias and geraniums, all in bloom, perfuming the dying
day.

To my relief we did not stop before the monumental ascent; I
was sure I could never get up the steps without stumbling.
Instead the carriage turned to the left and passed through a
gateway into a walled courtyard.

With the assistance of the driver we descended from the
carriage and stood looking about us. The courtyard was clean
and well kept, its surface neatly paved with stone set in
geometrical patterns. Shrubs and flowers fringed the perimeter
and grew about the edges of a small fountain. The doorway of
the house was surmounted by a carved stone crest, presumably
that of the Tarcontis, but I could not make out its details, for it
was badly worn by time and weather.

Interesting as these features were, they were overshadowed by
the strange collection of objects that littered the courtyard.
Broken columns and headless statues stood all about; fragments
of sculpture were fastened to the stuccoed walls. Even the pots
that held the plants were of antique vintage. In a spot of honor
near the stairs, sheltered under an awning, was the strangest
object of all: a great stone box, carved all over with reliefs, and

surmounted by the semireclining statue of a man. He was raised
on his elbow, and his loose robe had fallen away from one
shoulder. In his hand he held a cup, lifted as if in salute. The
intimate gesture, the warm terra-cotta brown of the material,
and the stiff, almost sinister smile that curved the carved lips
gave the figure a frighteningly lifelike appearance. He seemed to
be looking straight into my eyes; and I felt as if we had been
greeted, if not welcomed, by the presiding genius of the place.

Miss Perkins let out a cry of delight. "It is Etruscan—I have
seen engravings like it. An Etruscan sarcophagus, no less!"

"Yes," I said. "No less, and no more. Do you suppose he is
the only one who is going to greet us?"

I was learning to speak coolly in order to hide my real
feelings—which, if I had displayed them, would have made me
turn my back on the Etruscan gentleman's unpleasant smile and
scramble back into the shelter of the carriage. I might have done
it—for Miss Perkins, abandoning me, had made straight for the
carved coffin and was peering at the reliefs on its side—had not
the door of the house swung open.

Our driver, who had been unloading our belongings, straightened and called out.

The person in the doorway came trotting down the stairs. It
was not my grandfather, or any of the other members of the
family, but a stout, elderly woman whose face was the color of
oak and who wore a peasant costume—a white apron brightly
embroidered, a laced bodice, and a high, fluttering cap. She
came straight to me, dropped a stiff curtsy, and broke into a
flood of speech. My Italian was improving, but I understood
only a word or two of her dialect—enough, however, to believe
that my arrival had been expected. Miss Perkins understood a
little more. She looked as relieved as I felt.

"It is not courteous, though," she remarked, as we followed
the servant into the house. "One of the family might have come
to welcome you."

"To be truthful, I am too tired to care," I replied—though
not quite truthfully. "If there is a room prepared for us, and
some water with which to wash off the stains of travel, I will be
content."

Tired and worried though I was, my first impression of the
place was not unpleasant. There was no Gothic gloom in the

entrance hall, with its broad flight of curving stairs, nor in the handsome drawing room into which the servant escorted us. It was a room of considerable grandeur, in the French style, with large windows and light-painted paneling. There were paintings on the ceilings and on the paneled walls, and fine carpets covered the floor. The furniture was upholstered in rich velvets and brocades. A pianoforte of rosewood and a great gilded harp stood in a bay formed by the curved windows. Before the fireplace, like a throne, stood a big red velvet chair. The servant indicated the person who was sitting in this chair and immediately withdrew, closing the door behind her.

For some time no one spoke. I realized that the person who had received us was deliberately postponing speech in order to increase our discomfort. We stood there weary and travel-strained, like beggars come to ask a favor of a great lady.

It was a lady who sat there, and I had no doubt as to her identity. I had seen women of her type often; she was as typically English as the old servant had been typically Italian. We were in the presence of Andrea's Aunt Rhoda.

She was extremely thin and, I thought, tall, although the fact that she was seated made it hard for me to ascertain her exact height. Her face was long and narrow, her hair gray. Her eyes were gray too, almost colorless. She wore a gown of heavy black wool, with the latest-style hoops puffing out her skirts. Her hands, holding a piece of needlework, were so long and thin and white they looked like naked bone.

"Good evening, Aunt Rhoda," I said.

The lady, who had been staring curiously at poor Miss Perkins, turned her icy gaze on me.

"I am not your aunt," she said. "You may address me as Miss Rhoda."

I bowed my head without replying. I was beginning to be angry. She might at least have the courtesy to ask us to take seats!

Like a subaltern making his report, Miss Perkins introduced herself and explained how she had come to be employed by Andrea. She concluded by asking after his health.

"My great-nephew is quite well," said Miss Rhoda. She sounded a little less hostile, as if she had decided that this strange-looking female did know how to behave, even if her bonnet was not à la mode. "Unfortunately he is not here at present. He is an irresponsible young man. It was only last week that we learned of your coming. I have had rooms prepared for you. You will be shown to them shortly. I detain you now because it is necessary that you should understand the basis on which you are to be received here."

"Then," I said, "perhaps you will allow Miss Perkins to sit down. We have had a tiring journey."

Miss Perkins made a deprecatory noise. Miss Rhoda ignored her; she looked at me, if not with warmth, with a little more interest than she had hitherto displayed.

"She may sit. You, miss, will remain standing before your elders. And I suggest that you do not adopt that tone with me. Your status is not so secure that you can afford to be insolent."

"What is my status?" I inquired. Miss Perkins did not sit down. She shifted a little closer to me, and I was conscious of her approval and support. I knew I could not allow this woman to bully me or she would continue to make my life miserable. After all, she had less standing in the family than I. She was not even related by blood.

"That of a dependent," said Miss Rhoda bluntly. "You have a certain moral claim, no doubt; but it was not that consideration that prompted the Prince to receive you here. I pointed out to him that his family honor demanded that you be rescued from the disgrace and infamy into which you would descend without his charity. Your father—"

"My late father," I interrupted.

I could say no more. I hoped that would be enough to remind Miss Rhoda of the newness of my bereavement, for I knew if she spoke disparagingly of my father I would cry. I did not want to cry in front of her. As I was to learn, she was hard, but she had a strong sense of propriety. She nodded grudgingly.

"We will say no more of that. I only mean to warn you that your grandfather does not wish to see you. Avoid him. Do not expect from him affection or kindness. He means to support you and shelter you, but that is all."

"I understand," I said. "And now—pardon me, but it has been a tiring day."

"Very well." Miss Rhoda rose. She was even taller than I had thought; she towered over me. "Follow me."

As she swept toward the door, I glanced at Miss Perkins, who shook her head warningly. We would talk later—and, I imagined, with considerable warmth. Now at least we were assured of shelter for the night, and both of us were too tired to think beyond that.

But the surprises of the day were not yet over. As we crossed the entrance hall, preceded by the dignified black form of Miss Rhoda, I heard footsteps on the stairs. Miss Rhoda stopped with a start and muttered something under her breath. She turned quickly, as if to speak to me; but there was no time. A man came into sight around the curve of the stairs. Preoccupied with his private thoughts, his eyes fixed on the steps, he did not catch sight of us until he was almost at the bottom of the flight. He recoiled, so suddenly he had to catch with both hands at the railing to keep from falling; and there he remained, staring until the whites showed around his pupils.

He was elderly, but not old and fragile, as I had expected him to be. His figure was still broad-shouldered and vigorous, his gray hair thick. His features were marked by pride and temper, with harsh lines scarring his brow and framing his thin-lipped mouth. Yet there was something in the expression of his eyes—some vague wildness—that did not fit the general impression of severity. At the time I attributed this expression to surprise, for he certainly was not expecting to see us.

After Miss Rhoda's warning, and what I already knew of him, I would not have been surprised to see him turn his back in silent disdain, or hear an angry tirade. Instead, incredulously, I beheld the stern face soften. It took on a look of radiant joy.

"Larthia!" he whispered. His voice was that of a man welcoming back to life a loved one whom he has given up for dead.

II

The room that had been prepared for me was not good enough, my grandfather declared. Only one of the grand state apartments would suffice. Miss Rhoda's furious objections were brushed aside, and only my own insistence that I would prefer this smaller, cozier room to the dust-enshrouded grandeur of the great bedchambers persuaded Grandfather to leave matters as they had been arranged, until the larger room could be properly cleaned and redecorated. Another advantage to the original arrangement, in my eyes, was that Miss Perkins' room was next to mine. They were not quite servants' rooms; not quite. But it was clear that Miss Rhoda was not anxious to see me comfortably settled. She expostulated loudly with Grandfather. It was grotesquely comical to see them shouting at one another, for she did not use a word of Italian, and he answered only in that language. Yet they seemed to understand each other well enough. Finally Miss Rhoda was shouted down. She withdrew, and the angry look she gave me suggested that she blamed me as much as she blamed the old gentleman for criticizing her arrangements.

My grandfather followed her out, after summoning an army of servants, who were ordered to supply us with every possible comfort. He was oddly formal, almost shy, with me. There were no warm embraces; he bent over my hand, touched my hair; yet the affectionate smiles and glances he gave me were a welcome I had not hoped to receive.

At last Miss Perkins and I were alone. She dropped into a chair, her booted feet extended, and I followed her example. For a few moments we stared at one another; there were so many things to say, I hardly knew where to begin. Finally she sat up and examined the contents of the tray that had been brought for us, and a smile of pleasure spread over her weary face.

"Tea. Good India tea, I believe. We have Miss Rhoda to thank for that, at any rate."

"We haven't much else to thank her for," I said. "Imagine, her daring to tell me that Grandfather didn't want to have me here. She must have known I would see him sooner or later, and that his affectionate behavior would prove her a liar."

"Precisely why I suspect she was not lying," said Miss Perkins, pouring tea. She took a sip and sighed luxuriously. "Our first decent tea since London."

"But nothing could have been fonder than his treatment," I protested.

"Yes. Therefore we must conclude that between the time he gave her her orders and the moment when he saw you something happened to change his attitude. I observed that he addressed you by a name that is not your own."

"Name?" I frowned. "I thought it was an Italian word for welcome, or a term of affection."

"My knowledge of the language is fairly good, and I assure you that is a word I have never heard. It was not your mother's name?"

"Her name was also Francesca."

"Most peculiar. I don't know why I am so sure it was a name, unless. . . . Yes; I am sure I have seen or read it, in that context. But where?"

"I don't know." I drank my tea and felt the warmth relax my taut nerves. "Nor do I really care. I am limp with relief, Miss Perkins. I confess I was very much afraid of how we would be received."

"I know you were." Miss Perkins smiled at me. "You controlled your anxiety very courageously. And see how well it has all turned out! Now I suggest we make use of those basins of hot water the servants have provided. The Prince said he would see us at dinner—supper, I suppose I should call it—and we mustn't be late."

I agreed; and Miss Perkins retired to her own room, where, I hoped, she would have time for a rest before we were called to supper. I was no longer tired. The joy of finding that I was welcomed and wanted had restored all my energy.

It was a pleasure to loosen my tight stays and remove my travel-stained clothing. While I was doing so, one of the maids came to unpack for me and help me with my toilette. By means of gestures I persuaded her to return later. I wanted to be alone for a while—to think, and to explore my new surroundings.

As I have intimated, the room was small and somewhat shabby. However, the bed linen had been aired, and the huge armoire had been cleaned out, ready for my clothing. I hung up my few dresses, trying to decide what to wear. I had little choice, for there had been no time to have mourning made before we left London, and only three of my gowns had been dyed a suitable black. Then, unable to contain my curiosity any longer, I went to the window.

The room was on the third floor of the castle, so the view was splendid. Daylight still lingered, though the light was gray and melancholy in the deeper recesses of the uneven ground. The distant vista was empty of life; only steep hills, completely covered by dark pines and tangled underbrush, lined the horizon. Nearer at hand the castle grounds descended in a series of terraced gardens to the valley below. On the left, half hidden behind a clump of trees, was a small building too ornate for a shed or a servant's cottage. The roofline was like that of a miniature castle, with battlements and a tiny tower. As I contemplated this structure, straining my eyes to make out details through the gathering darkness, a light sprang up in one of its windows. So the little house was inhabited. I wondered by whom. It was the sort of place that might have belonged to one of the faerie knights in the French romances.

A knock on the door signaled the return of the maid, so I tore myself from my musings and let the girl go to work, unpacking and helping me dress. Teresa—for that was her name—was a pretty child, with the coal-black hair of the Roman native and a rounded figure that would one day be fat. Now it nicely filled out the short-sleeved white blouse and laced bodice she wore with a brightly embroidered skirt and apron.

Before long Miss Perkins joined me, and fell into conversation with Teresa, hoping to improve her knowledge of the local dialect. Her painstakingly learned Italian was of limited use, since the accent and vocabulary were so different. Miss Perkins' attempts to imitate her speech reduced Teresa to red-faced gasps, as she tried to restrain her laughter. Miss Perkins soon put her at ease by chuckling loudly at her own errors, and the two of them had quite a merry time.

Teresa was an efficient maid, as I would have expected a servant trained by Miss Rhoda to be. She would not allow me to do anything for myself, even taking the brush gently from my hands when I started to do my hair. As she brushed, she murmured, *"Bella—molto bella . . ."* and I smiled at her, for I recognized that word. When I indicated that the brushing had gone on long enough and started to pin my hair up, she objected, and indicated, by gestures, that I should allow it to flow loose down my back. I shook my head. I had not worn it so casually since I was a child.

Miss Perkins, who had followed the discussion with interest, said, "Do as she says, Francesca. She would not make such a suggestion on purely aesthetic grounds; either it is the local style, or it has been requested by someone who has a right to do so.''

"Do you think Grandfather—?"

"We will soon find out," said Miss Perkins, for Teresa was indicating that we should follow her.

We would surely have gotten lost without a guide. The room into which Teresa finally ushered us was not the formal parlor we had seen before, but a smaller, more pleasant chamber on the ground floor. It had French doors that stood wide open, admitting the perfumed breeze from the gardens. Darkness was almost complete, but the room was brilliantly lighted with dozens of wax candles. Two men occupied chairs on either side of a low table, where a chessboard was set out.

My grandfather rose quickly to his feet as we entered. His clothing was that of an earlier, more colorful era—knee breeches of brown velvet and a matching coat trimmed with gold braid. The hand he extended to me twinkled with jewels.

He frowned slightly at the sight of my somber bombazine dress with its simple white lace collar. My only ornament was a mourning brooch of jet with a lock of hair under glass. Father had had the brooch made years before, with Mother's hair. I had prized off the back and added one of his brown curls.

Grandfather's frown turned to a smile as he touched my hair, and I knew it had been by his orders that I was wearing it loose. His hand resting gently on my shoulder, he turned me to face the other man.

He had not risen from his chair. In the first moment of seeing him I had been misled by his curling fair hair; but my start of joyful recognition was premature. A second glance told me that this was not Andrea after all. It must be Stefano, his brother; the resemblance between the two could only be that of close kinship. Stefano's features were like his brother's, but his face was thinner and not so tanned. His eyes had the same sapphire sparkle, but their expression lacked Andrea's cheerful candor. His dress was quietly fashionable; the stark white-and-black evening garb contrasted with Grandfather's more flamboyant suit. He was balancing a slim black stick between his hands, and as I returned his critical stare with interest he lowered this to the floor and started to rise.

Then I realized the truth, and felt my cheeks turn warm with embarrassment. He was lame. Without the stick he would not have been able to stand up, and even with its aid he leaned noticeably to one side.

During the slow and obviously painful movement his eyes did not leave my face. Now the corners of his narrow lips curved slightly. I had the ridiculous impression that he had deliberately delayed rising from his chair so that I would have time to misjudge him, and then feel guilty for doing so.

When Grandfather introduced us, I found that my tentative identification had been correct. Stefano greeted Miss Perkins in English, and with perfect courtesy. Then he turned a satirical eye upon me.

"My dear Miss Perkins, are you sure you and Andrea found the right Miss Fairbourn? This infant doesn't look old enough to be out of the schoolroom. What on earth am I to call her? I don't know her well enough to use a pet name, and the more formal mode of address—"

"Francesca will do nicely," I interrupted. I had felt sorry for him when I saw his infirmity, but his sarcastic manner of speaking about me, as if I were the infant he had called me, irritated me very much.

His thin smile broadened.

"I see you have a mind of your own—and a tongue to go with it. But pray be seated, Francesca, and you too, Miss Perkins. There are several matters to be explained before you meet the rest of the family. From now on regard me merely as a voice. I am here to translate; the sentiments I express will be those of his Excellency. He understands English—better, I sometimes think, than any of us realize. . . ."

He turned his sardonic smile on the old gentleman, who glowered back at him without making the slightest indication that he had comprehended; but I rather thought that he did understand quite well.

"In any event," Stefano went on, "he refuses to speak the language. It is his way of annoying Miss Rhoda. So, I am here. And I must first tell you that initially he was opposed to your coming. When your father's letter arrived he was unbearable for several days—muttering curses like a stage Shylock. It was Andrea who persuaded him to behave sensibly. Andrea is the favorite here; Andrea can persuade him to do almost anything. It is to your advantage, Francesca, to keep on the good side of Andrea.''

"I only wish I could," I replied. "I had hoped he would be here."

"Oh, he has gone off on some jaunt or other," Stefano replied, with a curl of his lip. "He is quite a gay blade, my handsome, athletic brother. . . . But he was here long enough to tell us of the unfortunate situation in which he discovered you."

The tone and the implication were cruel. I felt tears of shame and vexation rise to my eyes. Before they could spill over and disgrace me completely, Grandfather burst into a torrent of agitated Italian. He even went so far as to shake a fist under his grandson's nose. Stefano laughed.

"The Prince says I must apologize. He also remarks that Andrea's conduct was worthy of his name. You see how it is? By murdering a man, my brother has raised himself in our grandfather's esteem. But''—as the old man began sputtering again—"perhaps we should abandon that subject. Andrea, in short, insisted that you could not be abandoned; and the Prince agreed that you might come here so long as you kept out of his way. Is it clear now to whom you owe your reception?"

I nodded and exchanged a meaningful glance with Miss Perkins, who had been listening as interestedly as I. She had been quite right about Miss Rhoda; however antagonistic the woman might be, she would not have risked a direct lie. Again Andrea had been my good agent. It was like his modesty to have given so much of the credit to his brother.

Stefano continued to watch me with the same fixed smile. His mouth was a contradiction; the lower lip was full, a sign of passion and sensuality, while the upper lip was so narrowly cut as to be almost invisible. If the laws of physiognomy were true, his was a nature in which the emotions warred with the intellect—and his sour, cynical look showed that resentment had overcome both his intellect and his other emotions.

"Very well," he said, after a moment or two. "The next question is this: Why did our esteemed ancestor change his attitude toward you? For I am to inform you that you are the new favorite. If Andrea doesn't take care, you will supersede him. I am myself in the dark as to this. Do you have any ideas?"

I said nothing, and after a moment the keen blue eyes moved from me to Miss Perkins. She shook her head.

"Hmmm," said Stefano. "The Prince refuses to explain himself. He always does. Well, then, I am to inform you that you are his dear granddaughter and the beloved daughter of the house. Pleasant, is it not? But I fear you must face some hostility, Francesca. Miss Rhoda is not well disposed toward you. She dislikes almost everyone, and she was very jealous of your grandmother, the Prince's second wife. Then there is Galiana—"

Here he was again interrupted by Grandfather, who had been listening with increasing signs of impatience. I had suspected that we were getting quite a few of Stefano's personal opinions, in spite of his claim to be merely a translator. I thought the Prince said much the same. Stefano continued to smile.

"I am relieved of my duties," he said, with mock distress. "We are to go in to the others now. What?" He turned to the Prince. "Oh, yes, I am to assure you of his affection; you are to come to him with any difficulties, and you are to tell him that you understand what I have told you."

I turned to the old gentleman, who was leaning forward in his chair watching me with affectionate anxiety. Words seemed too flat—especially English words—so I smiled and put my hand on his. He clasped it tightly, then raised it to his lips.

"A touching moment," said the dry voice I had already learned to dislike.

A footman appeared out of nowhere, as a good servant should, and opened the door. I cast an appealing glance at Miss Perkins. Imagine my surprise when I saw that Stefano was offering her his arm in a most gentlemanlike fashion. He walked with a perceptible limp, but more nimbly than I had expected, though he leaned heavily on his cane.

The hall was very long, lighted by candles set in heavy silver sconces. Grandfather chatted cheerfully, smiling down at me and patting my hand as we walked side by side. Stefano and Miss Perkins were behind us. They were speaking, but I was unable to overhear them.

At least Stefano had been courteous to Miss Perkins. She had been unusually silent during the interview; but then she had not been given a chance to speak. I was somewhat surprised that no one had questioned her about the trip and the arrangements Andrea had made with her. Well, but we were here, safe and sound; there was no need to go into unnecessary detail.

I was occupied with such speculations as we walked the length of the long, quiet hall, my hand on Grandfather's arm. With his affection to support me I was not afraid of meeting the other residents of the castle, but if Miss Rhoda was an example of what I had to expect I was not looking forward to the others.

Then the footman opened a pair of doors at the far end of the corridor, and stood back. There were several people in the great drawing room. Miss Rhoda I knew. The other two were strangers. My eyes fixed themselves on one of them. She was the most beautiful girl I had ever seen.

CHAPTER 4

Girls know when they are pretty. Mirrors may lie, but the eyes of young men do not, and even in our unworldly school atmosphere we had not been totally deprived of masculine company. Brothers, fathers, and uncles had been allowed to visit; the Misses Smith had entertained us with occasional evening soirees at which gentlemen of under thirty might appear; even in church, when our minds ought to have been on higher things, we had not been unmindful of the young men who took advantage of those occasions to survey the Misses Smith's students.

I knew I was not ugly. My complexion was the favored pink and white, my features were regular, my eyes blue. I also knew that my flaxen hair would be appreciated in a country where the people are predominantly brunette. I was, as my cousin had mockingly observed, of small stature. I had no reason to become stout. I must confess that I had a fairly good opinion of myself when I walked into the drawing room that night.

But this girl! A mass of coal-black hair, shining in the candlelight; great black eyes, soft as velvet, framed by feathery lashes and brows that might have been shaped by the brush of a master painter; a mouth. . . . Well, in my jealousy I thought her mouth a little too small, a little petulant. But it was a perfectly shaped Cupid's bow, and the features I have not mentioned were no less exquisite.

As we entered, she moved her embroidery frame out of the way and rose. Her height and her figure were as perfect as her face. She bent in a curtsy that displayed the grace of her movements and the abundance of her flowing locks.

The older ladies had to be presented first. I was forced to turn my eyes away from the girl, but I was conscious of every move she made.

Miss Rhoda had not risen in deference to my grandfather's rank. From her expression it was clear that nothing less than the presence of royalty—British royalty—would have brought her to her feet. She wore a magnificent gown of plum-colored velvet with skirts so wide they completely hid the chair in which she was sitting, giving her a startling appearance of sitting on air. A Gorgon would have looked less grim.

The other elderly lady's gentle face was in pleasing contrast to Miss Rhoda's. She wore mourning that was extreme even by the severe standards of her class. Not a touch of white or color, not even the deepest purple, lightened the somber black of her gown. Her jewels—bracelets, rings, and a collarlike necklace—were of jet beads. From her widow's cap hung a heavy black veil that framed her magnificent pure-white hair. Her face was almost as pale as her pearly hair, without a trace of color in lips or cheeks, but her eyes, though sunken, were as bright and black as the jet beads. She was a striking study in moonlight and shadow, and I could see that once she must have been as lovely as the dark girl—her daughter, if resemblance was any clue.

So fascinated was I by this study of past and present beauty that I was slow in hearing the name by which the two were introduced. When I realized what Grandfather had said, I started. The lady of pearl and jet smiled faintly.

"It is a pleasure to meet you, signorina," she murmured.

"Contessa." I made a rather clumsy curtsy and turned to acknowledge the introduction of her daughter. "Contessa. . . ."

I could not say the name. I knew it well from my father's stories of the past. Count Fosilini, the pursuer of my mother, the cruel rival of my father. . . . Could these two be his widow and daughter? The two families had been friendly, distantly connected, if I remembered correctly. This was a shock I had not expected in all my worst forebodings.

Then I told myself firmly that I was being foolish. The old rivalry was far in the past. Neither of the Fosilini ladies showed any signs of recalling it. The younger countess smiled in a particularly friendly manner and indicated a chair near her own, which I took. She did not speak at first; but after the others had begun to converse, she leaned toward me and said softly in French,

"I hope you will be happy here, Mademoiselle Fairbourn. It will be a pleasure for me to have a young lady of my own age to talk to."

Her French was not very good, but her accent was adorable. I thought she seemed shy. I was soon to learn that this impression was erroneous, and that the young lady was far from subdued when her mother was not present.

"You are very kind," I said, returning her smile. "If we are to be friends, as I hope, you must call me Francesca."

"Ah, a good Italian name! Mine is Galiana. It was the name of a famous beauty of olden days, a lady so lovely that her native town went to war to keep her safe from the evil man who wanted to marry her against her will."

Her tone was so complacent, and her pretty face so smug as she told this little anecdote, that I was forced to laugh. I laughed too loudly; Miss Rhoda broke off her interrogation of Miss Perkins and stared balefully at me. I lowered my voice.

"How nicely you embroider," I said admiringly, leaning forward to examine the square of ivory satin on which Galiana was working a design of flowers in bright silk thread.

"Thank you. My mother has tried to teach me, but I will never embroider as well as she. That is the second altar cloth she is making for the chapel."

Then I realized that the Contessa had been watching us. She smiled sweetly as I looked at her, and turned her embroidery frame so that I could see what she was doing. The work was certainly marvelous. The background was a rich crimson velvet, on which her ingenious fingers had fashioned little figures of saints and prophets. Their robes were done in gold thread, with such intricate stitchery that the folds of the drapery looked three-dimensional. Tiny pearls and brilliants adorned the crowns of the female saints, and a border of Latin verse surrounded the whole.

"It is lovely," I said respectfully. The Contessa inclined her head but did not reply, and I was groping wildly for some means of continuing the conversation when the door opened and a servant announced that the meal was served.

Just at that moment, when I ought to have been relaxing and appreciating the fact that still another apprehension had proved groundless, I was conscious of a strange sensation. It was almost physical in its intensity, like an insect sting squarely between my shoulder blades. I had risen; now I turned, unconsciously defensive, and met the intent stare of a woman who had appeared as if by magic behind the chairs on which Galiana and I had been sitting.

She was short and squat, with a broad peasant face. Her features were coarse and unprepossessing; they were rendered even less attractive by the abundance of hair distributed about her countenance. The hair on her head was as coarse as black wire and as lusterless as the fur of a dead animal. Her eyebrows were half an inch thick; they grew together in a single bar and were paralleled by a distinct moustache. She was clad all in black, of a peculiarly rusty appearance, and her expression, as she stared at me . . .

I decided I must have been mistaken about her inimical look. As soon as I turned, her black eyes lowered submissively. Moving with a stealth surprising in so large a woman, she picked up the Contessa's embroidery frame and workbag. She moved bent over at the waist, as if in a perpetual state of obeisance, and the Contessa paid her no heed whatever. No one else seemed to see anything out of the way, either, except for Miss Perkins, who was staring at the woman as openly as I was.

Grandfather had offered his arm to the Contessa, while Stefano escorted his aunt. That left Galiana and me and Miss Perkins to go in together. As we followed the others, I whispered to Galiana, "Who is that woman?"

"What woman?" said Galiana.

"The one in black, who took your mother's work for her."

"Oh, Bianca," said Galiana indifferently. "She is the Contessa's maid."

"That unsightly creature?" Miss Perkins exclaimed. "Not that I mean to be unkind, but—"

"Oh, she is ugly, very ugly," Galiana said cheerfully. "She is also dumb, and very stupid. But she adores my mother; she would do anything for her."

"One of the Contessa's charities?" said Miss Perkins. "How

good it is of her to protect someone whom no one else would employ."

"My mother is a saint," Galiana said seriously. "She would have entered a convent after Father's death, if it had not been for me. As it is, she works endlessly for the Church. Her charities—"

But here she was forced to stop. We had entered the dining salon and were shown to our places.

The main meal of the day was in the early afternoon, so this was supposedly only a slight repast before retiring. As course followed formal course, I began to think that if this was a sample of a light meal, I should soon become plump. Fish, soup, game, poultry, salads of all kinds, fruit, elaborate sweets. . . . We were waited on by half a dozen footmen and served a different wine with each course.

I sat next to Grandfather, who kept urging me to eat. Conversation was general and rather stilted because of the presence of the servants; but there was one lively exchange, when Miss Perkins, in response to a question about our journey, described our encounter with Captain De Merode. She censored the account considerably, avoiding any mention of acquaintance with the two "brigands" whom the Captain had been pursuing, but even in its abridged version the story produced shocked exclamations from the audience. Grandfather was indignant until I explained that the Captain had been quite courteous after he learned who I was.

"Ah," Grandfather said, somewhat mollified. "Then it is excusable. I will speak to the Captain, all the same."

"He is a man of good family, devoted to His Holiness," said the Contessa, who had scarcely spoken up to that time. "His zeal is excusable—admirable, even—your Excellency."

Miss Rhoda demanded a translation of the last two speeches. That is how I know what was said. When Stefano had obliged, Miss Rhoda shook her head.

"Such rudeness could never happen in England," she said. "Do tell me, Miss Perkins, what is being worn at court these days."

"That should be a safe topic," said Stefano. "We don't discuss serious matters at table, do we, Aunt? Only dull banalities. I feel sure Miss Perkins can hardly wait to describe the latest fashions.''

Miss Perkins did her best, but this was one topic on which she was not well informed. The rest of the meal passed in comparative silence, and finally we returned to the drawing room.

I could hardly wait to be alone with Miss Perkins, to talk over these new people and experiences. Before long, however, the fatigues of the day caught up with me. A yawn which I was unable to suppress drew Grandfather's attention, and he immediately dismissed us. The military term is appropriate; it was clear that this household was run on patriarchal terms. Swaying with weariness as I was, I was amused to observe the nightly ritual, as each person stood before the Prince to bid him good night. The ladies curtsied and Stefano bowed formally. Grandfather acknowledged these gestures with as much condescension as a reigning monarch might have exhibited; but after I had curtsied he took me by the shoulders and kissed me gently on the brow.

Teresa was waiting for me when I reached my room, and I was glad of her help. I could barely keep my eyes open long enough to undress, and I slept instantly, without dreaming.

I always slept well in that cozy little room, and it was as well that I did, for the next days were so busy and so full of new impressions that I needed all my strength to keep up with the plans Grandfather made for me. He had the energy of a young man and the arrogance of an emperor.

He was also a busy man. The life of a leisured dilettante was not to his taste, and much of his wealth came from various business enterprises which he himself controlled. But he spent considerable time on my concerns. First and foremost was the refurbishing of the apartment he had selected for me. It had been my mother's, and since it had not been touched since the day of her elopement, considerable work was necessary to make it habitable. The rooms—bedroom, salon, and several smaller chambers—were to be completely redecorated. Servants were sent riding posthaste to Urbino and Parezzo carrying the Prince's instructions to linen drapers, cabinetmakers, and painters; and the following weeks were enlivened by the arrival of huge wagons bringing the new furnishings. In the meantime servants cleaned, painted, plastered; a wispy-looking little man arrived from Florence to restore the ceiling paintings, which had been damaged by rainwater.

I also had to have an entire new wardrobe. My grandfather's vigorous criticism of my drab clothing required no translation. Among the battalions of servants—who were tucked away when not required, somewhere in the sprawling attics like unused tools—was a resident seamstress who was immediately set to work. It was during this long and, I must confess, most enjoyable procedure that I became better acquainted with Galiana.

I couldn't help liking her. Her dark, somber beauty did not match her personality, which was as cheerful and gay as she was dark. We communicated in an odd mixture of languages, mostly French, although she did know a few words of English and helped me to improve my Italian.

"From the first I knew we should be friends," she told me, in her prettily accented French. "You cannot know how good it is to have another girl here. Always when I come I am bored, bored!"

"Then you and your mother don't live here?" I asked.

We were rummaging among the fabrics in a storeroom, trying to select something for a morning gown. I held up a length of rather faded lilac print.

"No, no," Galiana exclaimed. "That, it is for housemaids, peasants." She snatched the fabric from my hands and threw it on the floor with a theatrical gesture of disgust. "Live here? No, we have a house over the mountain; but we come here often to stay, since our roof leaks—is that the word?"

"That is the word," I agreed, smiling. "But why don't you have the roof mended?"

Galiana opened her big black eyes even wider.

"But there is no money. My father was not a sensible man. He spent it all, all. He was your mother's lover, you know."

I would have remonstrated with her regarding this term, but I realized that Galiana did not know its implications, in English or in French. So I said nothing, and she went rattling on.

"I am glad your mother did not marry him, for then I would

not be here, eh? Perhaps I would have been you! Ah, but that is
funny, is it not? I would be you, and you—you would not
exist.''

The oddest little chill ran through me when she said that. For
a moment I almost fancied that the merry black eyes had lost
their sparkle and were regarding me with cold dislike.

But the next moment she was laughing heartily as she draped
herself in a piece of heavy gold brocade, and stalked up and
down the chamber pretending to be Cleopatra.

The castle was a vast storehouse of treasures, including
enough fabric to clothe an entire boarding school, but Galiana
declared that most of it was too old-fashioned, or too worn, or
inadequate in some other way. So another messenger was sent
off to merchants in Florence. Of course I should not have
expected to wear colors for another year; but I told myself it
would not hurt to have the fabric on hand. If Grandfather should
insist that I disobey society's rules about mourning—which he
was quite capable of doing, since he preferred to ignore my poor
dear father's very existence—then filial duty would require that
I obey.

I don't like to think how shallow and vain I was at that age. In
fact, when I look back on my behavior during those first weeks
in Italy, I am heartily ashamed of myself. My painful experiences ought to have taught me that the vanities of this world are
not to be relied upon, but I did not want to think about the past.
All the happy memories of my father had been overshadowed by
the final revelations, as a spreading ink stain can spoil a pretty
gown. There were moments when—I confess it with shame—I
thought of him almost with hatred. It would have been better for
my character if I had been received by Grandfather as he had
originally intended to receive me; then I would have had to win
his affection with patience and good behavior. But he gave me
his love and I accepted it complacently—as we always accept
things we have not earned.

I am glad to say I had enough decency to be concerned about
Miss Perkins. It was not selfishness that prompted my interest in
her—not entirely—for by then I had smugly decided that I
needed no companion. Was I not the spoiled darling of a
wealthy prince? I had a friend of my own age in Galiana; and if
there was some patronage in my attitude toward the girl, I wasn't

aware of it. I thought of myself as being very kind. . . . Oh, dear. It is so depressing to look back on one's past failures.

At any rate, I saw little of Miss Perkins in the days immediately following our arrival. I wasn't worried about her, for I knew she could amuse and entertain herself anywhere; if she went to Purgatory instead of Heaven, she would poke her head into all the dark corners and interrogate the attendant imps about the various methods of torture. Of course we met at meals, but I did not speak to her at length until one bright afternoon a week or so after we arrived. Galiana was with her mother, who spent many hours in her room reading and meditating and praying. I went out into the courtyard looking for amusement, and there I found Miss Perkins seated on a fallen column. Her hands rested on her knees and she was staring solemnly at the great sarcophagus with its statue of a reclining Etruscan.

"Did you know that his Excellency your grandfather excavated that object himself?" she demanded, motioning for me to take a seat beside her. "Your cousin the Count informs me that there is an entire Etruscan cemetery not far from here. I do hope I shall have time to see it, and your grandfather's collection of treasures, before I leave."

"Leave?" I stared at her. "But, Miss Perkins—"

"Well, my dear, I was hired to bring you here and I have done it," said Miss Perkins.

She turned her cheerful smile on me. I was conscious, all at once, of paler streaks in her iron-gray hair, and of the deep lines in her face. Impulsively I threw my arms around her.

"Miss Perkins, please stay. There is a great deal more for you to do. I need you. Please don't leave me alone."

"But, Francesca, you are not alone. You have a whole new family, and you are the pet. Why do you need me?"

"I don't know," I mumbled. "That is—I know I have been very fortunate. But I would like you to stay. Unless you have duties, connections, in England—"

"No, I am quite independent. However—"

"Oh, splendid. I will ask Grandfather now."

"Wait—Francesca, don't be so impetuous—"

I paid no attention. Leaving her staring after me, I ran up the steps and into the house. I did have the courtesy to knock before

I entered the library; and the gruffness of my grandfather's voice as he shouted "*Avanti!*" made me think that perhaps I ought to have waited. But it was too late to retreat now; I opened the door.

As soon as he saw me, Grandfather's scowl turned into a beaming smile. Stefano, who was seated beside the desk, did not look so pleased. He lifted his black cane in a mocking salute.

"How charming," he exclaimed, as I stood with Grandfather's arm around me. "Curls flying, frills and ribbons fluttering, the fresh young face flushed. . . . We must have your portrait taken in just that pose, Cousin."

Grandfather's right hand moved in one of those eloquent Italian gestures, and Stefano subsided, with a vulgar wink at me.

The relationship between my cousin and my grandfather was a curious one. Grandfather regarded Stefano with a mixture of respect and contempt—respect for his cool intelligence, contempt for his physical weakness. There were times when his infirmity troubled Stefano a great deal, and then he kept to his own rooms, not even appearing for meals. At other times he served as a useful adviser to Grandfather in business matters. The two of them spent long hours in the library. The discussions were not always amicable; one could often hear voices raised in anger, even through the heavy carved door. Voices, did I say? No; Grandfather was the only one who shouted. Stefano never lost his temper, he only incited other people to lose theirs.

I was determined not to let him incite me, so I ignored the wink and plunged into my speech. I knew some Italian by then, but in my excitement I forgot what little I knew. Grandfather always seemed to understand me anyway.

"It is about Miss Perkins," I exclaimed. "I would like her to stay here. Couldn't she be my governess or companion, or something like that?"

For once Grandfather didn't understand. He turned a bewildered look on Stefano, who was watching me with his familiar narrow smile. He translated what I had said and added, in English, "What a high-handed young person you are, Francesca. It is in your blood, I suppose. Interesting, how quickly personality can adjust to changes in fortune."

He would have gone on with more sly digs at me if Grandfather had not waved him to silence.

"You may have anything you wish, child," he said. "If you want her to stay, it is settled."

"Just a minute," said Stefano. "You can't dispose of a lady's person so easily. Suppose Miss Perkins doesn't want to stay."

"Oh, she does," I said eagerly. "She told me she had no relatives in England and she is fascinated by Italy—especially by Grandfather's antiquities. Couldn't she help you with that, Grandfather? *La vostra collezione—antichità*—er—"

"*Sì, sì, carissima.* She will be very useful."

"*Grazie!*" I stood on tiptoe and kissed his cheek.

He patted me on the head. Courteous as he was, I could see he was anxious to get back to his interrupted work. Before I could take my leave, Stefano spoke again.

"One more question, Cousin. Why are you so anxious to have Miss Perkins remain? She can't be of any use to you."

"It is just barely conceivable that I might be of use to her," I replied sharply. "She is not young. I don't suppose she is rich—"

"Ah, it is sheer benevolence on your part, then." Stefano nodded. "What a beautiful thing to see."

That was the day when I realized how thoroughly I disliked my cousin Stefano.

It was also the day when we received a formal call from Captain De Merode. I had almost forgotten about him; and when he was announced, I was fool enough to be flattered. He must be interested in me after all, I thought.

We ladies were sitting in the main drawing room—the Salon of the Sybils, as it was called, from the paintings that covered the ceiling. This was a penance I paid daily, unless I could think of some excuse for not joining in the teatime ritual—a ritual long established and insisted upon by Miss Rhoda. I must say that she had trained the servants to prepare the beverage and its accompaniments quite nicely, and I found the delicious little sandwiches and cakes some compensation for the dull conversation. I don't know what moved the Contessa to join us; it couldn't have been the food, for she ate like a bird. She displayed no especial warmth toward Miss Rhoda, only her usual gentle courtesy, and since she spoke no English and Miss

Rhoda no Italian, conversation between them was severely limited. Galiana told me that teatime was much less dull since Miss Perkins had arrived, for that indomitable lady did her best to converse with everyone, translating when possible, and carrying on a cheerful monologue when no one else spoke. She found it heavy going, however; Galiana was too intimidated by her mother to risk a remark often.

Usually the gentlemen did not join us for tea, but on this particular afternoon Grandfather and Stefano were both present. The latter, seated next to Miss Perkins, was discussing antiquities with her, and Grandfather was giving me an Italian lesson, to our mutual amusement, when the Captain was announced.

Grandfather rose. He was usually punctilious about such courtesies, but I could see that he was honestly pleased to see the young man. De Merode was in full dress uniform, and looked quite handsome. His spurs, sword hilt, and decorations shone brilliantly; his boots had been polished to a mirror finish, and his tall helmet, which he held under one arm, had a lovely white egret plume.

He bowed over the hand of each lady, leaving mine till last. There was design in that, I thought, and when his warm lips lingered on my fingers, instead of brushing the air above them, I was sure.

Grandfather—who could speak adequate French when he had to—immediately took De Merode to task for his rudeness, but his smiling manner showed that he was prepared to forgive and forget.

"My dear Prince—have pity!" De Merode covered his eyes with his hand in mock repentance. "Credit me only with too much zeal in my profession. I have come to beg forgiveness. I would have come earlier, but we have been on duty day and night this past week."

"Ah." Grandfather leaned forward, forgetting his mock displeasure in his curiosity. "Then the tales I hear are correct? That wretched mountebank has appeared again?"

"You mustn't refer to our hero so rudely, Prince." De Merode smiled meaningfully at me. "I believe the ladies find him very romantic."

"Oh, certainly we do," Galiana exclaimed. "I am sure he is

young and handsome; aren't you, Francesca? I wish I could see him!''

''Galiana.'' The poor girl jumped at the sound of her mother's soft voice. The Contessa went on, ''I know you speak in jest, but on this subject mockery is profane. This wretched man is defying not only the law of man but God's vicar on earth. You should pray for his soul and deplore his actions.''

''Yes, Mama,'' Galiana muttered, lowering her eyes.

''What has he done now?'' I asked.

''Rescued his printing press,'' said the Captain.

I had been expecting some tale of human interest—a poor peasant freed of his taxes, a bandit snatched from prison—and this anticlimax, I regret to say, struck me as very funny. I began to laugh, and after a moment Galiana joined me. The Captain frowned.

''The press is more important than you realize,'' he said. ''An informer—that is to say, a patriotic peasant—gave us information which enabled us to locate the abandoned hut in which the machine was concealed. Unfortunately we arrived too late. Oh, the press had been there, the evidence was unmistakable, but that demon had somehow gotten wind of our intentions and anticipated us.''

''But most of the peasants can't read,'' Grandfather protested. ''How stupid these revolutionaries are, to waste print on such animals.''

Stefano coughed gently. All eyes turned toward him. Sitting at ease, dressed with his usual severe elegance, his only sign of disability was his black cane.

''The gentry can read. It is this class, one supposes, that your bird of prey wishes to convert.''

''Precisely,'' De Merode agreed grudgingly. ''Besides, it is not only words he prints. I suppose, your Excellency, that your people don't want to show you this inflammatory nonsense, but you ought to know what your peasants are seeing.'' With a flourish he pulled a scroll of paper from the breast of his tunic and unrolled it.

It was a drawing. Crudely done, but immediately apparent to the meanest intelligence, it showed a figure dressed in flowing robes and a papal tiara. One hand was raised in blessing under a celestial glory (in the shape of a fat cloud). But the other hand was employed in snatching a loaf of bread from the hand of a miserable-looking peasant. A dead or dying child lay at the feet of this man; beside him crouched a woman, menaced by a leering figure in the same uniform Captain De Merode wore with such distinction.

Someone, I did not see who, gasped sharply. My grandfather's face turned purple with rage; he snatched at the drawing.

"Wait," I said, putting out my hand. "May I see it, Captain? I know something of drawing, and I think. . . . Yes; this sketch is a piece of deception in itself. Its first impression is one of crude vigor, effective but unsophisticated. Yet this is not the drawing of a man untrained in art. The perspective, and the anatomy of the figures, is quite good."

I had forgotten myself in my interest and had spoken in English. Stefano tapped his stick on the floor and gave me a mocking smile.

"Clever," he said condescendingly. "But I fear your analysis doesn't help the Captain. This need not be a masterpiece from the hand of the Falcon himself. He numbers educated men among his followers."

He then proceeded to translate my comment. The only one who seemed to be impressed or interested was Galiana, who looked at me admiringly. The Captain merely nodded.

"As the Count has said, this tells us nothing."

"I fail to see, however," said Stefano, "why you brought it here. Surely my grandfather needs no urging in his dedication to the cause?"

"But, my dear Count, how can you even mention such a thing?" De Merode's eyes widened. "I desire only to be of service to his Excellency."

I doubted that, and so, from his skeptical expression, did Stefano. What the Captain's real motive was I could not be sure, but the result was disastrous. Grandfather was very upset. Before his anger could subside, De Merode introduced another sensitive topic.

"I had hoped to greet Count Andrea," he said, accepting a sandwich from a tray that was offered to him. "Where is he?"

"You know Andrea," Stefano said casually. "Always the gadfly. Actually, he has been in Rome on family business."

"Really? That's strange. A mutual friend mentioned to me that he had seen the Count in Genoa a few weeks ago."

Genoa, as everyone knows, is a northern Italian city. There was no apparent reason why the name should have struck that assemblage of gentlefolk like a cannonball. Grandfather's face had lost some of its ominous color; now the blood rushed back into his cheeks. Stefano's eyes narrowed; Miss Rhoda made a sudden movement, her skirts rustling; and Galiana let out a little squeal.

Thanks to Miss Perkins' interminable lectures, I knew why they had reacted as they did. From that northern port, in the darkness of night only two weeks before, the Thousand volunteers had set forth with Garibaldi for the liberation of Sicily. That they had landed, and had had some military success, we all knew, for Grandfather subscribed to the official Roman newspaper. It was always several days late in reaching us; and, as Miss Perkins liked to point out, its reporting was far from unbiased; but even the papal press was forced to admit what all the rest of the world knew—that Garibaldi's ragged forces were making amazing headway against the trained troops of King Francis of the Two Sicilies.

"But surely," I said—careful now to speak French, so that everyone would understand—"surely it is possible to visit Genoa for innocent reasons. Your zeal carries you too far, Captain."

The Captain, of course, made quick disclaimers, and the conversation turned to harmless topics. Miss Perkins had been reading Manzoni's novel *I Promisi Sposi*, which had become a minor classic in the thirty years since its publication. She and Stefano managed to carry on a dialogue about the book. The rest of us were silent, for the most part; Galiana and I because we had not read the book, the Contessa because she seldom spoke at any time, and Grandfather because. . . . Well, I thought I knew his reasons.

When the Captain took his departure, he bowed gracefully over my hand, but this time I did not let it linger in his. The man was somehow sinister. I was forced to admit that my foolish vanity had led me astray. This tight-lipped fanatic, as Miss Perkins had called him, had no interest in me as a woman. He had barely glanced at Galiana, whose beauty would have held the admiring gaze of most men. He cared only for the cause in whose name he was willing to commit acts of horrible cruelty. But why had he come to visit us? Unless . . .

Knowing Andrea's ardent temperament, I could imagine him taking up the cause of liberation, even though it was anathema to Grandfather. Had not Miss Perkins said that some young aristocrats followed Garibaldi? Yes, I could admit the possibility; and I am ashamed to say that my reaction to the idea was one of irritation. Surely Andrea wouldn't be so foolish! Life was pleasant here in the castle; would he risk losing all that comfort and luxury for a hopeless cause? Nor was that all he stood to lose. I had not forgotten young Antonio.

II

I found the Captain's visit even more disturbing in retrospect than it had been in actuality. Thoughts of Andrea wounded, lying in pain on the dusty plains of Sicily haunted me. The weather did not help my mood. Wind and rain brought unseasonable cold, and darkness set in early. My little room, once so cozy, seemed cramped and shabby. When Teresa had finished dressing me for supper I paced restlessly around the small chamber. Then it occurred to me that I would see how the repairs in my new rooms were progressing. I was anxious to move into them. Perhaps Grandfather would let me do so before the work was finished, if the rooms were at all habitable. The bedchamber, at least, might be ready for occupation.

Snatching up a candle, I set out along the corridor. A stair, another long hallway, a second stair—all gloomy in the half-light, melancholy with the sound of the wind moaning around the windows. The rooms themselves, unlighted and desolate, only increased my gloom. It was clear that they were a long way from finished. Wood shavings, pots of paint, stained cloths lay all about. The high-ceilinged, empty rooms echoed to my footsteps. A gust of air from one of the uncurtained windows lifted a corner of a dust sheet and I started nervously. Imagine, then, my horror when I heard the sound of footsteps rapidly approaching. There was no reason for anyone to come here at this time of night, and in such frantic haste. The workmen had left long ago.

I worked myself into a regular melancholy fit, and was prepared for the worst. My relief was exaggerated when I saw a familiar form in the doorway.

"Grandfather," I cried, with a nervous little laugh. "Heavens, how you frightened me."

He was as pale as a sheet; the candle he held trembled violently. He said nothing, only stared at me with a wild, haggard look.

Then I realized why he looked so. The doorway of the sitting room was visible from his own room. Seeing a light where there should be none—a frail, flickering shadow of light—in a room that had not been inhabited since his adored daughter left, never to return, he had thought. . . . I dared not contemplate what he may have thought.

"I came to see how the work is going," I explained, taking his arm. "Come, let us go; it is dark here, and cold."

"*Sì, sì,*" he muttered, yielding to the pressure of my hand as a child might. "*È molto freddo qui. . . .*" And he accompanied me into the corridor with a faltering step quite unlike his usual brisk stride.

Once out of the room, he recovered some of his spirits, but as we went on I saw that he was studying me with a frown. Suddenly he said, "Your gown. It is not right."

Puzzled, I looked down at my frock. As I had half expected, Grandfather had objected to my wearing black all the time, so I had allowed myself to be persuaded to relax the rules just a little. I was proud of this dress, which the seamstress had finished only the day before. It was of gleaming white satin with an overskirt of black lace and scallops of the same shadowy fabric around the sleeves.

Grandfather touched my jet mourning brooch, which fastened the lace bertha.

"Jewels," he said slowly. "A princess should wear jewels. Come. I will give you the ones that are yours."

"But—" I began.

"Yes, yes, it is necessary. I have wanted so long to see you wear them. For me, *carissima?*"

It was impossible to refuse him; and, to be honest, I was vain enough to be easily persuaded. I assumed he meant to offer me, only for that evening, some of the family jewels that would have been my mother's. Few women are strong enough to resist the lure of gems, and I was no exception.

We strolled arm in arm to the library, and there he seated me in a chair while he went to the Raphael madonna that hung between the windows. I watched while he lifted the picture. Behind it was the utilitarian gray face of a wall safe.

From the aperture Grandfather withdrew box after box of crimson leather stamped with the family arms in gold. They were of all sizes and shapes, and my anticipation mounted as he piled them on the desk. Not until all had been removed and the safe closed and hidden again did he begin opening the boxes.

The first was almost a foot square. When he took out the contents I caught a great solemn flash of gold, and eagerly put out my hand. Grandfather shook his head and with his own hands put the ornament around my neck. I had no opportunity to examine it before he came toward me with the next—a large golden brooch, which, with some fumbling, he fastened to the lace at my breast. They came thick and fast after that—a bracelet several inches wide, carved all over with tiny figures of crouching animals; other armlets of sheet gold; a second necklace, from whose woven gold chain hung the head of a fanged dragon; gold filigree earrings so heavy they dragged at my earlobes. . . . I held up my hand, filled with a mounting sense of oppression as the massive gold pressed against my flesh.

"Please, Grandfather. . . . It is so heavy!"

"One more." And on my brow he placed a diadem of twisted gold wires.

I knew the jewels were not family treasures, but the parure of an ancient Etruscan lady, excavated, no doubt, from one of the tombs on his property. The chill I felt from them was not solely physical; it was eerie to reflect that the last warm flesh they had touched was now dust. But I told myself not to dwell on such thoughts, which were, after all, pure superstition. Had not the Princess of Canino created a sensation by appearing at the ambassador's fete in the parure of Etruscan jewelry excavated by her husband?

Grandfather's strange mood had lightened as he took out the jewels; now, standing back to admire the effect, he smiled and said something I did not understand. When my hands went automatically to my head, to adjust the diadem, he laughed and spoke again; this time I recognized the word "mirror."

There was a tall, gilt-framed mirror on the wall. It had been chosen for the beauty of its carved frame, and the silvering of the glass was somewhat worn. Perhaps it was this quality, or the dim light—for the room was lighted by only a few candles—but the sight of myself in the muddy surface of the mirror made me start back.

My face was annihilated by its frame of gold—around my throat, at my breast, on my brow. For the most part the ornaments were far too massive for modern tastes. But the workmanship was superb. The first necklace was my favorite. The chain was composed of half a dozen tiny individual chains woven into an intricate web. From it hung loops of even finer chain, and a series of flower pendants, each covered with the minute balls of gold, tinier than grains of sand, which were a distinctive sign of Etruscan gold work. It was quite lovely, and by itself would have been a charming ornament. I touched it gently and said aloud,

"This must have been her favorite. Oh, Grandfather, may I wear this tonight, just this one? I promise I will take the greatest care of it."

I gave another start as Grandfather's face appeared in the mirror next to mine. The distorting surface gave him such an odd look—all staring eyes and smiling mouth. He understood my request, but I did not find it so easy to understand his answer. He wanted me to wear the entire parure to dinner! I expostulated. Not only was the jewelry quite uncomfortably heavy, but I felt I should look ridiculous. But Grandfather did not brook argument. So we started down the hall, my hand on his arm; and the well-trained servants who lighted our passage showed no sign of surprise at the sight of me.

Our entrance into the drawing room was sensational. The others were gathered there waiting for dinner to be announced, and when we came in Galiana bounced to her feet, knocking her embroidery frame over. Even the imperturbable Miss Perkins exclaimed in amazement, and Miss Rhoda let out a snort.

"How vulgar," she said loudly.

Grandfather took my hand and stepped back; he was displaying me, like a newly purchased statue, and for a moment I resented his possessive attitude. But the admiration in Galiana's face reassured me; I made a careful curtsy, so as not to disturb the weight that dangled from me. While Galiana fluttered around me, touching the ornaments with greedy little fingers, I looked at the others. The Contessa might have been in another room; she had not lifted her eyes from her embroidery. As for Stefano . . .

I had not expected we would see him that evening, since he had favored us with his presence for tea, but there he was, with that black stick balanced in his fingers, looking me over with a cool stare. Well schooled as his face was, I thought I detected an even more fiery emotion than usual in his blazing blue eyes, and I made him a mocking little bow. As the heir he probably regarded everything in the castle as his own property. He would not like to think that Grandfather would give me objects of such value.

"Well, Miss Perkins," I said, turning to that lady, who was walking around me with her head cocked, in the same style in which she was wont to examine works of art. "Have you ever seen anything so lovely?"

"Hmph," said Miss Perkins, rubbing her nose. "Rather overpowering, don't you think? Those earrings will tear your flesh, child."

"Not for one evening. They are only a loan, Miss P. After all," I added, as she still seemed uncommonly sober, "what better way to display jewelry than on a model? I thought you were anxious to see these."

"True, true." Miss Perkins stopped abusing her nose and looked more cheerful as her antiquarian zeal overcame whatever scruples had vexed her. "They are fascinating! Even lovelier than the Regolini jewelry, if the description I read is to be trusted. This giant brooch, or fibula, as it is called, is an amazing piece of workmanship. Look at these rows of tiny animals, sphinxes and lions. . . ."

A servant came to announce supper; I swept in on Grandfather's arm, feeling like a queen. It wasn't easy to eat, since a jangle of gold accompanied every movement I made, and the bracelets kept slipping down over my hand. And throughout the meal, whenever I turned to Miss Perkins, I found her watching me with the same puzzled frown.

III

There was rain in the night, but morning dawned clear and bright. By noon the sun had dried all but the deepest puddles, and I decided to go out. I was restless and bored. Miss Perkins was in the library pursuing some antiquarian search; Galiana had excused herself to attend her mother, whose health, always delicate, seemed to be worse that day.

I wandered out into the gardens in search of amusement, but found none, only the usual small army of gardeners at work clipping and raking and weeding. The acres of formal planting required constant attention, especially at this time of year. The roses were at their best, exquisite blooms of every shade from silvery white to a crimson so deep as to be almost purple. This garden, less formal than the others, had been laid out as a compliment to the Prince's English wife. I could picture her, in the softly flowing gown and broad-brimmed hat of half a century ago, walking along the graveled paths with her spaniels, or sitting on one of the marble benches breathing in the scent of the blooms.

The other gardens were in the Italian or French style, with flowing water ingeniously employed to create a feeling of coolness, not only in innumerable fountains but in water stairs and quiet pools where lilies bloomed. There were artificial grottoes, with statues standing in mosaicked niches. Peacocks strutted along the terraces, shattering the somnolent summer air with their harsh cries.

The gardens were so extensive that I had not yet explored them completely. I was in no mood to do so that morning—fountains and flowers are not exciting enough for restless youth—but in lieu of anything better to do I went on through alleys of close-grown box higher than my head, under fantastic arches of greenery. Passing along a tunnel of vines, I suddenly found myself in an open area bathed in sunlight. All around were flowers growing in delightful confusion—phlox, stock, roses, snapdragons; the tall blue spikes of delphinium, carnations of mammoth size. Their spicy perfume filled the air, which rang with the hum of insects seeking the nectar.

Before me were the walls and turrets of a little house, which I recognized as the one whose fantastic roof I had seen from my bedroom window that first night. Several times since I had watched the distant casements turn gold as lights sprang up within to combat the dark of evening, and I had idly wondered about the identity of the occupant, but had never had the time or the inclination to pursue the question.

Now I started along the path between beds of pansies and dahlias. The little house was quite charming. Leaded windows broke the austere lines of the stone facade. An octagonal tower at the left front corner had a steeply peaked roof, like a dwarf's cap, and a quaint little carved balcony. My curiosity aroused, I lifted my skirts in order to ascend the steps leading up to the front door. Before I reached it, the door opened and a man came out.

The dreamlike, fairy-tale look of the place had me half convinced that it was unoccupied. I fell back with a cry of surprise. Stefano—for it was he—also started violently.

"What are you doing here?" he demanded.

"I was unaware that this was forbidden territory," I replied, recovering myself. "Even Bluebeard warned his wife not to intrude on the chamber of horrors; if you wish to be undisturbed, you might have said so."

"I am saying so now," Stefano replied, in a tone of haughty irony. He folded his arms and leaned against the doorjamb.

"So this is where you hide, like a cross old hermit," I said. "It is a pretty little cell, Cousin."

"I'm glad you approve," Stefano said, still blocking the door.

"Aren't you going to invite me in?"

"No."

"You aren't very polite."

"That is a virtue I am seldom accused of possessing. Don't sulk, Cousin, it spoils the shape of that charming mouth. I am not discriminating against you in particular. No one comes here without an invitation from me."

"Not even Grandfather?"

"Not even he. There is nothing to see," he added, shifting

his weight carefully from one foot to the other. "Only bachelor quarters, austere and extremely untidy. No murdered brides, hanging by their hair, no evidence of weird, evil rites; not even a woman's forgotten shoe or ruffled garter, little Cousin."

I blushed furiously. I don't know which I resented more—the crudity of the hint, or the fact that he had read my unladylike thoughts with such precision. Stefano smiled.

"I'll give you a proper tour some other time, Francesca. At my convenience."

"But I'm bored now," I said.

"Then you are a young woman with very few resources. Read, embroider, play on the pianoforte, sketch, ride. . . . The Prince has given you the gentlest mare in his stables."

"I can't ride alone. Why don't you come with me?"

There was some malice in the question. I wanted revenge for his rudeness. But I swear I had no idea that I would be probing into such a tender spot. Stefano's smile vanished; his face grew dark with anger.

"Oh, well done, Cousin. However, lest you think your triumph too complete, I must tell you that I did remount the horse that threw me—two years ago, after my bones had healed in the inadequate fashion you see. But I ride, in my own clumsy way, privately. I certainly do not intend to give you the pleasure of jeering at me."

And with a lurch that almost threw him off balance, he plunged into the house and slammed the door.

The echoes were still reverberating as I ran down the flowery path. Tears of shame and anger clouded my vision. I had assumed—though I don't know why I should have done so—that Stefano had been crippled for years, perhaps since birth. That was bad enough; but for a man to be struck down in the full flush of his youthful vigor was certainly tragic. How he must rage against the cruel fate that had injured him and left his brother untouched!

As I have said, I am not proud of my thoughts during this period. As I went on, dabbing at my eyes, rage won out over shame. After all, he had mocked me first; no gentleman should even hint of such matters to a lady! And how was I to know he was so sensitive about his affliction? A truly noble character would have risen above it!

I went into the yew garden, where Alberto, the head gardener, was delicately clipping the bushes which had been shaped into fantastic animals. It was precise, exacting work, one clip for every fifteen minutes of concentrated study; and it was very boring to watch. I wandered on in the direction of the stables.

One of the stable cats had recently had a litter of kittens. She was a lean, wild black beast, who was extremely suspicious of my overtures. The cats were not pets, but working animals, tolerated because they controlled the rats and mice that infested stable yards. But the kittens were adorable, and I had hopes of winning their mother with time. I thought I might also pay a social call on Stella, the little mare that had been assigned to my use. Not being accustomed to horses, I was only an indifferent rider, and I had managed to postpone the lessons Grandfather wanted to give me by pointing out that I had no proper riding costume. A very elegant one was even now in the hands of the seamstress, and I looked forward to appearing in the high plumed hat and black wool jacket, which was to be cut like a man's military coat, with gold buttons and a high collar. I had no intention of riding that day, certainly, but as a soft breeze stirred my hair, I rather wished I could.

I was delighted, therefore, when I found Grandfather in the stableyard, booted and spurred, watching his favorite steed being saddled.

"Where are you going, Grandfather?" I asked eagerly. "May I come with you?"

His stern face lightened at the sight of me, but he shook his head.

"I am going to the tombs."

"The tombs from which my lovely jewelry came? But I want to see them. You promised you would take me one day; why not now?"

"It is bad country," Grandfather said slowly. "Rough and wild. Your pretty dress. . . ."

"I'll change into an old dress. Please wait for me!" And since he said no more, I turned impetuously to the groom and asked him to saddle my horse. Then I ran quickly back to the house.

I put on one of the muslin dresses that had been dyed black, and found a bonnet and gloves. On my way downstairs I passed the room occupied by Galiana and her mother and heard from within the soft drone of the Countess's voice invoking the Virgin. I am sorry to say that instead of admiring her piety, I pitied her daughter. Poor Galiana; how weary she must be of so much praying.

The library doors opened as I passed them, and Miss Perkins appeared, blinking and rumpled like a sleepy owl. She had a great thick book in one hand, with her forefinger inserted in the pages as a marker.

"Where are you off to?" she asked, seeing my outdoor attire. "Don't go far, Francesca; you still don't know the area well."

"It's all right, I'm going with Grandfather." I paused before a mirror to adjust my bonnet. "He is taking me to see the tombs."

"The Etruscan tombs? Oh, Francesca, I don't think—"

"I know you would like to see them too, and I would ask you to come, but I don't want to keep Grandfather waiting. He was ready to leave when I asked if I might go with him. Another time, perhaps."

"Wait." As I turned away, my skirts flaring, she caught my arm. I turned in some surprise, and saw that her face mirrored the urgency that had been expressed in her tight grasp. "Wait, child, I must talk to you. I have just found something—"

"I can't wait." I was not stronger than she, but I was more impatient; I pulled away. "Excuse me, Miss Perkins, but I really must run. As soon as I get back you can show me your great discovery."

I ran away, laughing, leaving her standing with her hand outstretched and her lips parted in a frustrated appeal.

The horses were saddled when I reached the stableyard, and Grandfather was pacing up and down switching at his boots with his whip. He said nothing, only swung into the saddle and turned the horse's head toward the gateway. Clumsily I followed suit. He seemed to be in a bad mood, and I thought it best not to annoy him with questions.

Conversation would have been difficult in any case. There was a trail, of sorts, but so narrow and overgrown and rocky that we had to go single file. I had sense enough to let the reins lie loose. My little mare had been chosen for her docility and intelligence, and she picked her way through the brambles with delicate steps. The shade of olives and firs softened the warmth of the sun, and the sky overhead was as blue as my cousin Andrea's eyes. The cloud shadows lay cool on the hillsides, dulling the brilliant green of the foliage.

Then we began to descend. Before long I regretted my enthusiasm and began to wish I had not come. The slope was so steep in places that I closed my eyes and clutched the pommel with both hands. Branches plucked at my bonnet. When at last the track leveled out, I dared to open my eyes and saw that we were riding slowly through a green twilight. The trees here were evergreens in whose perpetual shade the ground was damp and slippery. It was a strange, haunted place; one would not have been surprised to see the slender form of a wood nymph slipping through a ray of diffused sunlight.

The end of the ravine opened up into a wider area, though it was still below the surface of the upper plateau, and I began to see the gaping square-cut holes that opened into ancient tombs. The ground here was not so overgrown, so I ventured to urge my horse into a faster walk until I was beside Grandfather.

"Those are tombs, are they not?" I asked, in my careful Italian.

He turned his head. From under his frowning gray eyebrows his eyes contemplated me blankly, as if I had interrupted some train of thought.

"Yes," he said. "Tombs. But these are poor—the tombs of peasants. It is not here, the place we seek."

As we went on I was amazed at the extent of the ancient cemetery. There were tombs of all types; small primitive rooms cut into the rock, and larger ones of the tumulus type, in which mounds had been raised over the burial chamber. Bushes and small trees grew thickly over the swelling green slopes. In some places I could see the scars of digging, but vegetation had covered all but the most recent holes. It was not a place I should have liked to visit alone. The concealed shafts were like traps into which one might easily tumble. The atmosphere of the place was rather uncanny too. It was so still. No bird sang, no small animals rustled through the coarse grass. I remembered something Stefano had said the previous night at dinner, when he and Miss Perkins were talking about the cemetery. The peasants thought this was a haunted place, sacred to the dead.

The poor superstitious creatures believed in ghosts, and curses, and all manner of pagan horrors. We, of course, were above such fears. . . .

A little to the right of the rough path rose the towering slope of the biggest mound I had yet seen. It must have been thirty feet high. Around its curved base was a circle of masonry, big, roughly hewn blocks of pale tufa, like a stone girdle.

"Is that it?" I asked. "The tomb of the jewels?"

"*Sì, sì. La tomba della principessa.*" Grandfather dismounted and came around to help me down. For a moment he stood looking about with a puzzled air, as if he could not remember the way. Then, taking my hand, he struck off at an angle, straight through the weeds, toward the base of the mound.

It was hard for me to keep up with him. Once I tripped over a stone and would have fallen if he had not been holding my hand. We had gone halfway around the circumference of the mound before he stopped.

The bushes were thicker here, obscuring the masonry at the base of the mound. Grandfather pushed into them, tramping down weeds with his heavy boots, thrusting branches aside. While he searched, I tried to catch my breath. It was hot in the sun, and I felt all tumbled about. I took off my bonnet and pushed the heavy hair back from my face.

Grandfather turned. "Here," he said.

He had torn away some of the underbrush. There, in the slope of the bank, the horizontal blocks of the surrounding stonework had been cut out to form an entrance in the shape of a Gothic arch. A single monolith filled the opening like a great stone plug. So precisely had it been cut to fit the rounded sides that one could scarcely see the crack between door and frame.

I wanted to ask if this was the original door, or one he had placed there to keep vandals away. There were other questions I might have asked, for I was genuinely excited at being so close to my first ancient tomb. But my meager knowledge of the language failed; I determined to ask Miss Perkins, when I returned. How thrilled she would be by such an adventure! I felt a little guilty at having run off without her. Well, but I would tell her all about it, and we would come again another day.

I watched, fascinated, as Grandfather tugged at the stone.

There was no denying his antiquarian zeal; his suit was becoming dirty and snagged by the rough stone. I wondered if a man his age ought to be engaging in such heavy work. The stone must be weighted or balanced in some clever fashion, or he could never hope to move it. It must weigh hundreds of pounds—tons, perhaps, if it was very thick.

I didn't see the trick of the door, since his body was in the way, but apparently he found a catch of some kind, for the heavy block began to move. Without speaking or looking at me, he stepped through the opening.

It was as if he had vanished, so black was the interior. But when I peered inside, I saw him standing at the top of a flight of stone steps. On a shelf inside the entrance was a box of candles. He lighted one of these and held it up.

"Come," he said.

I hesitated. The candlelight was feeble; I could see nothing beyond the stairs. From the pitch-blackness came a breath of thick moist air, clammily cold and reeking of damp.

"*Avanti*," Grandfather repeated, beginning to descend. His voice came back, echoing hollowly. With a shiver I picked up my skirts and followed.

The stairs were few in number but slippery with damp. I touched the wall once for support, but pulled my hand back at once; the stone was slimy and cold.

At the foot of the stairs was a chamber some thirty feet long, but so narrow it was hardly more than a broad passageway. The walls were of stone. At shoulder height they curved sharply inward, so that the ceiling gave the impression of a long, high vault. The room was empty except for scraps of stone and rusted metal on the floor.

The candle burned blue in the dank air. I had already had quite enough of tombs, and would have retreated then and there—after all, there was nothing much to see—but Grandfather stalked on, holding his inadequate light high like an ancient priest. At the far end of the corridor-room were three openings, one straight ahead and one on each side. The side openings were quite low; peering through one, I saw a tiny stone-cut chamber, as empty as the first. The doorway straight ahead had been filled with blocks of masonry, which now lay broken and tumbled.

Grandfather stepped over these blocks and passed into the inner chamber. I followed; but I wished he had given me his hand. Climbing over the rubble was not easy with my voluminous skirts.

The far chamber was also the last; there was no other exit. It was a little smaller than the first, and had the same steeply vaulted ceiling, smeared with lichen and mold. At the very end was a low stone platform.

I think the musty air had dulled my wits; it took me several seconds to understand the function of this rude bier, and when I did, I felt a chill—a foolish qualm, since, after all, the purpose of the structure had been funereal.

"It is very interesting," I said, with a brightness I certainly did not feel. I didn't like the way my voice echoed in that chamber of the dead; when I spoke again, it was in a whisper. "Can we go now, Grandfather?"

"Here is where she lay," Grandfather said, his eyes fixed on the low platform. His hand was trembling. The candlelight flickered wildly across the stained ceiling. "Here. . . ." And then he said something else I didn't understand, something about remembering. He began to back away, as if he were retreating from the presence of a monarch—or from something he was afraid to turn his back on. I took one step after him, and then what I had feared happened: his shaking hand lost its grip on the candle, which fell to the floor and went out.

I cried out. The echoes of the scream went on for an inordinately long time. When they died, I heard Grandfather stumbling over the loose stones around the inner doorway. I was afraid to move, for fear of falling and hurting myself, or touching the foul slime that covered walls and floors. Naturally I assumed Grandfather was going to get another light. I could see the tomb entrance, or at least part of it—a square of brightness against the black of the interior. Grandfather's body blotted out much of the light as he climbed the stairs. And then—then.
. . . The light disappeared. I stared into blackness, unable to believe what had happened, although the dull, grating thud of the closing door confirmed the evidence of my eyes.

I don't know how long I stood there, waiting. . . . For the door to open, the beautiful glow of daylight, the sound of

Grandfather's voice apologizing, exclaiming, explaining how the accident had happened. . . . I don't know how long it was before the truth dawned on me.

I didn't really believe it. If I had done, I would have gone into hysterics. Instead, I began making my slow, careful way back toward that closed slab of stone. I couldn't bring myself to touch the wall, so I had to move an inch at a time, sliding first one foot and then the other along the slippery floor, stepping carefully over obstacles as my toe touched them, balancing for long moments on one foot while the other probed. Strain my eyes as I might, I could not see even a crack of light. Those ancient artisans who sealed the bodies of the dead away for eternity had known their business. Yet there was light in that dreadful place—patches of lichen that glowed with a faint greenish pallor, like the ectoplasm produced by mediums.

The tomb seemed very noisy. It wasn't until later that I realized that the hollow reverberation, like the beating of a far-off drum, was the pounding of my heart. My brain was too numbed to feel fear, but my body was wiser.

When I reached the steps, my knees gave way completely, somewhat to my surprise. But it was better to crawl up the stairs; they were steep and slippery. One patch of lichen on the right-hand wall looked exactly like the print of a giant, crippled hand. I thought, in the stupor arising from terror, that the twisted fingers pointed the way out. I followed their lead and crouched on the topmost step with my palms flat against the unyielding surface of the stone. I thought for a moment that it moved slightly. It was my arms that gave way; I was close to losing consciousness, and too benumbed to realize it. But the illusion gave me a moment of renewed hope. I rose cautiously to my feet, careful not to trip over my skirts, and threw all my weight against the slab. At least I meant to push. My body refused to obey me. A curious lethargy had seized my limbs.

Leaning against the stone, cheek and hands pressed against its roughness, I suddenly remembered what Grandfather had said just before he dropped the candle.

"Here is where she lay. . . ." But the Italian word for "she" is *lei*; and that is also the word for the formal version of the pronoun "you." One would use the formal version when addressing royalty—a princess. . . . And with that realization other unnoticed clues fell suddenly into place. The last, and most formidable of them, was the very fact of my entombment. It had not been an accident. If he had dislodged the slab by some ill-judged movement, he would by now have opened it again.

I realized that I was being overcome by some miasmic atmosphere in that long-sealed place. I seemed to feel the door move again, and knew this time that my senses must be deceiving me.

The door swung open.

Sunlight blinded me. A rush of warm, sweet air—how heavenly sweet, after the horror of the tomb—filled my straining lungs. For a moment I stood swaying on the threshold. I thought I must have fainted, and that this was a dream; for before me, his white shirt dirt-smeared and torn, his eyes wide with horror, his fair hair curling damply—was Andrea. With a long sigh of relief I fell forward into his outstretched arms.

CHAPTER 5

"You were never in serious danger, you know." How he knew I was awake I could not imagine. I lay still, my eyes closed, sensuously enjoying the touch of the sun on my upturned face. There was something soft under my head, but I did not mind the hard ground, or even the pebbles that pressed into my back. I would have endured greater discomfort and felt myself fortunate.

I did not need to open my eyes to know that my first impression had been incorrect. It was not Andrea, but Stefano, who had released me. I had made that error once before—stupidly, for the brothers were not that much alike. Certainly no one could confuse their voices. Stefano's cool ironic tones were unmistakable.

I opened my eyes. He was sitting on a rock a few feet away. The soft bundle of cloth under my head must be his coat. He was in his shirt sleeves. Perspiration streaked his face and his bared throat.

"If I was not in danger, why are you so pale?" I inquired.

"Exhaustion," Stefano replied coldly. "The exertion of moving the stone was strenuous, for a cripple."

"I can't imagine how you did it," I murmured, letting my eyes linger on the breadth of shoulder, displayed by his wetly clinging shirt. Unperturbed by my regard, Stefano smiled.

"Because my leg is injured does not mean all my muscles are atrophied. Can you stand?"

"No."

"I can lift you," Stefano said, "but I cannot carry you any distance. So, unless you wish to remain here all day. . . ."

"Oh, stop baiting me," I cried. "It was a horrible experience! You may say I was in no danger, but I am still shaken; I must rest a little. . . .''

I turned my head so he wouldn't see me crying. Now that the danger was over, I felt drained of all strength. After a moment Stefano spoke in a gentler voice.

''I know it must have been frightening, Cousin. You are no coward, I'll say that for you; I expected to find you screaming with hysterics, or in a swoon. Rest a while. But Miss Perkins will be pacing the floor until she sees you safe and sound.''

''Then it was Miss Perkins who sent you? Or did you know he would do this?''

''In God's name, how can you suggest such a thing?'' Stefano demanded in a rough voice, quite unlike his usual smooth tones. ''Do you suppose I would not have warned you if I had suspected for an instant. . . . It was an accident,'' he added, controlling his voice. ''You can't believe it was anything else.''

I raised myself on one elbow and looked earnestly at him.

''Stefano, you must tell me the truth.''

Stefano studied me thoughtfully. Then he nodded.

''You are right. The truth is probably less frightening than the things you are imagining. It all began here, you see—five years ago, when he excavated this particular tomb. It is a very old one, dating back to the early days of the Etruscan kingdom—the seventh or eighth century before Christ. How it remained hidden so long, I don't know. Many of the other tombs had been robbed. But this was untouched; the rich treasure was still here. Weapons, lamps, pottery—and the jewels you wore the other night. Also—the bodies of the dead.

''Those in the outer chamber were mere heaps of dust. But the inner chamber had been sealed. The Prince had to demolish the barricade himself. He had difficulty forcing his people to come here at all. Only a few of the bravest entered the tomb with him, and at the sight of that enigmatic, walled-up door, they fled, screaming of curses and vampires. So Grandfather took up chisel and hammer and attacked the wall. His imagination had been fired by the fine things in the outer chamber; as soon as one block had been removed, he thrust his head and one hand, holding a candle, into the aperture.

''The air in such places is usually bad. One might expect that the candle would not burn. But this one flared up, and the scent that reached his nostrils was not noxious; it was dry and strangely, spicely perfumed. As the candle flame leaped, he saw—her.

"She was lying on the stone bier at the far end of the chamber. At first he thought it was a statue he saw, one of those marvelous chryselephantine statues of gold and ivory, like the great Minerva of Phidias described by ancient writers. She was all gold, from her glittering gown and jewels to the golden hair streaming over her shoulders, down her ivory arms and breast. Her face was one the great Phidias might have claimed as his masterpiece, pale and unmarred. The Prince stood transfixed; and as he watched, her pure perfection suddenly crumbled. She fell into dust before his very eyes. The golden scales of her gown collapsed, with the faintest of musical chiming, and her diadem dropped into the hollow that had been her face."

I let out a little sound of horror, and Stefano nodded gravely.

"It must have been an appalling sight; I remember my own reaction when he described it to us, days later. He fell into a swoon after that dreadful vision. One of his most courageous attendants, venturing into the tomb in search of his master, found him lying on the floor, cold and still as a dead man. He was ill for days, but as soon as he could move, he insisted on returning to the tomb. We helped him demolish the wall, Andrea and I—for the story had gotten about and not a man on the estate would go with us, threaten as we might. There was nothing on the slab, only the eerie suggestion of a vanished form, outlined by the positions of the jewels that had fallen from it."

"I don't believe it," I muttered. "Such things don't happen. He must have been dreaming. He was ill. He saw the jewelry, fallen, as you saw it, and collapsed. In his delirium he imagined the rest."

"That is what I myself believe," Stefano said. "But it doesn't matter, does it? What matters is what *he* believes. And he believes he saw her—the Etruscan princess, the ancestress of our race."

I lay back, flat on the ground, and stared up at the blue vault of the sky. Never before had I so appreciated the simple joy of being alive, under the sun.

"There is one more thing," Stefano said slowly. "Among

the objects we found in the inner chamber were some silver jars that had contained perfume or cosmetics. They were inscribed with a name.''

"And the name was—"

"Larthia."

"So," I said, after a moment. "It *was* Miss Perkins who sent you in search of me."

"Yes. She had no real cause to fear for you, only a vague foreboding. But when she told me he had called you by that name, when you first arrived . . . You have the golden hair, the family blood. Such a fancy might explain his sudden reversal of feeling toward you. He has had . . . odd spells since the discovery, times when he doesn't seem to be himself. They don't last long, they are infrequent, but. . . . I thought he looked strange last night, when he had decked you out in his treasure. And so I came. I—I met the Prince between here and the castle. When I asked him where you were, he looked surprised and said he had not seen you since breakfast."

"You saved my life," I said. "If I had been there longer, I would have broken down."

"Don't thank me, thank your Miss Perkins. She has quite redeemed my opinion of the English—which has been somewhat prejudiced by Aunt Rhoda. A remarkable woman! She told me she had been haunted by that name since you came. Seeing you wearing the jewelry last night revived her memory. She spent the morning in the library looking for the reference. Dennis mentions the tomb and the name in his book on Etruria."

I sat up. My head spun for a moment, but soon I was able to get to my feet. I felt exhausted.

"Can you mount without help?" Stefano asked, still seated.

"I am afraid not," I said apologetically.

He rose. Limping badly, he came toward me. He did not have his stick. I knew, by the fact that he had forgotten this essential aid, that he had been more alarmed than he implied; but his face had settled back into its usual cold mask.

He helped me into the saddle, not without difficulty. His horse was cropping the sour grass nearby, but he made no move to approach it.

"Ride on," he said curtly.

I started to object, and then I understood. He did not want me to see him struggling to mount. So I turned the mare's head and set her into a walk. I heard nothing and I did not look back. After an interval Stefano came up beside me, and, as the trail narrowed, went ahead. We did not speak again.

I was not so resilient or so brave as I had thought. For some time I had horrible dreams of being shut into dark places or being pursued through underground passages by invisible horrors. I said nothing to Galiana about the experience. In fact, no one knew about it except Stefano—who never again referred to it—and Miss Perkins, who brushed aside my emotional thanks with gruff embarrassment. Grandfather behaved as if no such thing had happened and when, several days later, he made a casual remark about taking me to see the cemetery, ". . . which you have not yet seen," I realized that the episode had been wiped from his mind. I did not need Miss Perkins to tell me not to go in that direction with him again, yet strangely I was not uneasy with him.

I had plenty to occupy my mind, and before long the incident had faded in my thoughts, except for the occasional dreams. The work on my new suite of rooms proceeded apace, and the dressmakers from Florence arrived with cartloads of lovely fabrics. Galiana and I forgot our other concerns when that rainbow assortment was carried in; we reveled in India muslins and silver lace, in flame-colored taffeta and azure moiré.

I had become fond of Galiana, although I often thought in my smug way how typically Italian she was with her volatile moods—one moment convulsed with mirth over some schoolgirl joke, the next pensive and sad as she described her mother's failing health. Her black eyes could snap with anger when one of the servants failed to obey quickly enough, but her rages passed as quickly as a summer storm, leaving her sunny and cheerful again.

Some of her traits annoyed me, however. One of the most annoying was the way she behaved toward Stefano, when he chose to grace us with his presence. It would not be quite accurate to say she flirted with him, for she seemed a little in awe of him; but she hung on his words with a breathless attention I found disgusting. He was not particularly responsive; in fact his attitude was reminiscent of the way a man might look at a favorite puppy or kitten, if the little creature should suddenly break into human speech.

One evening she chose a seat on a footstool next to his chair and never took her big black eyes off his face as he discussed antiquities with Miss Perkins. Stefano left early that evening; and next morning, as Galiana and I were preparing to go out, I spoke to her about it.

"I didn't realize you were so interested in ancient history, Galiana."

"I am not." Galiana giggled. She had a sweet, high-pitched little laugh. "No, not at all."

"Then it must be Stefano who interests you," I said, concentrating on tying my veil.

"But he is the heir," Galiana said calmly. "One day he will be Prince Tarconti."

"Isn't that rather mercenary?" I exclaimed.

She didn't understand me at first. Neither of us spoke French all that well, and we often had slight difficulty in communicating. I was somewhat hesitant about explaining myself; my exclamation had been made in the warmth of surprise; but when she understood my meaning, she laughed and shrugged.

"It is always done," she said. "Oh, to be sure, *l'amour— c'est belle, certainement, mais n'est pas pratique*. Perhaps I will have a lover after I am married. And Stefano is not ugly. He is not as handsome as Andrea, but he will do quite well."

I found this terribly cold-blooded, but I had to admit it was the acceptable attitude for her nation and social class. In fact, it was the common attitude in England as well. I had often listened to the older girls at school discussing marriage; the question of dowries and settlements and titles entered into the matter pretty frequently.

Galiana hummed to herself as she studied her reflection in the mirror. I felt a stab of jealousy run through me. My new riding costume was finished and I had thought I looked rather well. The black wool was becoming and the dashing cut of the jacket set off my too-slim figure quite nicely. The swoop of the plume and veil against my fair hair was good too. But next to Galiana I looked like a child. She was deliciously plump. I knew her neat little waist owed a good deal to tight lacing, but the effect was excellent. Her riding costume was a daring shade of crimson that set off her vivid coloring. It was a little shabby, and if I had been more generous I might have been moved to suggest that she share in the bounty of new clothes I was getting. Grandfather would never have objected. But I was not noble enough to rise above the challenge of her bouncing black ringlets and rosy cheeks. Feeling a little out of sorts, I turned from the mirror.

"Let's go," I said. "The sky is clouding over; I don't want to be caught in the rain."

We were going to the village. It was not far away, at the foot of the hill where the castle stood, and I couldn't see why we were not allowed to go alone; but whenever I rode out, a groom in the Tarconti livery followed at a discreet distance. This was not only a question of propriety, but also of safety; for there were bandits in the hills, not only the mysterious Falcon's followers, but men who had taken up a life of crime as a result of poverty or their own vicious inclinations.

A trip to the village was a treat only because we got out so seldom. According to Galiana, it had little to offer. We had hoped of getting to Viterbo, or even Florence, eventually, but in the meantime even Isola Turna was a novelty to me. The shop in the village (there was only one of importance) had ribbons and buttons, sufficient excuse for two bored girls to seek it out.

The sun had gone under the clouds by the time we reached the town, making it look even more somber than it ordinarily appeared. The houses were of dull gray stone, with narrow, suspicious-looking windows. There were no trees and no flowers, not even window boxes, such as I had seen in other Italian towns. A few lean dogs sprawled in the dust of the main street. The central square was not unattractive, but it was very dirty. The fountain had floating debris of all kinds in the water, and the statue in its center was streaked with bird droppings.

The church, dedicated to Saint Sebastian, had a facade of the same gray stone. A single window and a flight of stairs leading up to the door were the only features that broke the monotony of the flat front wall. Even the bell tower was short and squat. Apparently the church wall served as a sort of public notice board; a few tattered papers flapped loose corners in the wind.

One side of the piazza had houses a little more pretentious than the others we had seen, with stone balconies and handsome windows. There were also a few small shops. One was a café with rusty iron chairs set out on the stone paving. When we came into sight the chairs were pushed back, conversation stopped, and the patrons—roughly dressed, bearded men—stared at us as hard as they could.

The shop we entered was dimly lighted and so filthy that no respectable English merchant would have admitted to owning it. I found Signor Carpaccio, the owner, unpleasantly obsequious; and I could not help contrasting him with crusty old Mr. Peters, who had owned the sweetshop in the village in Yorkshire.

The ribbons were not very pretty, but we bought several yards of lilac twill, just to be buying something, and Galiana found a crude little statue of Saint Sebastian for her mother. Poking around on a shelf filled with carved stone figures, I selected a rather nice little image of a cat. So we had several parcels when we came out of the shop.

The clouds had thickened, and we made haste to remount. Galiana shivered. She was a creature of the sun, and often complained of the cold at temperatures I found pleasantly mild.

"Brrr! It is going to rain, I think. Let us hurry, Francesca."

She set her horse into a canter at once and I followed, with the groom behind me. We were almost out of the town when a child darted out of a side street, no wider than an alley, right under my horse's feet.

I jerked on the reins so suddenly and so awkwardly that even my gentle Stella was forced to rear, and I came close to tumbling off. I dismounted as quickly as I could, without waiting for the groom to help me. The child lay still, face down in the dirt.

I should not have moved it. Miss Perkins told me that, later, but I was too frightened to be sensible. I caught the little thing up and lifted it onto my lap. I use the indefinite pronoun because I couldn't tell whether it was a boy or a girl. It wore the loose robe-shirt all tiny children wore before they graduated to skirts or trousers, and its hair was cropped crudely around its ears. It was very slight; its bones felt as fragile as a bird's under my hands.

Its face was pale under a solid coating of dirt, and its eyes were closed. My heart gave a great leap and seemed to stop. Then the eyes opened.

"Thank God," I cried, forgetting my hard-won Italian in my agitation. "Are you hurt, child?"

The groom, a stocky young fellow named Piero, was now beside me. His Italian was difficult to follow, he spoke only the harsh local dialect; but after he had passed his hands over the child's body and limbs, he smiled reassuringly and spoke slowly. I caught the word "*bene*." That, and his smile, made me feel better. The child continued to lie in my lap, staring up at me with great velvety eyes. It looked very solemn for such a young child. It was also very dirty.

Galiana had not dismounted.

"Come along, Francesca," she said impatiently. "It will rain any moment. We will be soaked."

"But the child," I began.

"You heard Piero say it is not hurt. Put it down and hurry."

Angrily I gathered the child into my arms and stood up. It weighed nothing at all. I was looking around, wondering how to ask Piero if he could locate its home, when the door of a nearby house opened and a woman ran out. The shawl had fallen back from her gray hair, and her lined face was anxious. She limped as she ran. I thought it must be the child's grandmother. The small face came alive at the sight of her. Stretching out two bony little arms, it cried, "*Mamma.*"

The woman took the child, an operation made slightly more difficult than it needed to have been because she was simultaneously trying to curtsy. When the exchange was effected she pressed the infant to her bosom and wrapped her shawl around its bare feet and legs. I was still stunned by the revelation of the child's cry; the woman looked far too old to be the mother. When the woman looked up at me she was smiling, and I saw, with another shock, that her teeth were brown and broken. I had expected her to rail at me, and I wouldn't have blamed her; the child had moved too quickly for me to avoid it, but a mother's concern is excusable. Instead she snatched at my hand and tried to kiss it. I fumbled in my purse and pressed a coin into her hand.

"For medicine," I said. "Or a doctor, if. . . . Oh, Galiana,

tell her, will you, she doesn't understand me. A doctor should
see the child.''

"Doctor?" Galiana looked baffled. "There is no doctor in
the village, Francesca. Do come! Such a fuss over a peasant
child. They are just like animals, my dear, they aren't easily
hurt. If you don't come now, I shan't wait for you.''

Tossing her head, she rode away.

The woman was retreating, bowing with every step. The child
lay in her bosom; it was placidly sucking its thumb and still
staring at me. I looked helplessly at Piero. With a smile, he bent
and held his hands for me to mount. There seemed to be nothing
else to do, so I clambered back onto Stella and followed
Galiana.

I made no attempt to catch up with her immediately. I was
puzzled and shocked by her attitude. It made me feel quite
unfriendly toward her. But she reined up and waited for me with
an angelic smile on her pretty face.

"I have just thought of something very amusing," she said.
"Did you hear what the woman said to you when she was
mumbling over your hand?''

"I couldn't understand her," I said shortly.

"Why, she called you by the name these ignorant people give
to the harvest goddess. They have a festival in the autumn, with
games and feasting; one of the girls is chosen to be the
Principessa Etrusca, as they call her. Stefano says it is a . . .
What did he call it?" She frowned prettily. "Oh, yes. It is a
survival of the old religion, and the girl who plays the goddess
must bleach her hair yellow if it is not that shade already. I
suppose they confuse her with his Excellency's princess—the
one he found in the tomb with all her jewels.''

I jerked on the reins so hard that Stella stopped.

"What are you talking about?" I demanded.

"You must have heard of the princess," Galiana said.
"Everyone in the village knows about it, that's why they won't
go near the old tombs. You have yellow hair, like hers.''

I looked sharply at her, but her smooth face was quite
innocent.

"Yes, I have heard about her," I said. "How strange. I don't
think I want to be taken for a goddess.''

"It's your own fault," Galiana replied. "Getting involved with these people. You'd better take a bath as soon as we get back, Francesca. You look a fright, all covered with dust. And—" Her eyes narrowed with malicious laughter. "I'll wager you have fleas, too. The villagers all have them."

I lifted my chin in my most dignified manner and said nothing. I had been about to apply my nails to a spot on my neck that had developed a suspicious itch; but not for worlds would I have given Galiana that satisfaction.

II

The poets say that beauty is in the eye of the beholder. I never realized the truth of the statement until I next rode to the village. This time Miss Perkins was with me, and I felt as if I were seeing the place through new eyes.

Galiana insisted on coming. Any excursion was better than staying at home. She had taken a fancy to Miss Perkins, although the way she laughed at that poor woman's manners would have infuriated a less amiable person. Miss Perkins didn't mind. "There is no harm in the girl," she said, after I had indignantly described Galiana's callous behavior toward the child. "She is the product of her class, Francesca; she has never been taught to think of others. You mustn't blame her. Perhaps you can help educate her feelings and tastes."

I couldn't be so tolerant. But I had to admit that Galiana was not beyond hope. She came with us even though she knew my reason for going was to inquire after the child.

We stopped in front of the house and Piero went to knock at the door. A strange woman answered it. But she knew who I was, and what I wanted; in a moment the child's mother came running out of the house, whose windows and doorway were now fringed with staring faces. She tried to kiss my hand. I could hear Galiana giggling as I hastily pulled it away. There was no use trying to explain to her that it was a sense of fitness, not fear of fleas, that made me reluctant. I had been taught that one bowed the knee only to God and the Sovereign.

With Miss Perkins to interpret, I found that the child had taken no harm. It was even then at play in the piazza. So we rode that way, after I had given the woman a few coins. Her gratitude was so exaggerated that I was reminded of Galiana's remarks about the Principessa Etrusca.

I had told Miss Perkins about this theory and she was inclined to agree. As we rode off, she looked thoughtful.

"I am afraid, Francesca, that you are about to become a local saint. You must control your benevolence."

"Don't be sarcastic, Miss P.," I said sulkily. "You know I am not benevolent at all. Only the cruelest brute could be indifferent to an infant—and anyone would look like a saint next to Galiana."

The other girl was a few feet ahead, and I was speaking English, so I had no fear that she would overhear me. Miss Perkins shook her head.

"It isn't only Galiana. This country is ripe for a revolution. It is not quite as bad as France used to be; but the tumbrils and the guillotine, tragic as they were, arose out of bitter injustice on the part of the nobility."

She was surveying the mean little street as we rode, and her face was both sad and angry.

"Look about you," she went on. "There is no school in this town, no hospital, not even a doctor. Oh, yes, we have far to go, even in England; but this country is still in the Dark Ages. Do you know how old the child's mother is? Thirty-one! She looks sixty. She is so badly crippled with rheumatism she can scarcely walk—the result of living in damp, filthy old houses. Those houses belong to your grandfather, Francesca. How long has it been, I wonder, since he repaired any of them? Yet he is considered a kindly lord in comparison to others in the province."

I was too shocked to answer at first. Miss Perkins rode on, muttering angrily to herself, and I let her draw ahead.

I could hardly blame Galiana for laughing at the way Miss Perkins rode; she was a figure of fun on a horse, for she had never learned to post, and rolled around in the saddle like a two-year-old. But she rode as she did everything else, with a grim determination that overcame lack of skill, and that day her generous indignation lent her dignity. By the time we reached the piazza she had forgotten her libertarian sentiments, and the face she turned to me was beaming with admiration.

"What a beautiful old town!" she exclaimed. "Look at the

carved stonework on that balcony, Francesca. The church cannot be later than the fourteenth century. See the shape of the Gothic arches in the rose window.''

When she had finished exclaiming over the beauties of the piazza, it looked quite different to me. The sun was shining brightly, which may have helped. The fine weather had brought the townspeople out into the air. Women filled great jars at the fountain. A group of little children sat in the dirt playing some sort of game with pebbles and bits of stick. I saw my small acquaintance among them, but did not go to him (Miss Perkins had ascertained that the infant was of the male sex and was named Giovanni), fearing that my attentions might alarm him. I pointed him out to Miss Perkins, adding,

"His mother says there is nothing wrong with him; but see how quietly he sits there. Surely small children should be running around, shouting. . . .''

"They are all too quiet," Miss Perkins replied, her face darkening. "A diet of macaroni and vegetables gives one little energy. Even the women move slowly, with effort. As for the men . . .'' and she snorted contemptuously.

There were certainly a number of men lounging about doing nothing, while the women were carrying the heavy jars. Now that Miss Perkins had pointed it out, I could see the lethargy that affected all of them, even the busy women. They were not pale; no one who lived under the hot Italian sun could help but be burned by its rays. But they had a sickly look under their tans, and most of them were too thin.

Galiana was already before Signor Carpaccio's shop, calling impatiently to us. Miss Perkins paid no attention. She jerked her horse's head around and went bouncing across the piazza toward the church. Laughing, I followed her, leaving Galiana to do as she pleased.

Miss Perkins rolled out of the saddle before Piero could come to her assistance. He gave me a grimace of mingled amusement and chagrin. I grinned back at him (Galiana was forever reproaching me for my informal attitude toward the servants) and accepted his help in dismounting.

Miss Perkins was standing at the top of the steps, her head tilted back and her bonnet hanging by its ribbons as she contemplated the carved Gothic window.

"What is the interior like?" she asked.

"We didn't have time to visit the church before."

Miss Perkins shook her head. "Tsk, tsk. People come all the way from England, even from America, to see historic beauty of this sort. You should not ignore—"

Luckily for me, we were interrupted by Galiana at that point in the lecture.

"What are you doing?" she demanded. "Let us go to the shop."

"I want to see the church," Miss Perkins replied coolly.

"What for?" Galiana asked.

"Have you ever seen it?"

"No, of course not. There is a chapel at the *castello;* we hear Mass there, with Father Benedetto. Even you heretics must know that. . . ."

Galiana was beginning to learn that she could say such things to Miss Perkins, but her expression was rather wary until Miss Perkins burst into a shout of laughter.

"Heretics, are we? Well, for a good Catholic, you are singularly ignorant about your own faith, my dear. This heretic will help educate you, and we will begin by visiting this most interesting and ancient church. Ha—but, what is this?"

She turned and peered near-sightedly at one of the yellowed placards fastened to the facade of the church.

"It is a notice of taxes," Galiana said. She could read barely.

"So I see." Miss Perkins adjusted her pince-nez. "An inappropriate notice for a church, is it not?"

Galiana sighed impatiently. Miss Perkins proceeded to read all the notices, while we fidgeted. Finally she walked toward the door. We were about to follow when there was a shift of movement all over the piazza. For a second everything froze. The women stopped in midstride, balancing their heavy water jars; the men looked like statues caught in a dramatic gesture; even the children stopped pushing the pebbles around in the dust. The next moment—it was amazing, how quickly it all happened—the piazza was half empty. The women and children had gone.

The troop of soldiers came into the piazza two abreast. They must have filled the narrow street from wall to wall. They carried long muskets, with bayonets attached. Behind them came the cavalry, a dozen or more mounted men—and Captain De Merode.

"What miserable-looking soldiers they are," I said, remembering the Queen's Household troops whom I had seen on parade in London. In comparison to their spotless uniforms and military precision, these slouching rascals looked like scarecrows.

Miss Perkins shook her head. "Don't you remember the Swiss mercenaries we saw in Civitavecchia—lazy, fat men whose muskets were rusted with disuse? These men may be dirty, but their bayonets are freshly polished. . . . Look at their faces—their eyes. The peasants call them *'lupi'*—wolves."

"How do you know all that?" I asked in surprise.

"I talk to people," said Miss Perkins. "What is more, I listen."

I took a closer look at the soldiers, who had spread out around the piazza like troops occupying a hostile city. The villagers had melted away; the chairs before the café were empty. But I was aware of watching eyes, flashes of movement in doorways and windows. The soldiers sensed the invisible watchers too. Now that Miss Perkins had alerted me, I saw the ferocity of the bearded faces, the animal keenness of the eyes.

The mounted men rode straight toward us. The Captain lifted his hand, and the little troop came to a ragged stop around the curving steps of the church. De Merode dismounted with a jingle of swordbelt and spurs. He swept off his helmet.

"Ladies, what a pleasure to meet you here. I would not have thought this wretched hole had any amusement to offer ladies of your sort. And you, Mademoiselle—Parker? I was under the impression that you had returned to England."

"Were you?" Miss Perkins did not bother to correct his mistake about her name. "You do your spies less than justice, Captain. I am sure you know everything that goes on in this district."

The word was ill-chosen—deliberately, if I knew my Miss Perkins. The Captain scowled.

"My spies"—he emphasized the word—"are less efficient than I could wish. I have not yet succeeded in the task my commander honored me with."

"Honored?" I repeated, glancing at his unkempt soldiers with a curling lip. I had learned this gesture from watching Stefano. Apparently it was just as annoying on my face. De Merode's cheeks reddened.

"Any service of His Holiness is an honor," he snapped. "To be assigned to clean out this viper's nest of traitors is a duty worthy of a soldier. There is no more dangerous post in the Papal States, I assure you."

"I can see that," I remarked, glancing around the empty square. "What dangerous mission have you come to perform, Captain?"

"Since you are here, you may watch," said De Merode. Turning, he snapped out an order. Two of his men came forward. One was carrying a roll of paper, the other a pot and a brush. Before long, the facade of the church bore a new notice. From where I stood I could see only one line of the printing—the number 10,000.

Miss Perkins scrutinized the notice. "So much money for the capture of one local rebel? But I suppose you need not pay it, eh?"

"The money will be paid," De Merode said. "It is a small price to pay for peace in this province; but a large sum for a poor man."

His voice carried across the quiet piazza. He spoke Italian, instead of the French he had been using; and Miss Perkins answered in the same language and in the same loud tone.

"Larger than the thirty pieces of silver Judas earned. . . . You will excuse us, Captain. I have brought these two young ladies to see the church. It is of great antiquarian interest."

She swept us before her through the heavy doors.

The interior was so dark, after the sunlight of the piazza, that I stopped short, gripped by a wave of panic. The darkness reminded me. . . . Then Miss Perkins caught my arm.

"Straight ahead. There is a heavy leather curtain between this entrance and the body of the church."

It was not much lighter inside; the high narrow windows were so encrusted with grime that little sunlight struggled in. Toward the altar, some distance away, a few tiny candle flames burned bravely.

Galiana muttered, "I want to go."

"So long as you are here, you may as well say a prayer," said Miss Perkins. "If I do not mistake my saints, that statue is of the Holy Sebastian; you observe the arrows protruding from his side, like the quills of. . . . Say a prayer, Galiana, while we examine the church."

Galiana obeyed reluctantly, falling to her knees before the statue. It was a horrid-looking thing, of painted wood, unpleasantly lifelike despite its crudity. Streaks of garish red streamed down the saint's body from his manifold wounds, and his face was contorted by a spasm of anguish.

Still holding my arm, Miss Perkins drew me to the far side of the church.

"The reward," I said. "Was it for the Falcon?"

"Yes."

"But why make such a great show of putting up the notice? One soldier could have done it."

"I don't understand that myself," Miss Perkins admitted. "I think perhaps we should go back to the castle. I have an uneasy feeling."

But when this proposition was put to Galiana, she made a loud outcry. She had followed our desires with regard to the church; the least we could do was let her visit the shop. Miss Perkins gave in, but I could see she was still uneasy.

I began to share her feelings as we crossed the square toward the shop. The mounted men had gone, but many of the foot soldiers were still there, relaxing like men released from duty. Some occupied the chairs outside the café. A waiter, wearing an exceedingly filthy apron, was serving them wine. The others strolled two by two or sat on the edge of the fountain.

At first the shop seemed to be deserted. Galiana called the proprietor's name and after a moment Signor Carpaccio appeared from behind a curtain at the back of the shop. He greeted us with his usual obsequiousness and ran to show Galiana a tray of trinkets newly arrived from Florence. They were cheap-looking things, shiny silver rings and pendants set with mosaic, but Galiana's tastes, like those of a magpie, were all for the cheap and shiny. She poked at the trinkets, bartering like a fishwife. I joined Miss Perkins, who was examining the ceramics I had seen before. The animal figures were rather appealing.

"Strange, how the talent survives," said Miss Perkins, holding up a small glazed statue of a stag. "The Etruscans were particularly skilled in the art of terra cotta."

While we were standing there we heard a burst of coarse laughter from one of the soldiers at the café next door.

"I can't understand why they are still here," Miss Perkins muttered. "They are stationed at Parezzo; from what I hear of that city, there are wine shops and—er—entertainment of other sorts more interesting than anything this poor hamlet can supply."

"Ask him," I suggested, indicating Signor Carpaccio.

When the question was put, the man shrugged.

"It is only this wretched outlaw, this Falcon. He has sworn to tear down a reward notice if one should be put up. The soldiers are waiting for him to come. But," he added quickly, as Miss Perkins made a movement toward the door, "there is no reason for the signorina to run away; the villain will not dare appear. He will certainly be captured if he does."

"Of course he will appear," Miss Perkins snapped. "His reputation depends on his keeping such rash, stupid promises. Girls—come, we must go."

"But surely, Miss Perkins, he will wait till nightfall, or till tomorrow, when the soldiers are less alert," I exclaimed. "It would be madness for him to come now."

"Publicity is his aim, not caution," Miss Perkins replied. "Where is Piero? We must leave at once."

Galiana, her eyes sparkling, joined me in pleading for a delay. She was as anxious as I to catch a glimpse of the romantic bandit. Unlike myself, she seemed to believe he would appear soon. I could not believe any man, even a romantic bandit, would be so stupid. No; the Falcon would steal into town after dark, that would be the sensible thing to do.

However, Miss Perkins was adamant. She herded us out into the piazza, where we found Piero waiting by the fountain. He was chatting with one of the soldiers. The mood had relaxed. The drinkers were still drinking, and some fluttering skirts could be seen among the uniforms. The girls—for they were all young—did not seem to share the fear of their fellow townspeople. They were giggling and flirting. One bold-faced, black-haired beauty was strumming a stringed instrument and smiling up into the face of the soldier who bent over her. As we stood waiting for Piero to bring the horses, the girl struck a ringing chord and raised her voice in song. It was a strange, wild strain in a minor key, like a lament. I expected Miss Perkins would want to listen, but she urged us to mount, and we turned toward the narrow street that led to the castle.

We had almost reached it when a thunder of pounding hooves was heard. A shot rang out. The voice of the singer rose to a scream, and broke off. I tried to stop and turn around. The horses reared and danced; and for a few seconds all was confusion. However, I saw him come.

Like a bullet from a pistol barrel, the great black stallion came plunging out of one of the narrow *vincoli*, or alleyways—a space so confined it was a wonder a horse could pass through it, much less at that speed. The soldiers, still milling about, were not expecting anyone to come from that quarter. Before they could aim their weapons, the rider had reached the church steps. Swaying sideways in his saddle, he thrust at the newly affixed placard with the blade of his sword. The glue had not yet set; the paper pulled free and wrapped itself around the blade. The rider whirled it once around his head with an indescribable air of mockery and disappeared into another alleyway, as narrow as the first.

It transpired in far less time than it takes to describe it, yet I was left with an indelible memory of horse and rider. The bandit's clothing matched the ebon hue of his steed. Even his head was covered with a close-fitting black hood. The only touch of color was the blood-red sash tied around his slender waist—the scarlet badge of rebellion. The somber colors were not depressing or sinister, however; on the contrary, I had never seen anything more vigorously alive than the man and his beautiful stallion.

I was still staring at the narrow orifice into which the rider had vanished, his dark attire blending with the gloom of the *vincolo*, when something struck Stella on the flank. She might have bolted if Piero had not snatched the bridle. I turned to see a jostling mass of horsemen filling the street behind me. The papal cavalry had been lying in ambush somewhere along that main thoroughfare—which, though narrow, was considerably wider than any of the other streets that led into the piazza. But the riders had been unable to follow the Falcon because of the impediment presented by our group. De Merode, his face livid with anger, was trying to lead his men through. It was he who had struck at Stella.

A few of the foot soldiers, less scatterbrained than their fellows, were already running in pursuit, but of course they had no hope of catching a rider—and such a rider!

We got ourselves straightened out finally, after considerable pushing and shouting. De Merode gave me a furious look before gathering his troop together and galloping off. I knew he must suspect us of deliberately barring his way, and I couldn't entirely blame him. Considering the circumstances of our first meeting, he had some reason to wonder whose side Miss Perkins and I were on. Doubly reassured by my awareness of my innocence and by my grandfather's unassailable position, I was quite willing to be the object of his mistrust rather than have that dangerous young man turn his attentions to the real conspirators —the girls who had been so friendly to his soldiers, distracting their attention and preventing them from reaching their weapons in time.

I expressed these ideas to Miss Perkins, not without difficulty, for we were trotting along at a rapid pace.

"Quite right," she gasped. "The girl who sang—a signal—"

She broke off with a grunt as our horses, urged by Piero, broke into a gallop. She had said enough, however; and I contemplated this new idea with growing amazement and indignation. Had our romantic bandit had the cold-blooded effrontery to use us as a shield? The girl's song might well have been a signal; and if so, then the Falcon must have been lurking in the immediate vicinity, perhaps in one of the walled courtyards of the houses near the piazza. That would suggest that he lived in the town, or very close to it. What really disturbed me was the fact that he must have known of our trip to the village in order to plan his strategy. He must have spies in the very stronghold of his enemies—in the castle itself.

CHAPTER 6

We were late returning, and the others were just sitting down to tea. It was in the Salon of the Nymphs that day; Miss Rhoda preferred to use the formal rooms in turn, to make sure they were properly kept up. This, one of the smaller salons, was particularly pleasant on hot days, for the water theme suggested by the ceiling paintings had been carried out in the color scheme and ornaments. The bas-reliefs of flowers and vines twining across the pale-green paneling had been done in soft silver gilt instead of the garish gold prevalent elsewhere. The draperies were of silvery green satin. The chandeliers of Murano glass, in delicate shades of blue and green frosted with crystal, suggested waves breaking in sprays of foam. The rugs, which had been specially woven in Persia, were of the same cool sea shades. Even the Nereids on the ceiling sprawled languidly in aquamarine shallows, although their curves were rather more prominent than slender sea nymphs ought to have had. As Miss Perkins once remarked, the artists had used mythological themes only as an excuse for painting unclothed female forms.

Galiana was the first to enter, rudely pushing past Miss Perkins in her anxiety to tell the exciting news. I thought Grandfather would have a fit. He turned an unbecoming shade of scarlet that clashed horribly with his mauve smoking jacket, and rushed from the room.

"Profanity is so useful to gentlemen in relieving their feelings," remarked Miss Perkins, gazing after him. "No, Francesca, don't follow him; he will not be able to express himself freely in your presence."

"My daughter," said the Contessa gently, "you should not have told the Prince."

Galiana, who was so brash and assertive with others, never contradicted her mother, so I came to her defense.

"He would have heard of it sooner or later. The village must be buzzing with the news, and Piero will spread it among the servants."

"It is certainly a most inappropriate time, however," sniffed Miss Rhoda. "He was on the verge of a tantrum already, after reading the newspaper."

"Ah," said Miss Perkins, reaching eagerly for the copy of *Monitore*, which lay on a table. "What is the news?"

"The worst possible," said Miss Rhoda, as the Countess sighed and shook her head. "That bandit Garibaldi has captured Palermo."

Miss Perkins, her face aglow, read of her hero's exploits.

"All of Sicily must be in his hands by now," she muttered. "The newspaper is a week old."

"Much good may it do him," snapped Miss Rhoda. "The largest Bourbon army is on the mainland; if Garibaldi dares to cross the straits, he and his hobgoblin crew will be annihilated."

"On the contrary," cried Miss Perkins. "This is only the beginning. The kingdom of the Two Sicilies will fall into his hands like a ripe plum. It is rotten with discontent. And then—"

"He would never dare attack the realm of His Holiness," said the Contessa in a strangled voice. "God would not permit such blasphemy!"

"God and Cavour," said Miss Perkins dryly. "The Prime Minister of Piedmont does not want Garibaldi to claim credit for liberating the Papal States as well as the Two Sicilies. Cavour is jealous of Garibaldi—"

"For heaven's sake, must we discuss politics?" demanded Miss Rhoda. "It is a most inappropriate subject. At least, Miss Perkins, I beg you to be silent in the presence of the Prince."

"But his Excellency and I have had several good heated discussions," exclaimed Miss Perkins. "I think he enjoys them."

"Well, I do not," said Miss Rhoda; and that was the end of that.

However, Miss Perkins received support from Stefano, who

joined us for dinner that evening. He immediately introduced the subject of Garibaldi's success, with a sly sidelong look at Grandfather; and although the old gentleman fumed, it seemed to relieve his spleen to pound on the table and shout. Stefano egged him on; but he didn't agree with Miss Perkins either. Like all moderates, he incurred the ire of extremists on both sides, and bore it with amused condescension.

The latest exploits of the Falcon amused him even more. Galiana, always eager to gain his attention, described the incident in her breathless fashion; and Stefano shook his head, with a sneering smile.

"The fellow is a clown. But how typically Italian. Conspiracy is in our blood. For the last fifty years the country has been crawling with secret societies, petty groups with poetical names, noble aims, and very little effect. The Sons of Mars, the Carbonari, and the White Pilgrims were just as absurdly theatrical as the Falcon. He is obviously ignorant of our history, or he would remember what happened to other incompetent idealists. Emilio and Attilio Bandiera, for instance."

He paused, sipping his wine; and although I knew he had done so deliberately in order to whet our curiosity, I could not refrain from asking the question.

"Who were they?"

"Young officers who took it into their heads to liberate the peasants of Calabria," Stefano replied. "They landed—if you can believe this—with sixteen men! They assumed, of course, that the peasants would flock to join them. The peasants did not object to being liberated, but they were not about to risk their skins for that illusory good. . . ."

"Pardon me, Cousin, if I object to your rhetorical style," I said, trying to imitate Stefano's tone of cool irony. "I think I can anticipate what you are about to say; the young idealists were caught and executed, is that right? How can you speak so callously of a noble aim, however misguided?"

My attempt at coolness failed; my voice broke on the final words. I don't know why—at least I did not then know why—I was so moved, but my emotion silenced the others for a moment. Stefano's fixed smile never left his face, but the look in his eyes indicated that I had touched him—probably evoked his contempt and annoyance. Surprisingly it was the Contessa who spoke first.

"The signorina is right about one thing, Stefano. You are too frivolous about serious matters."

Stefano bowed his head without replying, and Miss Perkins hastened to break the awkward silence.

"You are unfair to our friend the Falcon, Count Stefano. There is reason in what he does. The people here are not the peasants of Calabria, and this is 1860. A rebellion at this time might well succeed; at least it might produce more lenient laws, kinder treatment."

"Not at all," Stefano replied. "Last year's rebellions in Tuscany and Aemelia succeeded, to be sure, but only because they had support from Piedmont. No local uprising here can possibly succeed without outside aid, and Victor Emmanuel cannot challenge the Pope without risking war with France. Napoleon must defend Pio Nono; the clerical party in France is strong, and he needs their support, usurper that he is."

Once again Grandfather proved that he understood the abhorred English tongue quite well. He interrupted this speech with a growl and a comment about the valor of the papal troops. Stefano's lip curled.

"Oh, as for that, I consider De Merode's international rabble a greater danger than your foolish Falcon. The gutter scrapings of Europe and Ireland—"

"The De Merode family is one of the best in France," Grandfather interrupted.

"Impractical dreamers, like the other refugee nobles who fight for Pio Nono," Stefano said curtly. "They still dream of a restoration. France has seen the last of its kings. Not that the Buonapartes are any improvement over the Bourbons."

"Then you would support a republic?" Miss Perkins asked.

Stefano raised his eyebrows until they almost touched his exquisitely arranged curls.

"Heaven forbid, Miss P. The tyranny of the mob is as bad as the tyranny of a noble class. Look at what happened to France when she tried that solution."

At that point Miss Rhoda let out a loud "hem!" and rose. The other ladies followed, leaving Stefano and Grandfather to their argument. The only one who was reluctant to depart was Miss Perkins.

II

I remember the following Thursday for three reasons. It was Galiana's saint's day, and we were to have a little party; one of my lovely new dresses was finished; and Andrea returned.

I was trying on the dress when he arrived and he made such an uproar that all of us flew downstairs to see what was happening. We followed the sound of music—the grand piano in the Salon of the Sybils, which was being played in great crashing chords. The music was more notable for volume than for beauty, but it had a fine martial ring; and somehow I was not surprised when I ran into the room, with Galiana on my heels, to see my cousin seated at the instrument pounding away at a great rate. He bowed when he saw us, but did not rise. Instead he began to sing.

> "Si scopron le tombe, si levano i morti,
> I martiri nostri son tutti risorti! . . ."

I needed no interpreter to understand. The ghosts of the martyrs were rising, with swords in their hands, to join in the fight for Italy's freedom. They were thrilling words. Andrea fairly shouted them, his golden curls tossing, his eyes shining. He ended with a mighty crash and bounded to his feet. He seized my hand and planted a hearty kiss upon it; then he turned to Galiana and caught her up in his arms. She shrieked with delight, her little feet dangling.

Still the same impetuous Andrea—but there were several significant differences. The blond moustache was new, and so was the bronzed hue of his skin; but the most striking change was in his attire. The loose red shirt, and the bandanna tied rakishly around his throat—how well I knew them, from Miss Perkins' descriptions! Not an official uniform, but as distinctive as any regimental facings, this was the costume worn by Garibaldi's soldiers—by the Thousand (as they were called) who had set sail from Genoa for the liberation of Sicily.

I was endeavoring to assimilate this startling new development when an outraged exclamation made me turn. Miss Rhoda stood in the doorway, her lavender satin skirts filling it completely. Over her shoulder I saw the pale face of the Contessa; her eyes were fixed on her daughter, still clasped in Andrea's red-shirted arms. And behind the Contessa was her omnipresent shadow—the maid Bianca.

Andrea lowered Galiana to the floor as Miss Rhoda swept into the room and bore down on the young pair like a battleship. The Contessa swayed, as if seized by faintness. Bianca's muscular black-clad arms supported her mistress instantly. After a moment the Contessa recovered herself and waved the maid away, but Bianca continued to stand in the doorway, her eyes fixed on her mistress with a look of doglike devotion that was very curious to see.

Andrea grasped Miss Rhoda's hand and pumped it so enthusiastically that her intended lecture turned into a series of stutters. His manner changed completely as he greeted the Contessa; he took her hand gingerly, as if it would break, and raised it to his lips. Then, with obvious relief, he turned to me.

"Cousin, it is good to see you. I am sorry I could not greet you on your arrival; but as you see, I had more pressing matters to attend to."

"I do see." I could not help smiling at the twinkle in his eyes. "But what a way to announce yourself, Cousin. Is that the new anthem of Italy?"

"It may well be that. A stirring song, eh? We call it Garibaldi's Hymn."

"Sing it again," Galiana begged.

Andrea was willing to comply, but as he went to the piano the Contessa said softly, "Galiana, you forget yourself. Andrea, you must not offend your grandfather in his own house."

Galiana drooped, as she always did when her mother reprimanded her. Andrea looked abashed.

"Where is my grandfather?" he asked.

"Here!"

He entered the room as he spoke. His face was set in a scowl that would have daunted most erring children, but not Andrea; he ran to greet his grandfather with outstretched arms, as is the Italian custom. The old gentleman received him with an arm extended, not to embrace, but to repel. He gave Andrea a hearty shove and burst into speech. I caught references to the red shirt, and words like "traitor" and "rebel."

Smiling, Andrea again tried to embrace the Prince, who swung his fist in a blow the younger man easily avoided. Then the old man turned and rushed out of the room. Andrea winked at us and followed.

III

They made it up, somehow, before dinner, which was a gala meal in honor of Galiana's saint's day. But Andrea was the center of attention. He had abandoned his red shirt in favor of formal evening attire, which was only to be expected; but I fancied that the disappearance of the uniform of insurrection was a concession on the young man's part. As for Grandfather— well, men are very peculiar. He glowered at Andrea from his position at the head of the table, and spoke in a gruff voice, when he spoke at all; but the light in his eyes as he looked at this grandson gave him away. I suspected that in spite of his lack of sympathy with the cause of independence he thought all the more of Andrea for fighting.

The meal was a succession of elaborate dishes, including Andrea's favorites, and it was the gayest supper I had enjoyed since my arrival. Andrea's bubbling good spirits infected almost everyone. Even Miss Rhoda smiled now and then, and Galiana was transformed. Her eyes shone and her mouth was constantly curved in laughter. Andrea directed his wittiest jokes at her.

The Contessa was silent, but then she always was. And Stefano, at the foot of the table, watched his brother with an enigmatic smile. I wondered what he was thinking. Did he return the love and admiration his brother felt for him, or did he resent the fact that Andrea was the favorite, even with his grim English great-aunt? Did he, too, yearn for the excitement of battle? It was impossible to tell for sure; but I thought it would not be surprising if Stefano failed to relish his role as business adviser.

After dinner we retired to the Salone dei Tritoni and had an evening of music. Both brothers played; I had heard Stefano once before, and had admired his precise touch with Bach and Vivaldi. Andrea played with more bravado and less finesse; he did not repeat the stirring hymn, but sang a series of romantic ballads in a rousing baritone, rolling his eyes at me during the most sentimental passages. It was all in good fun, and I enjoyed it as such; but as the evening went on I wondered if Andrea was not becoming overexcited. His cheeks were so flushed he looked feverish.

The Contessa was the first to rise. Her departure—with Galiana, of course—ended the entertainment, and soon afterwards we all said good night.

It seemed to me that I had hardly fallen asleep when I was awakened by sounds outside my door. I heard Miss Perkins' voice—subdue it as she might, it was a resonant, resounding voice—and footsteps moving quickly. I got up and slipped into a dressing gown.

Miss Perkins' door stood open. Her bed was not occupied. Now I began to be alarmed. I went to the end of the corridor, and below, at the bottom of the stair, I saw light. I descended into the west wing. The family apartments were on that floor, and there were more lights in that direction. I felt sure now that something had happened.

The door of one of the bedchambers was open and a beam of yellow candlelight spilled out into the hall. The room was filled with people. One of them was Miss Rhoda, almost unrecognizable with her hair up in curl papers and her bony figure undisguised by the limp folds of her dressing gown. As I peered in, she gave a sharp order.

"Get out, all of you. I don't need any of you except the signora."

The signora—a courtesy title—was Miss Perkins, who was looking down at the bed with an expression of concern. I could not see the occupant of the bed for the servants who stood around—two of the footmen and several maids. These people obeyed the order to leave, and as they came toward the door, I saw Andrea.

His eyes were half closed and their blue brilliance was dimmed. On his brow and his bared breast were white cloths; as I watched, Miss Rhoda removed one of these and replaced it with another, which she had wrung out with water from a basin. I caught a glimpse of Andrea's tanned body before the cloth was replaced, and at first I thought he must be wounded; there was a small reddish mark, roughly circular, on his right side just under the collarbone.

As I moved aside to let the servants out, Miss Rhoda saw me. "This is no place for you, Francesca," she said sharply. "Go back to bed."

"Is he wounded?" I asked anxiously. "Can't I do something to help?"

"No, no, child." Miss Perkins was helping to place the cold cloths on Andrea's head. "He isn't wounded, but he is feverish; some illness he contracted in Sicily. It is very unhealthy country. He may be infectious, so don't come any closer."

"But you," I began, unwilling to leave the poor sufferer until I had been assured he was not in danger.

"I sent for Miss Perkins because she told me she had had nurse's training," Miss Rhoda said. It was quite a condescension for her to explain anything; I knew she must be too worried to maintain her usual haughty dignity, and that increased my anxiety.

"I am too tough to catch anything," said Miss Perkins with a smile. "Go back to bed, my dear. There is nothing to worry about. The Count is in no danger. He is young and healthy; I have seldom seen so splendid a physique."

With that I had to agree. I gave the handsome invalid one last look and reluctantly departed. I would have liked to nurse him; it would have been a fitting return for his gallantry to me. If we had been in a novel, no doubt that is how it would have transpired. Instead he had two middle-aged ladies working over him, and I am sure he recovered much more quickly as a consequence.

He was better next day and on his feet again within the week, seemingly unhurt by his illness and as energetic as ever. Our quiet lives became full of activity, as Andrea invented schemes for our amusement. He took me to task, in his quaintly humorous fashion, for being so lazy about my riding, and under his brisk tutelage I soon became a fairly competent horsewoman. Scarcely a day went by that we did not ride out, visiting various beauty spots in the neighborhood. Andrea was quite a keen naturalist and knew a lot about the flora and fauna of the region. To see him holding a delicate flower in his big brown hand, earnestly discoursing on its beauty, was a most engaging sight.

Sometimes Galiana accompanied us. More often her mother found reasons for her to remain at home. The poor girl's morose face, on these occasions, should have cast a slight shadow over my selfish pleasure, but I'm afraid I didn't let it bother me much. I wondered if the Contessa suspected that the two young people were becoming too attached to one another. I could see no basis for such a suspicion. Andrea was charming to Galiana, but he was charming to everyone. Of course I fancied myself in love with him. Why not? He was a delightful companion, he had saved me from a fate worse than death and had risked his life to avenge me; he was incredibly handsome, brave as a lion, romantic as a hero of legend. I yearned to see him again in his dashing red shirt, and I tried to question him about his adventures in Sicily.

But on that subject Andrea's facile tongue failed him. He told me about Garibaldi, whose men thought of him as superhuman —about the General's courage, his tenderness toward the wounded, his cheerful acceptance of danger and discomfort. He narrated comical little anecdotes about the camp and the soldiers. But he would not talk about the fighting, and I finally came to realize that his memories were not the sort he could share with a young girl. I had sense enough to leave off questioning him when his face assumed an uncharacteristic expression of grim sorrow. But I did not have sense enough to realize that there were depths in him that I had not fathomed; that I had fallen in love with a handsome face instead of studying the real man.

Being in love is great fun, however, and I had a wonderful time. Miss Perkins often accompanied us on our expeditions; even Stefano joined us when the activity was not too strenuous for him. On the occasions when he was present, Galiana usually made one of the party too, but I could not decide whether she was allowed to go with us because Stefano was there, or whether it was he who sought out her company. Frankly, the subject did not interest me. It was no pleasure to have Stefano along; whenever he came there was an argument, usually about politics.

It was a dangerous topic at that time, and in our house. The Prince's method of dealing with what he regarded as Andrea's criminal folly in fighting with Garibaldi was characteristic of him; he simply ignored the subject as if no such thing had ever happened. Andrea went along with this. The brave, bright uniform did not appear again, nor was Garibaldi's Hymn heard within the castle walls. He even shaved off his moustache. Outside the walls Andrea spoke freely enough, especially when Stefano egged him on.

Grandfather might be able to erase unpalatable truths from his mind, but I suspected that the rest of the world might not be so accommodating. Ever since Andrea's return I had been worried for fear the soldiers might ride up and arrest him. But when I expressed this worry, the others laughed at me. Andrea laughed loudest of all.

Stefano was more explicit.

"Andrea is protected by the outmoded feudal system he fought against in Sicily," he said, with a mocking glance at his brother. "The Princes Tarconti are above the law; one might even say that, like ancient Roman tyrants, they *are* the law. Andrea had sense enough to misbehave outside the borders of Umbria. His actions would not be precisely favored in Rome, but they can be ignored—for favors rendered. Now if he had chosen to lead a band of rebels against Pio Nono, he might be in serious trouble. Not even our grandfather's influence could protect him."

Andrea's eyes flashed blue fire.

"I do not expect the Prince or anyone else to answer for me," he exclaimed. "Nor will I subdue my conscience to his. You may make jokes, Stefano, but you know Italy must be unified. Dismembered as we are, we are the plaything of the great powers. If you had seen the arrogant Austrian soldiers strutting down the streets of Florence, ogling the women—"

He broke off there, whether from delicacy or indignation I did not know. For a short while no one spoke.

We were sitting on the ground—or rather, on a handsome rug spread on the grass—in the sunshine. Galiana's tumbled curls shone like a blackbird's wings; the wild daisies she had twined in her hair looked like little stars in the night sky. Andrea, his coat discarded, his shirt sleeves rolled up to display his muscular brown arms, was flushed and handsome in his enthusiasm. Miss Perkins, too, was flushed, but not with enthusiasm. She had gotten sunburned on our last outing, and her nose was peeling.

Only Stefano sat upright, on a small chair that a servant had brought for him. His controlled features showed little emotion, but I thought he had frowned slightly when Andrea mentioned the Austrians in Florence—perhaps because he did not like being reminded that he was no longer free to travel about as his brother did.

"What a tiring fellow you are, Andrea," he said, with an affected yawn. "Do try to control your zeal; you are boring Galiana and Francesca—"

"He doesn't bore me at all," I broke in. "And I agree with everything he has said."

"How can you agree with something you don't understand?"

"I do understand!" I rose to my knees—and had to snatch at my skirts as my hoops bounced higher than decency allowed. Stefano laughed, and I went on indignantly, "This country is still in the Dark Ages, it is ripe for revolution! Why, I heard of a case, this very year, in Civitavecchia. Some young men had asked permission to show their respect for a deceased friend by carrying his coffin to the grave instead of allowing it to be carried by the religious society in control of funerals. They were granted permission, but several days after the funeral they were all arrested and sent to the state prison without trial. Such a stupid petty offense—even if it had been an offense, which it wasn't, because they had asked and been granted—"

"Yes, yes, I heard of the matter," said Stefano, speaking with difficulty through his laughter. "If you would stop to take a breath occasionally, Cousin, your speeches would sound more professional. The voice is the voice of Francesca, but the words, I suspect, are those of Miss Perkins. Dear lady, you mustn't turn my little cousin into a revolutionary. Life is very pleasant here; why don't you both enjoy it and forget your radical ideas?"

That ended the argument for the day; Galiana began to pelt Andrea with daisies, and a mock battle ensued. But it did not end the subject, for Stefano seemed to delight in stirring up controversy, and Miss Perkins was always ready to debate her favorite cause.

We received several newspapers. Grandfather pretended to read only the official organ of the Roman government, but occasionally he might be caught peeking into the Tuscan *Monitore* or even the *Gazzetta Piemontese*. Miss Perkins read them all, from front page to back. As the summer wore on, she became more and more excited. Garibaldi had been proclaimed dictator of Sicily, and there were rumors that he planned to attack the mainland. King Victor Emmanuel of Piedmont and his wily Prime Minister Cavour had spoken out against this move. Cavour was reluctant to have Naples owe its freedom to the guerrilla leader. He wanted his king to be the liberator of Italy. But there was a report that Victor Emmanuel, though publicly forbidding Garibaldi to cross the Straits of Messina, had privately written to the General encouraging him to go ahead. At the same time Piedmontese agents were trying to promote an uprising in Naples, so that Victor Emmanuel would have an excuse to march into Neapolitan territory himself in order to restore law and order.

Ironically, we were less well informed about what was happening in our own province than we were about events as far away as Sicily. The reasons for this were obvious; censorship ruled with an iron hand in the Papal States, and the wildest rumors flew about in lieu of facts. "Our busy friend the Falcon," as Stefano sarcastically called him, was busy indeed; his illegal newspapers and pamphlets blew about the province like snowflakes. They reached a wider audience than one might have supposed. When we rode to the village we would sometimes see a group of people clustered around one of the tables at the café, listening intently as one of their number read aloud from a crudely printed paper. The paper would disappear and the group would disperse as we approached, but none of us doubted what the subject of the paper had been.

A few of the posters even reached the castle. They were found in the most unexpected places; one morning the major domo discovered one pinned to the front door. There was a tacit conspiracy to keep these papers from Grandfather, but the rest of us read them avidly, and Miss Perkins was loud in her admiration of the writer's skill. Stefano enjoyed reading them aloud and commenting on the grammatical and rhetorical errors of the text.

Politics were not our sole concern, of course. Miss Perkins was almost as interested in antiquities, and one day, at her urging, we agreed to make an expedition to the Etruscan cemetery. I shrank from returning to the place where I had had such a terrifying experience, but I could hardly have avoided going without appearing conspicuous, for the entire household was to take part in the plan. Grandfather was eager to display his family treasures to Miss Perkins, and even the Contessa agreed to make one of the party. It was possible to reach the spot by carriage if one followed a long roundabout road through the hills. The older ladies and Stefano took this route, accompanied by a wagonload of servants carrying all the requisites for a formal meal alfresco. The rest of us rode by the direct path.

We set out early in order to do our exploring before the greatest heat of the day. It was a glorious morning, sunny and bright; but as we rode along the rustic trail, one could see the first hints of autumn in an occasional branch of reddening leaves. Taking a shorter path, we riders reached the spot before the others did, but agreed to wait for them before exploring the tombs.

Grandfather was in fine spirits. It was obvious that he had no recollection of having been here with me. I knew I had nothing to fear; Galiana and Andrea were with us, not to mention half a dozen servants. But I confess I felt a cold chill as I saw the high green mound that concealed the tomb of the princess.

Galiana looked lovely in a gown of white printed with scarlet flowers and a wide-brimmed straw hat tied under her chin with scarlet ribbons. Andrea was teasing her because this was her first visit to our celebrated cemetery.

"All these years," he exclaimed, "and you have never had the energy to come. Shame!"

"But how could I come alone?" she asked, fluttering her eyelashes at him. "Besides, I don't see anything very nice about the place. What is so exciting about weeds and broken stones?"

"I will have the honor of showing you, my dear," said Grandfather kindly. "But we must wait for the others. Sit down and be very still, and I will show you something that may interest you more than broken stones."

The servants spread rugs on some flat rocks so that Galiana and I could sit without spoiling our dresses. Then they withdrew, at the Prince's command, and for a long time we sat in silence.

In the warmth and the pastoral stillness my nerves began to relax. My earlier impression of the place as uncanny and frightening must have come from my sensitivity to Grandfather's strange mood. It really was quite a pretty place. Wildflowers bloomed everywhere. Birds sang in the trees; as we continued to sit quietly they began to flutter about and swoop from branch to branch. Then a rustle in the underbrush made Galiana start. Andrea put his fingers to his lips and shook his head, smiling. A rabbit hopped out into the clearing.

It was the biggest, fattest, whitest rabbit I had ever seen, and the least timid. It hopped out onto the path and stood still; it was so close that I could see its whiskers quiver as it sniffed the air. It must have scented us or seen us, but it did not seem at all disturbed by our presence. With a negligent air it began to nibble at the rank grass.

Galiana broke the spell by giggling. The rabbit gave her a sideways look and retreated, but not in a blur of motion as these wild creatures usually exhibit when startled. It bounced along in a leisurely fashion, as if it had just remembered a not very important engagement.

"How tame it is," I exclaimed. "Was it a pet at one time?"

"No," said Andrea. "All the rabbits here are wild; all are white; all are as unconcerned about man as that one you saw. It is because they have never been hunted. The peasants think they are supernatural creatures—the souls of the old Etruscans, perhaps."

"You don't hunt them either?" I said. "I'm glad, Andrea. They are so pretty and so trusting."

"They do not challenge a hunter," said Andrea, with a laugh. "Besides, the Prince has a fondness for them; eh, Grandfather?"

Grandfather shrugged; he disliked being accused of sentimental weaknesses, though he had quite a few.

"They are a curiosity," he said.

It was not long before we were joined by the rest of the party. They had to come the last few yards on foot, leaving the carriage at the road, and it was an amusing sight to see Miss Rhoda being respectfully propelled along by two sturdy footmen. The Contessa leaned on the arm of her maid, who lifted her over the rougher parts as easily as a man might have done. Stefano brought up the rear. He obviously found progress both painful and difficult, but no one volunteered to help him or expressed sympathy.

The tomb of the princess was the greatest attraction, so we went there first. Miss Perkins was fascinated by the monolithic stone door.

"How wise of you to have left it in position, your Excellency," she exclaimed. "So many excavators simply blast their way through by means of battering rams and explosives. I am amazed at how clever these ancients were in devising such things."

"It is a curious structure," Grandfather said. "You see how carefully it is balanced. Once the trick of opening it is known, it can be moved by one man. This crevice in the rock . . ." He slipped the fingers of his right hand into a crack that was in no way distinguished from other irregularities in the rock facing. "This crevice is the point of pressure. There is a rude catch, a sort of lock. One pushes . . . and *voilà!*"

And with the word—like the "Open Sesame" of the fairy tale—the great slab slowly swung out.

We were standing in a semicircle before the entrance, at a safe distance from the swing of the door, but as the great stone moved, several of us involuntarily stepped back. A breath of cool, dank air issued from the opening.

Stefano was watching me with his faint sardonic smile. He and Miss Perkins were the only ones who knew of my brief incarceration in this dreadful place, and I was determined that no one else should know of it. I thought I concealed my agitation rather well. I might even have forced myself to descend into the tomb if Grandfather had not, in all innocence, made a fatal gesture.

In our exploration of the tombs we had to manage without the assistance of the servants. They were reluctant to come into the valley at all; into the tombs they would not go, not even under threats of the direst punishment. The only exception was the Contessa's maid, who followed her mistress like a squat black shadow—counting, I suppose, on that lady's saintly character to shield her from spiritual dangers.

So, when the door of the tomb swung open, Grandfather assumed the role of guide, lighting one of the candles and preparing to lead the way. It was then that he struck down my faltering confidence by simply holding out his hand to me. Of course he meant to assist me on the narrow slippery stairs. His face was wreathed in a kindly smile. I had actually extended my own hand to take his when suddenly I realized that I was unable to move.

"No," I gasped. "No, I cannot—"

"*Moi, aussi,*" said Galiana, putting her arm through mine. "Oh, that horrible dark hole! We will stay here, Francesca; you brave gentlemen may descend into the dirt and the dark without us."

Thanks to her, my refusal was considered no more than a typical feminine weakness. The others tried to persuade us. Grandfather demonstrated several times the method of blocking the door so that there was not the slightest danger of our being trapped inside. A wooden wedge, inserted into the crevice, prevented the stone catch from slipping into place; the door could thus be completely shut and still yield to pressure from within. I watched this demonstration with shivering interest, wishing I had known of it on that other occasion; but even this, and Andrea's offer to carry her, did not persuade Galiana to risk her embroidered skirts on the stairs.

In the end only Grandfather and Miss Perkins, assisted by Andrea, made the descent. Miss Rhoda declined with a sniff; I doubt that she could have squeezed her crinoline into the space anyhow. The Contessa stood watching. The beads of her rosary, which was always in her hands when they were not occupied with embroidery, slipped slowly through her fingers.

The others stayed underground for quite some time. We could hear their voices, grotesquely distorted, and an occasional laugh from Andrea. When they finally emerged, Miss Perkins was beaming and repeating her favorite word.

"Fascinating. Absolutely fascinating. Your Excellency, do you consider the date of 800 B.C. reasonable for this tomb?"

The two of them continued their discussion while we visited several other tombs. I found that I was able to enter these without a qualm, although they had stairways even steeper and narrower than those of the tomb of the princess. These tombs were later in date than the first, being of the fifth and fourth centuries before Christ, and I found them more interesting.

The rock-cut ledges on which the bodies of the dead were laid had been carved in the shape of beds, with stone pillows and posts. One of the tombs had walls ornamented in bas-relief; shield and spears, helmets and pieces of armor showed that the occupants had belonged to a family of warriors.

Interesting as it all was, it was also a dirty, depressing experience, and even Miss Perkins had had enough when we emerged from the tomb of the warriors into the pleasant sunlight. While we explored the tombs, the servants had set out a magnificent repast, covering a stone slab that served as a table with snowy damask cloths, and bringing chairs from the wagon. We all ate too much—except the Contessa, who nibbled in her birdlike fashion—and after dining we were glad to sit or recline for a while before returning to the castle.

The Contessa decided to return to the carriage, where her embroidery was awaiting her attention. She and her maid went off, the slight form of the older lady leaning on the arm of the younger. They were both wearing their usual unrelieved black, yet no two persons could have been more different. Bianca's rusty black skirts were like molting plumage, and even the hoarse caw which was the poor creature's only mode of expression resembled the cry of a crow. As for the Contessa . . . There was one black swan among all the white ones that swam in the pond in the garden. The Contessa was like that swan, in her slenderness, her gliding movements.

After a while Miss Rhoda followed the Contessa, declaring that she had had enough of picnics and was ready to return to civilization whenever the rest of us were. Miss Perkins begged for a delay; she was ready to explore again, and Grandfather, flattered by her interest in his ancestors, offered to show her another tomb at a little distance. They invited me to join them, but I was having trouble with one of my boots and said that if I could fix it I would catch them up. So they went off; Grandfather offered Miss Perkins his arm, but she was gesticulating so animatedly that she failed to observe the gallant gesture. I looked about and realized that Galiana and Andrea were no longer with us. Even the servants had gone, after tidying up the remains of the banquet. Stefano and I were alone.

He had settled himself in the only patch of shade, under an

overhanging rock ledge, so I joined him. It was too hot at this hour to sit in the sun.

"I wonder where Andrea and Galiana have gone," I said, lifting my foot and inspecting my boot. The heel was loose. There was nothing I could do about it; makeshift repairs would not serve.

Stefano, leaning against the rock with his arms folded and his eyes closed, said shortly, "Leave them alone. They have few enough opportunities to be by themselves."

"Do you think they are—er—fond of one another?" I asked, conscious of a strange little pang.

"What gossips women are," Stefano said irritably. "Of course they are fond of one another. They have been friends since infancy."

"That isn't what I meant."

"I know." Stefano opened his eyes and stared at me. "Are you jealous, Cousin? I suppose that like all the females who pass through Andrea's life you fancy yourself in love with him."

"If I were, I certainly would not confess it to you," I replied angrily.

"Very wise of you," said Stefano, and closed his eyes again.

We sat in silence after that. I knew Stefano was not asleep, but I had no intention of arousing his biting tongue. After a while the heat and the quiet made me sleepy. I was beginning to doze when suddenly Stefano flung himself at me, knocking me off my rocky seat onto the ground and falling heavily upon me. A loud crash shook the air.

For a few seconds I was too dazed to move or cry out. The weight of Stefano's body robbed me of breath. Then he rolled to one side and I struggled to a sitting position. The angry words I was about to say died on my lips as I saw the heap of tumbled rock on the stone where we had been sitting.

"Good heavens," I exclaimed, putting my hand to my stinging cheeks. My fingers came away red.

"It is only a superficial cut," said Stefano. He was sitting up too, in a strange, twisted position. One leg was bent under him.

"You are quick to minimize other people's injuries," I

snapped; and then, seeing his pallor, I repented of my sharp tongue. "Are you hurt, Stefano?"

"How should I be hurt when you cushioned my fall so sweetly?" inquired my cousin.

His acrimonious reply did not wound me this time. I looked at the great heap of rocks, several of which were large enough to have dashed out my brains, and began to shiver.

"What a miraculous escape! I must thank you again, Stefano. How were you able to move so quickly?"

"I happened to glance up and see the rock tremble." With a grimace he could not repress, Stefano tried to straighten his leg. "It was foolish of me to sit there. Such rock falls are not infrequent."

"It was an accident then?" I asked in a small voice.

Stefano's eyebrows lifted.

"What else could it have been? Oh, but perhaps you are an heiress in disguise or an agent of the British government, so that some unknown villain is trying to destroy you. . . ."

He would have gone on in this vein if the others had not come running, alarmed by the crash. My only injuries were scrapes and bruises on the left side of my body, where it had struck the ground; so I was not too distracted to fail to notice that Galiana and Andrea returned together; nor too alarmed to wonder where they had been and what they had been discussing to make Galiana's cheeks so rosy red and her eyes so bright.

CHAPTER 7

Stefano had sprained his ankle; he retired to his lair, as I called it, and we saw nothing of him for several days. Our accident had one other consequence. The near fatality confirmed the servants' abhorrence of the valley of the tombs. To a man—and woman—they regarded it as an unlucky place and refused to enter it again.

Grandfather would never have admitted to being superstitious, but the incident had shaken him. That very day, pleased by her enthusiasm, he had given Miss Perkins permission to do some archaeological digging. But after the accident he refused to allow her to dig in the valley. He had a reasonable excuse, since the sinister reputation of the place made it virtually impossible to hire workers. Instead he suggested that Miss Perkins should attempt an excavation at the base of the hill on which the castle was situated. He had observed unusual rock formations there and had meant to investigate them himself at some future time. Miss Perkins accepted the suggestion with pleasure. Oddly enough, there was no problem about hiring workers. Apparently it was not the ancient tombs themselves but one particular cemetery the peasants feared.

This new pursuit amused all of us for a few days. We visited the excavations and I derived pleasure from watching Miss Perkins enjoy herself so thoroughly. She was always disheveled and dusty, since she was perfectly capable of snatching a shovel and digging at a promising spot. Her complexion was one of the unfortunate sort that burns but does not tan, so she was usually peeling. None of these inconveniences disconcerted her in the least. She actually discovered a few tombs, for my grandfather's calculations had been correct; the rock formations *were* man-made. The tombs were all poor ones, though, and all had been robbed in antiquity. By the end of the week all of us had lost interest except Miss P., who went out every morning to her excavations with her skirts hitched up and her eyes shining.

Toward the end of that same week, if my memory serves me correctly, our social life was enlarged by a rare event. Stefano invited us all to supper.

He had been speaking the literal truth when he told me that no one visited him without a formal invitation. Andrea often joked about his misanthropic tendencies and declared that he himself had not set foot inside the garden wall for months.

"He has traps set," Andrea said solemnly. "Last year he caught two poachers and Aunt Rhoda. She limped for weeks. The last time I attempted to call on him, a bullet narrowly missed my head. His servant, Piero, is one of the best shots in the neighborhood. I do not accuse, you understand, but—"

He broke off, throwing up his hands in pretended terror as his brother fixed him with a cold stare.

"Someone *will* shoot you if you continue to make such bad jokes," said Stefano. "I insist on privacy, it is true. I can enforce it only by being rude. If I did not, Aunt Rhoda would be bustling in every day to make sure the servants were cleaning properly, and all the bored inquisitive young ladies in the neighborhood would find pretexts to interrupt me."

Galiana turned red at this remark. So she, too, had attempted to invade Stefano's citadel! Stefano was not looking at her, however; he was smiling nastily at me.

"I can't imagine who would want to bother you," I said loftily.

"No? Unfortunately, Cousin, not everyone has your delicacy. At any rate I am giving you a chance to exorcise your curiosity. I will show you over my domain and my servants will give you an excellent meal. Will you come?"

"Oh, certainly," said Andrea. "We must encourage your coming out of seclusion, Stefano. You are becoming very social."

In truth we had seen a great deal of Stefano since his brother returned. I couldn't imagine why he spent so much time with us, for he didn't seem to enjoy himself.

I did look forward to seeing his house, and that evening I

dressed with special care. I had given up my mourning altogether. It was not hard to find an excuse for doing so; there had not been a single bolt of black fabric in the collection brought from Florence, and Grandfather himself had assisted in the selection of my new gowns. Between fear of his displeasure and simple vanity—and other reasons—I had not objected to the pale-green silks, the ivory brocade, or the blue satin. Now I had a dozen lovely gowns to choose from, and even with Teresa helping me I wavered between a rose taffeta with flounces trimmed in lace and narrow black velvet ribbons, and a white satin embroidered with tiny rosebuds. Finally I decided on the taffeta, and then there was the difficult decision of what ornaments to wear. Grandfather had given me my mother's jewels. Among them was a lovely seed-pearl set—bracelets and necklace and earrings, and a set of ornaments for the hair. I decided to wear this, and at last Teresa had me turned out to my satisfaction.

Miss Perkins was the only one of the older people who was having supper with us. Grandfather seemed to like to see us four young people together; he had declined the invitation and overruled Miss Rhoda's protests, saying that it was foolish to talk of propriety when four cousins dined together on the family estate. Besides, Miss Perkins would be more than sufficient as a chaperone. Stefano had insisted on her coming, since she had never seen his house. The two of them got on well; she was one of the few people who was never disturbed by his sarcastic tongue. In fact, she made herself popular with everyone. Grandfather found in her an antiquarian as learned and as enthusiastic as he was, and even Miss Rhoda had succumbed to her countrywoman's amiable willingness to be of service.

When I was dressed I went to see how Miss Perkins was progressing with her own toilette. I had finally persuaded her to accept a new dress, since her wardrobe was not adequate for the state Grandfather kept, even *en famille,* and I was looking forward to seeing her in the soft gray silk we had selected. I found her seated before her mirror, her mouth screwed up, as one of the maids tugged at her hair.

"This is ridiculous," she remarked, as I entered. "I feel like a figure of fun. Every time I move my head, this young person swears at me in Italian."

"You look lovely, I assure you," I said, laughing. "The Queen herself has not more presence."

"Humph," said Miss Perkins. "Well, I suppose I must suffer in order to be presentable. That will do, that will do. I can't stand any more hair pulling."

She did look nice. The crinolines then in fashion were becoming to the slender and the stout alike. They gave older ladies dignity, and the modest hoops Miss Perkins wore balanced the considerable size of the upper part of her body. The gown was trimmed with bunches of artificial violets, and it had long pagoda sleeves and a white embroidered collar; for Miss Perkins had shouted with amusement at the very notion of a decolletage.

Galiana and Andrea were waiting for us in the drawing room. They sat stiffly in two chairs separated by the entire width of the room, under the watchful eyes of the Contessa and Miss Rhoda. Galiana also had a new dress. The color was stunning on her—pale yellow-gold trimmed with bands of darker gold velvet. I assumed her mother had provided it, since I certainly had not, and I wondered where the money was coming from.

The Contessa was in unusually good spirits. With a warm smile she bade us enjoy ourselves, and she even patted Andrea affectionately on the arm as he bent to kiss her hand. Miss Rhoda grumbled, as she always did; this evening she predicted rain and remarked that my gown was cut too low.

We set out across the gardens. Miss Rhoda's fears of rain were all in her own mind; it was a beautiful evening. Andrea had given Miss Perkins his arm and was amusing her by his florid compliments.

Stefano met us at the door of the house. He wore immaculate evening dress, with bloodstone studs and amethyst cuff links. We went over the house before dining, and my expressions of admiration were quite sincere. Everything was in miniature, but in perfect taste. My favorite room was the library. It was a perfectly proportioned chamber, with lovely stucco reliefs of classical figures on the ceiling instead of the usual paintings. There was a big hooded fireplace, with the family arms above it. Wide French doors opened onto a terrace beautifully planted with rose bushes and gardenias, and the little courtyard beyond was enclosed by high brick walls hung with vines.

"Bluebeard's den," said Stefano, glancing at me. "You see, ladies, how harmlessly I occupy my time. I am working on a family history for the Prince, and I amuse myself by writing on philosophical matters."

As we went through the other rooms, we had evidence of the other occupations with which he filled his time. An easel and a model's throne showed his interest in painting, but he refused to show us his work, saying it was too amateurish. The grand piano in the drawing room was frequently used, as I knew from hearing him play. He even had a small laboratory fitted up. We left this place hurriedly, wrinkling our noses against a strong smell of chemicals.

We saw only the ground floor. One of the rooms had been fitted up as a bedchamber, and none of us needed to ask why Stefano did not use the upper chambers.

We were to dine on the terrace. It was an exquisite setting, with a tiny fountain tinkling in the courtyard. The food was excellent, as Stefano had promised. I noticed that all the servants were men, and could not refrain from commenting on this.

"I told you he was a misogynist," said Andrea. "Even his housemaids are men! That is why the furniture is not dusted, eh, Stefano?"

"I defy Miss Perkins, wearing white gloves, to find a speck of dust," said Stefano, who was in an unusually amiable mood.

We had almost finished the meal, and the light was dying fast, when the peace of evening was broken by the sound of a gunshot.

"Poachers again," said Andrea calmly, as I turned a startled look on him. "I have told you, Brother, that you must enforce the laws. We may sympathize with the poor devils needing food, but they have no right—"

"It is not sympathy, but lethargy, that keeps me from enforcing the law," said Stefano, scowling. "The Prince is strict enough about his rights; I am surprised that any of the peasants dare invade his grounds."

All evening Miss Perkins had nobly refrained from talking politics, but this reference to an outmoded feudal right was too much for her; we were treated to a forceful lecture on the unfairness of the hunting laws. "You aristocrats hunt for pleasure," she exclaimed indignantly. "As if it were a pleasure to inflict pain on other living creatures! At the same time you forbid starving men to hunt for food for their families, when you have deprived them of the means to earn an honest livelihood by monopolizing the means of production."

"Don't scold me, Miss Perkins," said Andrea pathetically. "I don't deserve it. You know I agree with you."

"And you know I do not," Stefano remarked with a smile. "But I won't argue with you, Miss Perkins. You are too clever for me."

He did argue, though, and the two of them went at it hammer and tongs, while Galiana yawned and Andrea laughed. But Andrea was conscious of his pretty cousin's boredom, and as soon as possible he offered to escort her on a walk through the gardens. Stefano waved them away without interrupting the point he was making. I don't think Miss Perkins even noticed that they had gone.

When the moon rose in its silvery splendor, bathing the courtyard in pale light, Stefano finally ended the argument.

"That was refreshing," he said. "But now I think we had better find Galiana and Andrea. Shame on you, Miss Perkins, for failing in your duties as chaperone."

"I could do with a walk myself," said Miss Perkins calmly. "I am afraid I made a glutton of myself."

The young pair were not to be found in Stefano's small enclosed garden, so we went out into the grounds of the castle. As we passed into the rose garden, Stefano leaning heavily on his cane, another shot sounded. This one was much closer, and Stefano stopped with an angry exclamation.

"I must put an end to this. Moonlight is tricky light to shoot by; the fool may injure someone."

He had scarcely finished speaking when something buzzed through the air, passing between us so closely that I felt the wind of it on my hair, followed by a third explosion.

I would have stood there staring stupidly if Miss Perkins had not wrapped her arms firmly about me and dragged me to the ground.

"Lie still," she said, as I struggled to free myself. "That was a bullet. Another may follow."

"But—Stefano—" I began, and then saw that my cousin had

disappeared. Almost at once I heard him calling out, and the voices of the servants answering. Lights flared up and began to move through the darkened gardens.

Before long Stefano came back to us, accompanied by one of his grooms, who was carrying a lamp. His lips curved up when he saw us sitting on the ground in an undignified jumble of skirts and hoops.

"You can get up now," he said, gesturing to the footman, who extended a hand to help me and then hoisted Miss Perkins to her feet.

"Oh, dear," she said, looking sadly at her skirts. "My pretty dress. I fear I caught my foot in it; there is a sad tear."

"Better your skirt than your scalp," said Stefano. "I think the danger is over; my people are searching the grounds, but the idiot who fired those shots will not linger when he realizes how close he came to murder." Then he turned to me. "Really, Cousin, I begin to think you are bad luck for me. Are you *sure* you have not stolen the crown jewels, or kidnapped the heir to the throne?"

II

I knew Stefano's words were one of his peculiar jokes, but a few days later I began to wonder myself if someone had not mistaken me for the object of a family feud. Two accidents in one week might have been coincidence, but a third. . . .

A few days earlier I had moved into my new rooms. The dilatory workmen had finally finished; the suite gleamed with fresh gold paint and smelled of varnish and beeswax. I had never lived in such luxury. The great canopied bed was draped with silk finer than anything I had ever put on my back, and the carpets were so deep I enjoyed walking barefoot on them. Two great carved wardrobes bulged with pretty clothes, and the dressing table held new toilet articles—silver-handled brushes and heavy crystal bottles.

However, the castle had a few inconveniences that I have not mentioned. One of them was the variety of animal life that infested it. Not noxious insects—Miss Rhoda would never have tolerated the degree of dirt that breeds such creatures. But there were flies and wasps; and even Miss Rhoda's British housekeeping could not keep down all the mice, or the bats that hang about the eaves of such old places. I was not especially afraid of these creatures, but no one likes animals that are apt to swoop or scamper out at one unexpectedly. Once before, in my old room, I had fled screaming from a bat that came through my open window. The poor thing was as frightened as I was, I suppose; at any rate, it blundered back out the window before Teresa and Miss Perkins came running in, to find me in the wardrobe with the door shut.

Mercifully, Teresa was with me, helping me dress for dinner, when my second encounter with a bat occurred. The heavy draperies were pulled back from the balcony windows, which were open because of the heat, but the light inner curtains had been drawn, since the light attracted moths and other insects. Teresa was brushing my hair when the curtain suddenly billowed out. We both turned to look, and I saw the flapping black shape behind the thin white fabric.

"Oh, dear," I exclaimed, in more annoyance than fear. "Do chase it away, Teresa, before it gets in, I cannot stand. . . ."

As I spoke, the bat came in through the opening in the curtains. It was enormous, much bigger than the others I had seen, and at once I realized that there was something wrong with it. Unlike the other creature, which had fluttered in aimless panic, this one seemed to be moved by a demonic energy. Instead of seeking the window, and freedom, it flung itself across the room in a series of swooping loops and then darted straight at me.

With a shriek I fell to the floor, my arms over my head. Teresa's face had gone white as dirty paper. I could have excused her for fleeing; instead she ran toward me, swinging the hairbrush like a club. It was luck, not skill, I am sure, that enabled her to hit her target. The solid silver of the brush struck the creature down. It fell to the floor not three feet from me, but it was not dead; its wings continued to flap feebly, and I could have sworn that, crippled as it was, it tried to crawl toward me. I had one horrible, unforgettable view of its evil little face—the eyes glowing red, the fanged mouth open—before Teresa grabbed my shoulders and dragged me away.

Our screams—for Teresa had been shrieking mindlessly the whole time—finally attracted notice. Galiana was the first to burst into the room. She fell back with the most earsplitting shriek of all as she saw the black horror flapping on the floor. Andrea was right behind her. He did not hesitate; thrusting Galiana roughly behind him, he snatched a poker from the fireplace and began beating at the fallen animal.

I didn't faint, but I certainly lost control of my limbs and my powers of speech for a brief time. When I regained them I was lying on the chaise longue, with Teresa crouched at my feet, her teeth chattering like castanets. Miss Perkins was bending over me. My eyes went at once to the spot on the floor. . . . A towel had been thrown down there.

"It is gone," Miss Perkins said. "The Count took it away. Francesca, did it touch you?"

"I don't think so," I said. "Teresa . . ." She looked up when I spoke her name, and I smiled and touched her shoulder. "Teresa hit it with my hairbrush. Really, Miss Perkins, I am ashamed to have been so silly. It was only a bat."

Teresa, still paper-white, muttered something I did not understand.

"Nonsense," Miss Perkins said sharply.

"What did she say?" I asked. I felt better, and was about to sit up when Miss Perkins pushed me back.

"The word means 'vampire,'" she said. "Foolish; there is a variety of bat in South America that drinks blood, but it has never been seen in Europe. However. . . . Francesca, are you certain it did not touch you, not even brush you in passing? Lie back and let me examine—"

"I am quite sure, really. What is all the fuss about? Where is Andrea?"

He returned at that moment and came to my side.

"The rug will be burned," he said, addressing Miss Perkins. "Is she—did it—"

"I will scream in a minute if you don't explain," I shouted. "Good heavens, you are all talking as if it were really. . . ."

Miss Perkins and Andrea exchanged glances. "Tell her, if you think it wise," he said.

"It had hydrophobia," Miss Perkins said. "If even a drop of its saliva had touched you. . . ."

Then I did feel faint. Andrea smiled reassuringly.

"The danger is over, Cousin. You were almost the victim of a rare and unusual accident. I can only recall one other case of a bat having this dreadful disease. As you know, it is more common in dogs, but occasionally other creatures are afflicted by it. Only occasionally; you will never see such a thing again in your lifetime, I am sure.''

"Good God," I said faintly. Again I put out my hand and touched Teresa. "She saved my life, then. If she had not struck it with my brush. . . . Ask her, Miss Perkins, make sure she was not hurt. She is the one who took the risk.''

Miss Perkins insisted on examining the girl, but her plump bare arms and round face were free of punctures. The color had returned to her face and she was about to get to her feet when suddenly she let out a shriek and fell back, her eyes staring.

The Contessa had just come in accompanied by Miss Rhoda and the ever-present Bianca. They had been attracted by the noise and confusion; now Andrea explained the situation, and both expressed their horror and their relief. Then the Contessa went in search of Galiana, who had returned to her room, overcome. Bianca followed her, as a matter of course, and as they left I saw that Teresa had extended one hand in a strange gesture, her fingers rigid.

Andrea saw it too. With an angry exclamation he struck at the girl's hand.

"Andrea," I cried. "What are you doing? After what she has done for me—"

"Forgive me," Andrea muttered. "You don't understand. I—you had better rest now. I will have the servants remove the rug." And he ran from the room.

"Send Teresa away," said Miss Perkins. "She should rest too, she has had a shock.''

I did so. When we were alone I turned a look of bewilderment on my friend.

"I don't understand."

"It is simple enough," Miss Perkins said with a sigh. "Superstition; the curse of the uneducated. These poor peasants explain everything that is uncommon as supernatural. The gesture Teresa made was the ancient defense against the evil eye. Afflicted persons such as hunchbacks and cripples are often regarded by the ignorant as agents of the devil. In medieval times women like Bianca were burned as witches. This country is still in the Middle Ages in many respects. I understand that the Contessa actually saved the poor creature from persecution in her home village. I think she is weak-witted, perhaps as a result of her affliction. It is no wonder that she regards the Contessa as a saint.''

"I still don't understand why Teresa should have made that gesture."

"It is only a theory, of course," said Miss Perkins modestly. "But I suspect that Teresa, like her ancestors, believes in a world which is infested by malevolent spirits. There is no such thing as accident. Therefore the rabid bat was a demon in animal form, a sort of witch's familiar. And since Bianca is regarded as a witch. . . ."

"That is ridiculous," I said. "I must talk to Teresa. But I can't forget, Miss P., how brave she was in defending me."

"She deserves even more credit for facing what she believed to be an emissary of Satan," said Miss Perkins with a smile. "Well, thank God it turned out as it did. We can forget the incident and go down to supper."

We went down, but I did not quickly forget the incident. Of course I did not believe in witches or curses or vampires. It was equally impossible that any human agent could have sent the infected creature to attack me. All the same—three "accidents" . . . it was surely stretching coincidence rather far.

III

Some day—if I should live to see it—I will probably tell my grandchildren that the accident of little Giovanni was the turning point in the development of my youthful character. It may be so. But I suspect the change was more gradual, the result of a series of incidents, each one of which wrought a small but meaningful alteration, until finally the accumulated influence exploded into my consciousness.

I well remember the day when the explosion occurred. It was a hot afternoon in August, and I was drowsing over a book in the rose garden when the summons from the village reached me.

I had been to the village several times, driven by I know not what vague impulse; I hesitate to call it kindness or charity, for charity should be more courageous. I crept there surreptitiously, fearing Galiana's mockery; and the things I took, small baskets of food, worn-out clothing, were pilfered from the kitchens and storerooms, though I might have asked Grandfather for anything in the castle. The villagers were so poor that they accepted anything gratefully, and even as I was handing out my scraps I felt guilty for not doing more.

I spent most of my store on little Giovanni and his family, since I had a particular interest in them, and also because of the mother's delicate condition. Heaven knows there was nothing delicate about the conditions of her life; she worked like a man, hoeing and harvesting in the fields when she was not working in the house. In spite of my contributions she did not look in good health, so when the messenger—one of Giovanni's innumerable brothers—came running to me, I had a premonition of what had gone wrong. The child was gray-faced and incoherent in his alarm, but Piero, who was ubiquitous in those days, popped out from behind the shrubbery and explained enough to make me anxious to leave at once.

With Piero to accompany me I needed no other escort, and I wanted none. I did not even want to search for Miss Perkins; time was already of the essence, if the urchin was to be believed, and I was afraid—oh, God, my stupid vanity!—I was afraid of being found out by the others. As I was mounting my horse, however, I remembered Miss Perkins' skill in nursing, and paused long enough to scribble a hasty note, which I gave to one of the stablemen—who would hand it to one of the scullery maids, who would hand it to an upper maid, who would pass it to a footman. . . . Eventually it would reach the recipient, and I urged haste with as much eloquence as I could command.

With Piero behind me and the child on his saddlebow, I galloped to the village. The main street was drowsing in the heat of afternoon; most of the dwellers were taking the siesta that is common in this country. But there was a group of silent watchers before the door of the house where Giovanni lived, and they all turned, their faces brightening, as I dismounted and flung my reins to Piero.

I had been inside the house before, and had found it hard to conquer my aversion to the foul filth of the interior of what had once been a comfortable medieval townhouse. But never had the abysmal poverty of the place struck me so forcibly as when I entered the darkened chamber where the mother lay. The windows were tightly shut and the stifling heat was enough to make me giddy. I tried to tell the hovering women to open the shutters (there was, needless to say, no glass in any of these houses); but they only stared blankly.

I managed to get one of the shutters open. The rush of clean air was unbelievably welcome. It roused the sick woman; as I knelt beside her, she opened her sunken eyes and smiled feebly. But I had seen death before. I knew its signs, and I saw them on the bloodless face.

Then I cursed my selfishness. If I had brought Miss Perkins, she might have been able to do something. I was helpless. I could only take the woman's gnarled hand in mine. That seemed to please her. She was beyond speech; but she tried to raise my hand to her lips. That gesture broke me down. I knelt, sobbing, with bowed head, while the woman died.

Miss Perkins found me there, only minutes later. Her firm hands on my shoulders roused me and lifted me to my feet. She sent me out of the room. One of the women had to go with me, I was so blinded by tears.

It was considerably later when Miss Perkins came out of the house. Her shoulders were bowed and she looked more than her actual age; but when she saw me she straightened up and tried to smile.

"Come now, Francesca, tears accomplish nothing. You did your best for the poor soul. You did what she wanted."

"I could do nothing," I exclaimed angrily.

"You came when she called. I don't think you realize how these simple folk think of you; your presence gave that woman comfort. No one could have done more."

My eyes were so swollen I had difficulty in seeing. The sunlight made them ache. I covered them with my hand, and heard myself saying,

"It is not right. They shouldn't live this way. I want to do something, Miss Perkins. Show me how to help! I have been selfish and stupid, but I will be different from now on."

Miss Perkins was far too sensible to respond to this outburst —genuine though it was—with sympathy or sentimentality.

"Splendid," she said, in her most matter-of-fact voice. "If you really feel that way, then stop crying, wipe your eyes, and think how you can help that orphaned family. Come, take your hand from your eyes; watch me try to mount, that ought to make you laugh."

I think she was clumsier than usual, on purpose.

So began my first exercises in benevolence. As I had expected, Galiana was very much amused by it all. Grandfather made no objections; charity, after all, was a suitable occupation for a lady. He let me rummage through the cupboards and storerooms for food, and watched with a smile while I laboriously sewed smocks and shirts for the children. I was a poor seamstress, and Giovanni wore my ill-made garments with a look of indignant suffering, but he did not complain. He was always a silent child. I think he was so used to having his thumb in his mouth he did not know that feature could be used for the purpose of speaking

On one of my visits to the village, a strange thing happened. I had gone down with a basket of bread, fresh from the oven. I was greeted with the usual smiles and genuflections (which I was frail enough to enjoy more than I should) but I was also conscious of a sort of bustling in the background that I had not encountered before. As I entered, I saw the figure of a man slip through a door at the back of the house. For a moment he was silhouetted against the sunlight, and I had an impression of someone unusually tall, wearing a slouch hat pulled down low on his head. Then the door closed, and the people of the house seemed to relax. When I went up to the room occupied by the Messana family I found them eating a haunch of veal. I knew these people never saw meat unless they were given it; and I certainly had not brought this roast. Poaching did occur, but it was extremely dangerous and was usually limited to small game such as rabbits. They would never dare kill a calf.

When I asked, they looked at me with the bland expression oppressed people learn in order to conceal their feelings. Finally Alberto, the eldest boy, said something about the priest. I knew better, of course. Father Benedetto was a good man, who tried to relieve his flock; but he was as poor and uninfluential as any of the villagers.

I could not help connecting the unusual food with the mysterious visitor. A thrill ran through me. Surely I had seen that tall, agile figure before. The twist of his body as he slipped through the door reminded me of a similar movement—a sideways slip from the saddle, a sword arm extended. . . . I needed no further evidence to be convinced that I had seen the Falcon on one of his errands of mercy.

I was learning a little sense, though; so I said nothing to the Messanas. Miss Perkins was my only possible confidante. I sought her out as soon as I returned home, and she listened to my story with interest, but with a twinkling eye.

"My dear child, you are hopelessly romantic. It is very unlikely that your hero would occupy himself with such trivia. I know he is said to help the villagers whenever possible; he seems to have a special interest in this district. But surely he would send one of his men on such an errand."

"I suppose so," I said, disappointed. "He has been very quiet these last few weeks, hasn't he? Since Andrea came home, in fact."

Andrea's stay was about to end, however. According to Galiana, he had already remained longer than he usually did. He found the castle very boring and went off frequently to seek amusement elsewhere.

"It is you he came to see," said Galiana, looking at me slyly. "I think he will marry you, eh?"

"Why should he?" I inquired.

"It would be most suitable. The two parts of the family united; the two pets of your grandfather. He would be happy to see it, I think."

"Would you be happy to see it?"

Galiana turned away, her face unusually sober.

"He is not for me. I must marry an elder son. We have no money, it is for me to restore the family."

"That's silly," I said. "Andrea won't be a pauper; he will have quite enough to live comfortably. Do you—do you care for him, Galiana? Lately I have thought. . . ."

"If I did, it would make no difference," said Galiana sullenly. "I must marry an elder son. But you—you love him too."

The betrayal in a simple three-letter word! I couldn't smile, she looked so sad; and in fact her statement made me consider the question more seriously than I had done.

"I love him," I said thoughtfully. "Certainly I do. But do I love him as a cousin, a kind friend—or as a man? I don't know, Galiana.''

"Then you are a fool," said Galiana. "Sometimes I wish you had never come here. Sometimes I almost . . ." And as I stared at her in shocked surprise, she burst into tears. "Oh, pay no attention to me, I never mean what I say," she sobbed. "I am not in love, I must marry—"

"I know," I said, putting my arms around her. "An eldest son. You are a bigger fool than I am, Galiana, if you really believe that."

Andrea left us the next day, to visit a friend whose villa was located near Lake Como. I was sorry to see him go, and yet, after my conversation with Galiana, it was almost a relief to have him out of the way for a while. We slipped back into our old quiet ways. When the blow finally fell, it came all the more painfully for the calm that had preceded it, like a thunderclap out of a smiling blue sky—that unheralded thunder that was regarded by the Romans, and their Etruscan mentors, as a sign of the gods' displeasure.

CHAPTER 8

One breathlessly hot afternoon a week or so after Andrea's departure we were having tea in the drawing room. I remember thinking—how ironically, as events were to prove!—that the day was very dull. The heat seemed to have stupefied our wits, and the group that had never been noted for vivacity seemed even duller after having known Andrea's laughter.

Then the bombshell fell. It was heralded by the bursting open of the great doors, and the appearance of Grandfather, flushed and panting. He was waving a paper. At first he was too breathless to speak.

The face of a scandalized footman appeared over his shoulder. I don't think I had ever seen one of the family open a door since I arrived; a servant always appeared when he was needed. This time Grandfather's unusual haste had anticipated the servant, but the man consoled himself by slamming the doors smartly after Grandfather had entered the room.

I rose and went to take his arm.

"What is it, Grandfather? Is something wrong?"

"No, no; it is good news, excellent news." He waved the paper, his face aglow. "They have caught him! At last the rascal is behind bars!"

Miss Perkins made a queer gurgling sound and rose slowly to her feet. The others stared. It was Galiana who exclaimed.

"Il Falcone? I don't believe it. Who is he, then, your Excellency?"

Some of the color faded from Grandfather's face.

"Most unfortunate," he said gruffly. "One of our best families. . . . It is the Cadorna boy—Antonio."

I caught Miss Perkins' glaring eyes in time to suppress my cry

of distress. I had forgotten; I was not supposed to be acquainted
with Antonio Cadorna. But Galiana did cry out.

"Antonio? *Non è possible!* He came to my parties, when I
was small. . . . Is he not a friend of Andrea?"

"I am afraid it is only too true," said Grandfather, ignoring
the last question. "Yes; unfortunate; a fine old family. But the
wretched boy deserves his fate. He was lucky to escape from the
affair in Perugia so easily. Apparently he did not learn from that
experience."

"Oh, dear."

I thought it was Miss Perkins who had emitted that particularly English expression of well-bred regret. Then I realized that
the speaker was Miss Rhoda. The Contessa looked at her
disapprovingly.

"I, too, regret the shame of a respectable family," she said.
"But Antonio deserves his fate. They will execute him, your
Excellency? His family's prominence will not excuse him this
time?"

"No. He is to be hanged in the square at Parezzo in three
days. This letter, from Captain De Merode, informs me of the
facts; quite proper of him, to notify me so promptly. He invites
me to witness the execution." Grandfather spoke firmly, but he
avoided our eyes. "I must go, it is fitting. As you know, I own
the inn in Parezzo; we will have a fine view from the front
balcony. You ladies can visit the shops. You will enjoy that,
eh?"

His air of forced cheerfulness told me he was not as callous as
he sounded. All the same, the idea that we could be bribed by a
shopping expedition into witnessing such a dreadful thing made
me angry. I turned away.

"No, I won't go."

"You may please yourself," said Grandfather stiffly.

"I will be honored to go, your Excellency," Galiana
exclaimed. "That is, if Mama—"

"But of course," said the Contessa. "It is proper, my child;
he is an old playmate. You must pray for his salvation."

"Good God," I burst out, and would have said more; but
again Miss Perkins caught my eye.

"I think we should all go," she said.

I knew her so well by then I could understand the way her

mind was working. She was right. There were good reasons why we should go. In my first horrified reaction I had not thought clearly.

"Very well," I said.

Grandfather smiled. He took my acquiescence for obedience to his will, and was relieved, like all domestic tyrants, that he did not have to reprimand someone he loved.

"Excellent," he cried, rubbing his hands together. "I will go and tell Stefano the good news. He is in the library."

As soon as the doors had closed after him, Miss Rhoda rose to her feet. There was so little extra flesh on her bones that it was almost impossible for her face to wrinkle, but she looked extremely agitated.

"I don't understand this," she said. "I remember that boy; he was here for a visit a few years ago, at Andrea's invitation. He cannot be the bandit they are looking for."

"No, no." Miss Perkins was pacing up and down; her knuckles beat a veritable tattoo on her nose. "No, it is a trick—a trap. They mean to execute the young man, no doubt, but they hope to catch a bigger fish with him as bait."

"Good heavens," I exclaimed. "You have it, Miss P. The Falcon—the real Falcon—will not allow his friend to be murdered!"

Galiana clapped her hands; her face glowed with excitement.

"Il Falcone will come to his rescue," she cried. "Do you suppose he will ride into the piazza on a great black horse, as he did in the village? Only think, we will have a perfect view! The *albergo* faces on the piazza, and the balcony—"

I could endure no more. I ran from the room, out of the house, into the gardens. I needed air. As clearly as if I had seen it only the day before, the face of the young man came back to me—his soft brown eyes, the bravado of the big moustaches hiding his gentle mouth.

Antonio could not be the Falcon. All other factors aside, there was one overriding objection to the identification. I myself had seen the rebel leader rip the proclamation from the church door. He had held his sword in his right hand. Antonio had lost that hand. De Merode must know this as well as I did. Miss Perkins was right, the execution was a trap; it was just the sort of diabolical scheme De Merode would invent. The Falcon would not allow his friend to be hanged. Honor and affection alike would demand an attempt at rescue. No such attempt could possibly succeed, for De Merode would take every precaution. And we, as unwilling witnesses, might have to watch not one, but two, brave men die.

I was young enough to find the Contessa's character quite inexplicable. I had seen her weep over a dead canary, and she was unfailingly kind to poor clumsy Bianca; yet this same woman had once described, with vindictive pleasure, the torments meted out by the Inquisition to heretics and unbelievers. I know now that human nature is not consistent, and that morbid fanaticism is not limited to any single faith; but I still find such an attitude horrible. At seventeen I was not only horrified, I was incredulous.

Galiana's callousness concerning a boy whom she had known and played with as a child was just as repugnant. Miss Perkins would say that her upbringing was at fault, but to me it seemed like a complete lack of moral character. She was like her father, who had been a cruel, arrogant man. How could I have considered her my friend?

I was pacing up and down the terrace in a state of great agitation when Andrea came in sight on the path that led to the stables. He was in riding costume; his dusty boots and flushed, perspiring face betrayed the haste with which he had traveled. He came to me with long, angry strides.

"Is it true?" he demanded. "I heard the news yesterday and came straight back. Is it true about Antonio?"

"Yes," I said miserably. "Andrea, I'm so sorry."

"Others will be sorry," said Andrea between his teeth. He ran into the house.

I stared after him. A new, monstrous suspicion had leaped into my mind. Was it possible. . . . No, I told myself; it could not be. All the same, Andrea was not the man to stand idly by while a friend went to his death. Now I had a new fear to haunt me.

II

We were to leave early next morning, in order to be in Parezzo in good time. A messenger had been sent off to warn the innkeeper of our arrival, so that he could prepare the rooms required for the family and its servants. I assumed that the persons who occupied those rooms would be summarily evicted. The privileges of aristocracy are very convenient—for the aristocrats.

I had a long talk with Miss Perkins, but came away without being much encouraged. It seemed impossible for two women to do anything to aid the condemned man; yet we decided we must attend the ghastly ceremony on the remote chance that something might occur. Besides, now that I had had time to think it over, I knew I would die of suspense if I had to wait at the *castello* for news—even though the news would almost certainly be bad.

Later in the afternoon I went looking for Grandfather in order to ask which of the maids would be coming with us. There was really no need for me to ask him, for the servants were expected to move at a moment's notice, without any regard for their feelings or plans. However, my newly aroused social conscience had made me more aware of the servants' personal lives. I had learned, to my surprise, that Teresa was married to one of the footmen and had an infant whom her aged mother tended during the day. Teresa had to run back and forth to give the infant the nourishment only she could supply, and I thought she might like advance notice in case alternate arrangements had to be made.

At that point in my thinking I felt both amused and embarrassed. Were alternate arrangements possible? I assumed they were; but if Teresa would prefer to remain near her child, I might ask Grandfather to let me take someone else.

When I reached the library I found the door slightly ajar. This was so unusual that I paused and looked about, and saw the slightest movement, no more than a breath of displaced air, at the far end of the corridor. So one of the servants had been listening at the door. Galiana had told me they did, but this was the first time I had had any real evidence of the fact.

I was about to enter the room when I heard a voice I had not expected to hear, and the words it spoke were so startling that I stopped where I was and listened myself, quite unashamed.

Miss Rhoda was the speaker; soon I heard Grandfather's low growl, and also Stefano's voice. He was speaking English, as he always did with Miss Rhoda. Grandfather's grunts were in Italian, but I understood most of them.

"He will be killed!" This was the comment made by Miss Rhoda that had reduced me to eavesdropping. "So ill advised, so reckless—"

"It was certainly ill advised of him to rush in here bellowing threats and curses," said Stefano's dry, drawling voice. "But very characteristic of Andrea, you must agree. If he had kept his opinions to himself, he might have gone to Parezzo and done something equally ill advised—challenging De Merode, perhaps, or attacking the executioner."

Andrea must have gone straight from me to Grandfather and expressed himself with his usual vigor. I was afraid that if I went into the room, the speakers would not go on. Carefully I pushed the door open a little wider until I was able to see them. Stefano sat in his usual chair, his neatly shod feet extended, his cane balanced between his hands. Miss Rhoda leaned against the desk, her hands pressed to her flat bosom; her face was turned away, but distress was evident in every line of her body. Grandfather was trying to look unconcerned. He did not succeed.

"Something must be done," said Miss Rhoda. "He must be prevented from going."

Grandfather muttered something I did not hear; and Stefano, infuriatingly, burst into a laugh.

"Don't worry about your pet, Aunt Rhoda. Something has been done. The Prince has given instructions to two of the larger footmen. How I look forward to watching Andrea trying to kick down his door! His comments should be very amusing."

"Thank God," said Miss Rhoda, with a sigh.

"What are you saying?" snarled Grandfather, turning on Stefano as if he needed some object on which to vent his anger. "You will not see him, or hear him; you are coming with us."

"Oh, no." Stefano shook his head. "Unlike my impetuous brother, I know there is no hope for Antonio, but I am not sufficiently depraved to enjoy the spectacle of a former acquaintance choking his life out at the end of a rope. Besides, my presence will be needed here. You may lock Andrea in his room, your Excellency, but I am the only person who can keep him there. Andrea is appallingly strong when he is in a rage; he is quite capable of battering the door down and massacring several footmen—even if they are not susceptible to bribery, which they probably are."

"Hmph," Grandfather grunted. "Very well. Suit yourself."

He turned to the window and stood there with his hands clasped behind his back. Stefano looked at the tall, unyielding figure; and for a moment his face had an expression I had never seen on it before. Then he shrugged and gave his cane an expert twirl, catching it in his hand.

"Your commendation and thanks touch me deeply, your Excellency."

"Oh, Stefano, don't be so rude," snapped Miss Rhoda. "Can't you see we are all upset today? Your plan is a good one. I approve of it. I count on you to keep Andrea here, it would be disastrous if. . . . Well, then, I will go and pack."

As she surged majestically toward the door, I picked up my skirts and fled. Considering Grandfather's mood, it would be better for me not to talk to him. It is said that listeners hear no good of themselves; but my eavesdropping had been quite useful. It had relieved one worry. Andrea would be prevented from helping his friend. Did that mean, I wondered, that the mysterious Falcon would not make an appearance?

III

We reached Parezzo late on the following afternoon. It was a hot, dusty ride, through the heat of the day, and even with the windows wide open the great traveling coach had the approximate temperature of a baking oven. The first sight of the old city would have aroused a cry of admiration from people less preoccupied than we were. Like San Gimigniano, Parezzo is a city of towers. Square and massive, they are a grim reminder of the troubled days of yore, when only the thickness of a man's walls protected him from the avarice and cruelty of his neighbors.

Frowning and formidable despite their age, the medieval walls followed the steep contours of the plateau on which the city stood. Only in one section, where a precipice plunged sheer into the green valley below, did the walls disappear, as if admitting that here man's handiwork could not improve on nature's own defenses. On a higher ridge above the town was the silhouette of battlemented walls—the old fortress, built in a remote age by a tyrant who commanded the streets of the town from that impregnable site. As a state prison and military barracks it still dominated the unfortunates who lived in its shadow.

After a steep ascent we passed under a great stone archway whose fourteenth-century masonry was guarded by modern soldiers. A crowd of people eddied around the gate. The soldiers were stopping everyone who sought entry to the city, checking papers and identities. The Tarconti arms on the side of our coach were a sufficient passport; we were waved on without delay.

Miss Perkins continued to point out architectural and artistic attractions until Miss Rhoda irritably asked her to stop blocking the window and cutting off what little breeze there was.

We were all crumpled and cross when the horses stopped in front of the Albergo Tarconti. It had once been a town house. One of the earlier Tarcontis, alive to the commercial interests of the family, had converted it into a hotel. We had the entire first floor to ourselves. It was a large, rambling structure, so there was more than enough room. Grandfather and his valet occupied one wing, while another was assigned to us ladies. A large central chamber, handsomely decorated, was to be used as a communal sitting room. It overlooked the piazza and had a long stone balcony running its entire length. The furnishings were amazingly fine for an inn—velvet settees and armchairs, marble-topped tables, porcelain lamps and a crystal chandelier. The beams of the ceiling had been carved, painted and gilded; one motif, repeated over and over, was the crest of the Tarconti family—a boar rampant on a field of blue.

A sponge bath and a change of clothing restored me to the state in which I had begun the day—one of physical ease and extreme mental disquiet. I went at once to the sitting room, where refreshments had been set out. Miss Rhoda had brought not only her favorite tea, but a maid who knew how to prepare it, and the scene that awaited me was, except for the setting, quite like the normal afternoon ritual. Miss Perkins, cup in hand, was standing at the window, so I joined her.

"Tomorrow they will carry chairs and tables out onto the balcony," she said quietly. "The pots of flowers on the balustrades will be put on the floor so as not to impede our view. It is a beautiful old town, Francesca. The municipal hall is particularly fine, and so were some of the houses we passed on the main street."

"Yes, I particularly remember the butcher shop," I said bitterly. "Bloody carcasses hanging at the open door. . . ."

But the piazza was beautiful. Of considerable extent, irregular in shape, it was virtually walled in by buildings of at least six stories in height. The cathedral, Santa Maria della Consolazione, was directly across from the inn. The communal palace dominated the eastern side of the square. Under its Romanesque arcade the town market was held twice a week. Its square tower rose high in the air, higher even than the *campanile* of the church. In the center of the piazza was a handsome fountain with a group of life-sized statues—Neptune, trident in hand, with dolphins at his feet.

On this day the spectator's eye was held, not by the ancient beauties of the piazza, but by newer structures. The broad steps before the *duomo* were hidden by rows of wooden seats. Most were not more than long planks raised on temporary supports; but in the center was a sort of loggia, with luxuriously cushioned chairs shaded by a striped canopy. I was reminded of Miss Perkins' description of the emperor's box at the Colosseum, from which the cruel Caesars watched the murder of the early Christian martyrs; for the canopied loggia was situated so that its occupants would have a direct view of the gallows.

It was almost finished. Workmen were hammering at the high crossbeam from which the rope would hang. The platform was ten or fifteen feet off the ground, so that everyone could see well. . . .

After supper, which was served in the sitting room, the nervousness that afflicted us all became increasingly apparent. Grandfather sat stolidly in the great velvet armchair that had been reserved for him; he was pretending to read a newspaper, but he never turned the pages. Miss Rhoda's embroidery made no more progress than his reading, but the Contessa stitched steadily at the great altarcloth. The gold thread in her needle flashed in the lamplight as she drew it in and out of the velvet.

The rest of us didn't trouble to conceal our feelings. Miss Perkins tramped steadily back and forth the length of the room, from the fireplace to the windows and back. Galiana was on the balcony, leaning over the railing and calling back descriptions of the progress being made on the gallows. It was not quite dark outside, but soon the situation—especially the rhythmic pounding of hammers from outside—got on my nerves to such an extent that I determined to go to my room. I doubted that I could sleep, but at least the dreadful hammering would be muffled by distance.

I was gathering my work together when the landlord came to announce a visitor. I immediately sat down again. I would not have missed this visitor for the world. It was Captain De Merode.

I had never seen him so impeccably turned out. His boots shone almost as brightly as his gilded cuirass, and the beautiful white plume in his helmet would have graced any lady's bonnet.

He accepted a glass of wine and sat turning the crystal goblet slowly in his hands.

"Well," barked Grandfather. "How is it going, Captain?"

"_Bien, très bien,_" was the tranquil reply. "A pity that the young man must die; but he seems determined to end on the gallows. This is not his first offense."

"And is he really the Falcon?" Galiana asked.

"It seems so." De Merode sipped his wine.

"You know he is not," Miss Perkins exclaimed; and then abruptly turned her back as De Merode glanced at her.

"I don't know anything of the sort, mademoiselle. Naturally, he denies that he is. But one would expect Il Falcone to do that, even under the most strenuous questioning. . . ."

"You have tortured him," I burst out.

Grandfather crumpled the newspaper and hurled it to the floor.

"Francesca, be silent. Such matters are not. . . . It is sometimes necessary. . . . Whether the boy is or is not the man in question, he is a criminal who deserves death. Captain, what measures have you taken to prevent a rescue? For, no matter what the man's identity—"

"Oh, of course we have taken precautions," said De Merode readily. "The Falcon has a motley band of adventurers at his command; some of them might be foolish enough to attempt a rescue. To date, no such effort has been made. We have the prisoner in the deepest cell of the fortress, where he is guarded day and night by a dozen men."

The Contessa raised her head from the cloth she was making for the glory of God.

"His men must know the impossibility of rescue," she remarked. "The oubliettes of the fortress have guarded prisoners securely for centuries. The dangerous time, surely, is when the prisoner is removed to the place of execution."

"Your intelligence is admirable, madame la comtesse," said De Merode. "Naturally we know that, and have taken steps. May I say," he added, turning to Grandfather, "that I am honored to see you here, your Excellency. But I am sorry not to see the Counts Stefano and Andrea. Are they, perhaps, abroad in the town?"

I was certain that De Merode knew quite well where my cousins were; but he accepted Grandfather's palpably false explanation without the flicker of an eyelash.

"What a pity they are both indisposed," he remarked. "I had hoped that Andrea in particular would attend; his recent—er—indiscretion has been overlooked, thanks to the favor of His Holiness, but some small demonstration of enthusiasm for our holy cause might be well advised."

Grandfather stiffened.

"My grandson's indiscretions, as you call them, are my affair, Captain."

"I hope so, your Excellency. I sincerely hope so."

De Merode drained his glass, put it on a table, and rose, adjusting his sword.

"I must take my leave. There is much to do, as you can imagine; but I could not neglect your Excellency. May I bid your Excellency good evening? Ladies. . . ."

Finally he was gone. I felt as if some oppressive presence had left the room.

"What did he mean?" Miss Rhoda demanded. "About Andrea? You assured me, Your Excellency, that you had arranged—"

"This questioning is intolerable," shouted Grandfather. "I

will retire. I suggest you ladies do so too."

He went storming from the room.

IV

During the night, servants moved some of the furniture from the salon onto the balcony. Grandfather's crimson velvet chair occupied the central position. There were other armchairs, footstools, and several low tables. Because of the orientation of the *albergo*, the facade was in the shadow when I went out at nine o'clock, but the air was already uncomfortably warm and Galiana, who had been in her chair since eight, was complaining about the heat.

"It will be an oven by noon," she grumbled. "What a silly time for an execution! I thought dawn was the traditional hour."

"The Captain wants the greatest possible degree of publicity," said Miss Perkins. "He has a good eye for drama, you must agree."

The scene was certainly lively and colorful. The viewing stands on the steps of the cathedral had been decked with tapestries and cushions. In stark contrast, the gallows was draped in black cloth. The strands were as yet unoccupied; presumably these favored seats were reserved for dignitaries. I saw one man, with a gaudily dressed woman on his arm, turned away from them by a soldier.

The troops were already in position. The vivid reds and blues of their uniform jackets, the flashing brilliance of their weapons formed a continuous barricade all the way around the piazza. The poorer spectators, who did not rate seats in the stands, were beginning to congregate. One would have to come early for a good view.

I felt a little faint and turned away from the piazza with its ghoulish crowd. The servants were serving breakfast. I watched Galiana bite into a roll thickly smeared with preserves, and for a moment I thought I would be sick.

Then Miss Perkins, who was watching me, remarked, "You must eat something, Francesca. Unless you mean to fast as a religious exercise?"

Sarcasm was not one of her habits. I looked at her in hurt surprise. She gave her head a little sideways twitch, so I went to the serving table and took a roll. After a moment she joined me.

"Look at the stones in the facade of that house," she said, leading me to the far corner of the balcony. "Unless I am mistaken, they are ancient Etruscan tombstones. One sees many such examples of building materials being reused."

We stood with our backs turned to the others. Miss Perkins glanced around; then she reached into her ample bosom and produced a scrap of paper. Pantomiming silence, with her fingers to her lips, she unfolded it and showed it to me.

There was a single line of writing—emphatic, spiky handwriting, clearly disguised.

"Courage," it read. "He will not die."

Down in the lower-right-hand corner was a tiny hieroglyphic—a bird with a hooked beak.

Despite Miss Perkins' warning I almost let out a cry.

"What does it mean?" I whispered. "Where does it come from?"

"I found it under my door this morning," Miss Perkins replied softly. "The meaning is clear, I think."

"Yes, yes, but . . ." Hope and astonishment closed my throat. I crumbled the uneaten bread in my hand. "It is kindly meant, a gracious thought; but why should he take the trouble to reassure you? Miss Perkins, are you—"

"No." Her gray eyes were steady; I could not doubt her. "I swear to you, Francesca, I know no more about the Falcon than you do. I was about to ask you the same question. If he knows me well enough to be aware of my sentiments on this matter, he must have known that I would confide in you. It would be easier to reach me, in my cubbyhole near the stairs, than to get to your room; and you have a maid who might have found it first. Are *you*—"

"I am sure of only one thing, and that is that I am sure of nothing. Miss Perkins, I will go mad of suspense!"

"We must keep our heads, my dear. I was not joking when I said you should eat. Keep your strength up and be on the alert. One never knows."

And this amazing woman then proceeded to eat the note, washing it down with a long swallow of tea. I began to giggle hysterically, though I knew she had done what had to be done.

Encouraged by the note, though utterly bewildered by its import, I forced down some bread and tea and then took my chair, determined to miss nothing. My heart was pounding so hard I thought everyone must hear it; but no one was completely calm that day.

Except perhaps the Contessa. Dressed in her usual black, looking icy cool despite the heat of the day, she had for once abandoned her embroidery. Her head was bent over her prayer book, and her lips moved continually. It should have been an edifying sight—this saintly woman praying for a man she despised—but I found it chilling.

Galiana's giddy comments were scarcely less horrible. For once she had found enough excitement. Bouncing up and down in her chair, her bright eyes darting from side to side, she saw everything that went on, and commented on it.

As the sun mounted higher, the gaily bedecked stands began to fill up. As I had suspected, the occupants were distinguished persons; their clothing spoke of their wealth and social position, for all were dressed in their best. Several men wore gaudy uniforms with yards of gold braid, huge epaulets, shiny buttons, and the most fantastic hats. One portly gentleman, whose stomach was so large he could rest his folded arms on it, had a tricorne hat as large as that of the great Napoleon I, and rows of medals decorated the breast of his bright-blue coat. There were even a few ladies among those present. Some carried ruffled parasols to protect themselves against the sun.

There were so many soldiers that they stood literally shoulder to shoulder. The bright bayonets on the muskets formed a shining wall behind which the humbler townsfolk pushed and shoved for position. The central part of the piazza was kept clear, but the perimeter, behind the barricade of soldiers, was a jostling mass.

Beyond the spire of the *duomo,* on the high westward promontory, the stone walls of the fortress could be seen. I looked at them, thinking of the young man who lay there, in the deepest dungeon. Would they send a priest to him, before the end? I shuddered to think of the torments he had endured, of the mental torture suffered by one so soon to die. As the morning wore on with horrible slowness—yet so quickly for the condemned man—the hopeful mood inspired in me by the note began to fade. The Falcon might boast of his intentions, but how could he possibly succeed? The piazza was swarming with soldiers, all armed to the teeth. If the Falcon was contemplating a dramatic last-second rescue from the very foot of the gallows, he must be desperately foolhardy. There was no way out of the piazza. The stone-walled houses around it were like a barricade. Mounted soldiers barred the exits into the narrow streets and *vincoli*. Even the doors of the cathedral and the entrances into the other buildings were guarded. There were six soldiers at the inn door, under our balcony. Galiana, leaning over the balustrade, was exchanging remarks with them. Neither her mother nor Grandfather reproved her; they were too occupied with their own thoughts to notice, and she was taking full advantage of this unusual freedom.

I decided we had all been misled by the Falcon's earlier demonstrations of reckless action. There was no reason to suppose he would wait until the last minute to attempt a rescue. No, he would perhaps attack the party while it was on its way to the place of execution, from the fortress. The streets were narrow, walled in by houses; from one of these a party of determined men might rush out and snatch the prisoner.

Then Galiana straightened up.

"Ah, but the Captain is a clever fellow," she said, addressing me. "Guess what he has done now. The soldier just told me. He has moved poor Antonio from the fortress; it was done last night, in secret. He is now guarded in the new barracks, on the east of the town. The soldiers will bring him from there to the piazza, and now all the inhabitants of the houses along the route are being taken from their homes and imprisoned in the fortress until after the execution."

She returned to her conversation with the soldiers, and Miss Perkins and I stared at one another in consternation.

"The Captain is a brilliant fiend," she exclaimed. "Even if the Falcon learns of the change in plan, he will be unable to arrange an ambush. Oh, dear, oh, dear; this is dreadful!"

The blazing golden orb of the sun lifted slowly toward the zenith. The stands were completely filled. In the central box sat a stout, mustachioed man dressed in a bright uniform. There were other dignitaries with him, wearing formal clothes and top hats, with ribbons stretched across their breasts.

The piazza was now a solid mass of people, except for the cleared space in the middle. Almost all the standing spectators were men. Their cheap dark clothing made a somber frame for the brilliance of the decorated stands. Some of the windows and balconies of the houses were crowded with spectators. Other windows were significantly shuttered; soldiers stood guard on certain of the balconies, and even on the lower roofs. De Merode had not missed a trick.

Suddenly there was a disturbance in the crowd under the arch at the opening of the Via della Stellata. The instantaneous response of the soldiers in the vicinity showed their alertness; they pushed ruthlessly at the crowd, ignoring the cries of pain, until a small space had been cleared. In the midst of this open area two officers, armed with swords instead of muskets, were struggling with a single figure which looked very small and slight between them. It wore a long dark habit and hood like that of a friar; but as the soldiers roughly grasped it, the hood fell back; and I, like the other watchers, let out a cry of surprise. The face displayed was that of a woman—not the sunburned skin of a peasant, but the pale, proud profile of a handsome young lady. I caught only a glimpse of it, and its expression of anguish, before the uneven struggle was quickly ended and the slender figure was borne away. But Galiana had recognized her.

"Santa Maria, it is Elisabetta Condotti. How did she get here? Her family has had her locked up for weeks."

"Who is she?" I asked.

"Antonio's betrothed. At least she was betrothed to him before he became a revolutionary. She is supposed to be married next month to a rich banker in Florence."

"Good heavens," I whispered. "That poor, poor creature."

"They will lock her up again, on bread and water," said Galiana, staring with interest at the spot where the struggle had taken place. "How foolish it was of her to do that."

"She hoped to see him, one last time," I said softly. "Perhaps even to speak to him, or touch his sleeve. . . . And he would see her, and know that she had courage enough to be with him at the end."

Miss Perkins looked at me curiously but said nothing.

Through the long hot hours, Grandfather had sat like a graven image, moving only to accept a glass of wine or a biscuit from his valet. Even the incident of the young woman had not wrung a comment from him. I knew he was not as unkind as he seemed;

I knew he was not completely happy about what was going on. But in the conflict between his natural kindness and his pride of caste, the latter had to conquer.

Just when I thought my stretched nerves could not bear the waiting any longer, there was a stir and eddy among the crowd across the piazza. Here, under a lichened stone archway, the Via di Guistizia entered the square. The soldiers there were shoving at the crowd, clearing the way.

"But surely it is not time," I exclaimed, turning to Miss Perkins. She consulted her watch.

"It is twenty past eleven. That cunning devil De Merode has thought of everything."

"And the Falcon has not made his move. It is too late; he can never reach Antonio here."

Unconsciously we had both risen to our feet. So had the others. Only Grandfather sat stolidly, staring straight ahead. Even the Contessa was standing; her lips still moved and her rosary slipped through her slender white fingers.

The soldiers had cleared a path into the center of the piazza, a passageway walled with naked steel. Mounted men, a dozen or more of them, guarded the archway. Through it came the procession.

Two men on horseback led it. De Merode was not one of them. Then I saw him; his tall white plume stood up bravely above the caps of the soldiers who surrounded the condemned man. As they drew nearer, our vantage point above the heads of spectators and soldiers allowed us to see every detail. De Merode, his unsheathed sword in his hand, walked immediately behind the prisoner.

Antonio's head was bare. His arms were bound behind him. His white shirt was open, the collar turned under, in order to facilitate the hangman's work. There was a soldier on either side of him, half supporting him, for he could barely walk. His face was unmarked, but I did not doubt that De Merode had used all the methods at his disposal to wring a confession from his prisoner—not of his identity, but of his leader's plans. The torture had an additional subtle cruelty in its results; physical weakness deprived Antonio of the ability to walk proudly to death with his head held high. He was a pitiful sight, but not a gallant or inspiring one, as he was dragged along between the two soldiers. From the crowd came a low, sullen sound, like the rumble of far-off thunder. It died as De Merode's voice cracked out an order and fifty bayonets rose to position.

In the quivering silence the little cavalcade approached the steps of the gallows. A black-robed priest walked beside the condemned man; a low mumble of Latin reached my ears, but the priestly exhortations were wasted on Antonio, whose head had fallen onto his chest.

The sunlight was so bright it hurt my eyes. The heated air distorted objects; they seemed to quiver and sway. . . . No! It was not an error of vision; the stands before the cathedral really were swaying. Slowly the whole massive structure folded, as if a giant invisible knife had cut straight through the center. It collapsed in a horrible mixture of wooden planking and torn cloth—and human flesh. A great scream went up; dust and splinters flew into the air.

Before the dust had time to settle, another sound rent the shaken air—not human this time, the roar of an explosion. A cloud of smoke rose behind the roofs of the town in the direction of the barracks.

This second catastrophe, on the heels of the first, completed the demoralization of the crowd. There was no longer a cleared space in the piazza; it was jammed with screaming, struggling bodies. Some of the spectators tried to get away, others ran toward the wreckage of the stands, where fallen bodies writhed.

Above the din one voice rose—that of De Merode, shouting orders. By sheer force of personality he had managed to keep a few of his men under control; they stood fast around the prisoner. De Merode had Antonio by the arm. A new ray of hope had given strength to the injured man; he stood upright, swaying with weakness but alert, looking from side to side. Yet his position was still hopeless; the point of De Merode's sword touched his breast, announcing as clearly as words: One move at rescue and I myself will perform the execution.

The piazza began to clear as the terrified spectators fled. The place was like a battlefield, with bayonets flashing, horses plunging out of control, blood and fallen bodies everywhere. I had heard no shots. The soldiers could not fire into the turmoil for fear of hitting an ally; and indeed, at this point there was no enemy to be seen, only utter confusion. So far as I could see, the only ones injured were those who had occupied the viewing stands, and I thought vindictively: It serves them right, the ghouls. Yet the sight was terrible. Some of the soldiers were pulling away the debris in order to free those pinned beneath. Those who had not been caught were staggering or crawling away from the scene of the disaster. One very fat young woman did not appear to be badly hurt, for she was scuttling along quite fast on her hands and knees. The angle of her crushed hoops gave us a shocking view of ruffled pantalets and plump pink legs. She was more comical than terrible, but another person— the military gentleman I had noticed earlier—was a frightful sight as he reeled across the square clutching his head. He had lost his tricorne hat, his blue coat was torn, and his features were almost obscured by blood. The crimson streams must have blinded him, for he plunged straight at the little group that still stood fast—the condemned man and his guard. . . .

Where was the guard? The soldiers had disappeared as if blown away by a magician's spell. It must have happened very quickly, for De Merode recognized that fact at about the same time I did. A great flash of light shone, as his sword arm moved. It was crossed by another flash—the sword of the bloodstained man in uniform, who was staggering no longer. Straight as a spear, the padding that had disguised his body flung aside, he struck the Captain's point away before it could pierce the prisoner's breast. Antonio went staggering back and was caught by a man garbed in the same rough dark clothing the poorer townspeople wore. This man helped him into the saddle of a horse whose uniformed rider had vanished like the other guards.

The piazza was still a melee of struggling bodies, but the struggle was purposeless no longer; for every bright crimson uniform there were several dark-clad men—some of them masked—and a dozen miniature battles were going on. A few of the mounted soldiers still kept their seats, but one by one they went down before the assaults of those grim dark figures. Demoralized, virtually leaderless, the soldiers were no match for opponents who were obviously acting in accordance with a brilliantly detailed plan. The sharpshooters on the roofs and balconies dared not fire; the struggling bodies were too close together. Speed was on the side of the attackers, too. The entire attack was begun and ended within the space of a few minutes, and the plunging horses galloped away with their new riders.

One struggle still went on, at the very foot of the gallows. De Merode's face was contorted in a wolflike snarl, his sword struck sparks every time it moved. The other man's face was obscured by the ghastly crimson mask, but it obviously did not affect his eyesight. Every stroke was neatly parried, every step calculated. Now that Antonio had been saved, the Falcon's design was to keep the Captain occupied while his men made good their escape. How he knew when the moment arrived I cannot imagine, but at a certain time he moved to attack instead of passively defending himself. De Merode was no mean antagonist. The two were evenly matched, and the unknown was unable to penetrate that flashing guard. I let out an anguished shriek as the Captain's blade barely missed the other's body. The piazza was clearing rapidly; soon the soldiers would get their wits together, and it would be a hundred to one. . . .

Miss Perkins snatched up one of the pottery jars, planted with a lovely trail of salmon geranium, lifted it high above her head, and threw it.

The first time I saw her I was reminded of a man, and now her broad shoulders and sturdy frame carried out the task with almost masculine strength. The heavy pot, which I could not have lifted, came crashing down into the piazza. It did not come close to the duelists, but the sound made De Merode start. He recovered almost at once; but he was just that fraction of a second too slow to deflect his opponent's blade entirely, although his catlike quickness undoubtedly saved his life. The thrust was aimed at his breast. It pierced his arm instead, but the blow was enough to fell him. His adversary snatched the bridle of a horse that was being held for him. But instead of mounting he paused and surveyed the piazza with a sweeping glance.

"Hurry, hurry," shrieked Miss Perkins, jumping up and down. She was clutching my arm. I had bruises next day, five little black spots, but at the time I felt nothing.

It almost seemed as if the Falcon had heard her. His gaze turned toward the balcony where we stood. The drying mask of his face cracked as he smiled; he drew one finger down his cheek, through the scarlet stains—and put it to his mouth. From Miss Perkins came a breathless squeak of laughter.

"Tomato juice," she gasped. "Under his hat. . . . Hurry, you mountebank!"

The Falcon's narrowed eyes had already left her; they focused on the object for which they had been searching. One of the fallen bodies, dressed in rough homespun, was moving. The Falcon reached it in a series of leaps, dragging his horse with him. Bending, he swept the man up and flung him across the saddle. Then he mounted and turned the horse's head toward the Via della Stellata.

His sword was still in his hand and he used it ruthlessly, striking down the soldiers who snatched at his stirrups. He was almost at the archway, and safety, when De Merode rose to a sitting position. His right arm hung limp; he held the pistol in his left hand—leveled it—and fired. He must have missed at such a distance. But his shot was a signal to the other men with firearms. A rattle of ragged musket fire burst out, and one of the bullets struck the target. I saw it strike, saw a puff of dust go up from the back of the brilliant blue coat of the mounted man. The impact of the shot flung him forward across the horse's neck. The startled animal bolted into the Via della Stellata, followed by a dozen men.

CHAPTER 9

No one said anything to Miss Perkins about the flowerpot, though the others, including Grandfather, must have seen her throw it. But the Contessa's attitude toward my friend changed. She shrank from Miss Perkins after that as she would have shrunk from a vicious criminal.

The ride back to the castello would have been uncomfortable in any case, even without the Contessa's refusal to sit next to Miss Perkins. We left immediately. Grandfather was like a man possessed, he barely gave us time to pack, and the fact that we would not reach home before nightfall did not alter his decision. He asked De Merode for an escort—and was met with a curt refusal. Every man was needed.

The Falcon had escaped, but only for the moment. His horse had been found running loose, its flanks horribly streaked with drying blood—real blood this time, not a substitute. The two men it had carried had found refuge in a stable or cellar, protected, no doubt, by a sympathizer in the city. There were hundreds of hiding places in the old town, but they would all be searched, and until the search was completed, the town was sealed off. De Merode himself would have to vouch for any person who wanted to leave.

It was late afternoon before our coach reached the Porta San Giovanni. All the other gates were closed. This was the only exit from the town, and it was guarded by a detachment of soldiers. The coach stopped and I heard the outraged voice of old Bernardo, the coachman, expostulating with the soldiers. I tried to look out the window, and bumped heads smartly with Galiana, who was trying to do the same thing.

The first person I saw was Captain De Merode. His arm was

in a neat white sling and he was paler than usual; otherwise one would not have known that he was injured, for he was faultlessly erect in the saddle and his expression was the usual one of cool indifference. Grandfather's great black stallion stood next to the Captain's horse, and the two men were talking together. Finally Grandfather shrugged and turned aside. De Merode came toward us.

"Ladies, your pardon, but I must ask you to get out of the coach. I assure you, the delay will be as short as possible."

Miss Rhoda voiced loud objections, but to no avail. Grandfather said nothing. So we got out and the soldiers practically took the coach to pieces. There was no space, no matter how small, they did not look into.

The transaction took less time than one might have expected, and in a few minutes we took our places again. As soon as we were through the gate, the horses broke into a trot and they maintained this pace for the entire trip except when it was necessary for them to be rested. What with the heat and the jolting, the ride was physically most uncomfortable. As for our mental states, they may be imagined. Conversation was impossible; even Galiana gave up the attempt after a few disjointed exclamations of curiosity and frustrated interest; and since Miss Perkins and I could not talk confidentially, we did not try to talk at all. Darkness had fallen before we reached the castle. We went straight to our rooms, exhausted.

I found Teresa waiting in my beautiful new suite. The bed was turned back, warm water stood waiting to be poured into the hip bath, and a fresh nightgown was laid out. Grandfather had sent one of the footmen galloping ahead to announce our imminent arrival. He had also carried the great news. I expected that Teresa would be overflowing with questions, but I found she knew as much about the affair as I did.

If it had not been for Miss Perkins, I probably would have gone on thinking of the servants as obedient, convenient puppets instead of as human beings. To think of them in the latter fashion was not convenient; it raised too many uncomfortable questions. It was common knowledge that the servants in a great house knew all the secrets of the house, often before the master did. The masters took this for granted and joked about it, as they would have joked about the clever tricks of a pet. It never seemed to occur to them that this secret pathway of communication might have its dangers, or that the creatures they disregarded might threaten them. The barriers between the two classes were unbreachable. Teresa and I were on friendly terms; I thought she trusted me and liked me. But that night, when I tried to get her to express her reactions to the dramatic events that had transpired in Parezzo, she simply shook her head and made noncommittal noises. She had been taught to hold her tongue—and I was one of the enemy. I didn't blame her, but it was exasperating. I finally asked her point blank, "Can he escape? *È possible?*" She shrugged tactfully and rolled her eyes.

"Well, I hope he does," I exclaimed. *"Il è un*—what is the word for 'hero'?—*un eroe. Nobile, bravo, galante. . . ."* Here my stock of adulatory adjectives ran out. Teresa stared at me, her face a well-schooled blank, and I added, "I will pray for him." For a moment, then, I thought the girl's black eyes softened.

Teresa tucked me into bed and put out all the lights except a pair of candles, shielded against drafts by a clear crystal cover. The slim topaz flames were shaped like little hands lifted in appeal. I watched them through drooping eyelashes, and although I did not lift my own hands, I prayed, more fervently than I had ever prayed before.

II

I woke next morning feeling wretched, after a night troubled by strange dreams. The hovering bird had been a constant leitmotiv; now soaring high with beating wings, now swooping to strike; now plummeting earthward, its once powerful wings limp in death. The last vision woke me. I sat up with a stifled scream. Sunlight was pouring into my room and my sweat-soaked nightgown clung to me uncomfortably.

The day was steaming hot, one of the hottest of the summer. Teresa laid out the coolest frock I owned, a thin barred muslin of pale green with ribbons of darker green at the waist and elbow-length sleeves. I tied my hair back, looping the thick waves up off my neck and binding them with dark-green ribbons. The image that glowered back at me from my mirror was marred by the sour expression and by the drops of perspiration on my forehead.

There was no one in the breakfast room when I went down. I nibbled at a roll, but heat and anxiety had destroyed my appetite. I asked the steward whether he had seen Miss Perkins. He said she had breakfasted and left, he did not know where. The eternal, amiable Italian shrug and outspread hands had never irritated me more. I finished spoiling my food and wandered through the empty echoing rooms. I knew it was cooler inside the house than it would be outdoors, but I wanted air, so I went into the garden.

There was no sign of Miss Perkins in the rose garden, which was usually one of her favorite spots. Nor was she in the water garden, or the arbor, or the fountain room. Increasingly hot and disgusted, I walked along the path that led to Stefano's retreat.

The flowers were drooping and dusty; the little house was shuttered against the heat. I leaned on the gate, staring at the closed door. By that time I would have talked even to Stefano, but I was afraid to risk a brusque denial. While I stood there, the door opened and Piero came out. When he saw me he made as if to go in again, but I beckoned peremptorily.

"The signorina will ride today?" he asked. "I cannot go, but another groom—"

"No, it is too hot," I said, in my careful Italian. "Is *signor il conte* within? Can I—"

"He is within, signorina; he is not well today, he rests."

"I didn't want to see him anyway," I muttered, turning away. I had spoken in English. Piero said, "*Come?*" I smiled and shrugged and walked away, thinking, "There, I am doing it myself. I wonder if it irritates Italians as much as it does me."

I went back to the rose garden, and there at last I found Miss Perkins. She had been looking for me; we had missed each other all morning. She was trying to look cheerful, but my heart took a downward plunge as I noticed the worry in her eyes.

"Don't tell me there is bad news," I exclaimed. "Have they—have they captured him?"

"No; in fact there is good reason to believe that he has escaped from Parezzo. A messenger arrived this morning, early.

The Prince is deeply concerned; I heard him instructing the innkeeper to send news at once if anything happened.''

"But that is wonderful news," I exclaimed. "Why do you look so serious?"

"The very fact that he is known to have left the town is cause for concern. De Merode cannot have searched every nook and cranny by this time, so he must have gotten word from an informer. If the informer is someone the Falcon trusts, his every move will be carried back to his enemy."

"I think you are being too pessimistic," I said.

"I hope so; I sincerely hope so," said Miss Perkins, with a groan. "I am not good at concealing my feelings; I suppose everyone in the castle knows that my sympathies are with this young man. And, oh, Francesca—I fear he is badly hurt. How can a wounded man, weak from loss of blood, travel fast enough to elude a merciless pursuer like De Merode? What refuge can he find, with a price on his head and every soldier in the area searching for him? I wish there were something I could do!"

"So do I," I whispered.

"Why?" We had been pacing slowly up and down the paths between the roses. Now she stopped and turned to face me. "Is it just a girl's romantic imagination that makes you so interested in this man? Or do you know—"

"I know no more than you. But believe me, it is not only. . . . Oh, I think any woman would respond to the sheer romance of the man, but it is more than that with me; I have seen how these people suffer, from poverty and ignorance and disease. They deserve better. This man is trying to help them."

"You are not the thoughtless girl you were when you came to Italy," said Miss Perkins. "You have grown up a great deal in the last few months."

"Yes, I have. And," I added, trying to smile, "I must say I find the process very painful."

"Well, we must hope for the best," said Miss Perkins, beginning to walk again. "That is all women can do—wait and hope. Such a waste! We have more strength, more ardor than men realize; if they would only allow us to share in their struggles!"

"Some men appreciate your abilities," I said. "Andrea once

told me—'' And then I came to a stop, my hand at my mouth. ''Miss Perkins! I have been so distressed I forgot all about Andrea. Has he been released from his room? Piero said that Stefano is in his house, so I assume—''

''Yes, he is free. He went flying off in a perfect rage, according to the servants. By then it was too late for him to reach Parezzo in time for the execution, so I don't know where he has gone. Off to drown his disappointment in some tavern, if I know men.''

''That is a relief. Do you know, Miss Perkins, I was silly enough. . . . For a while I actually wondered if Andrea might not be the Falcon.''

''Did you,'' said Miss Perkins thoughtfully. ''Did you, indeed?''

III

For the remainder of the day I haunted the Salone dei Divi. This formal, seldom-used chamber had one conspicuous advantage—it was near the library, where Grandfather was brooding like a lion in his lair. From this salon I would hear immediately if a messenger arrived, and I vowed that I would brave the lion if necessary in order to get the latest news. But the morning wore on without event, and when the *colazione*, the midday meal, was announced, I went to the dining room. Grandfather was not present. Miss Rhoda said he was dining alone. She seemed disturbed about something—her precious Andrea, perhaps, for he had not returned. Galiana was silent too. Her eyes were suspiciously red, and from the way she kept glancing piteously at her mother, I deduced that she had been scolded for some misdemeanor or other—perhaps for her bold behavior on the previous day. The Contessa did not look at her. Obviously Galiana was in disgrace, and I couldn't help feeling sorry for her.

It was a relief when the meal was finished and the others scattered to their rooms for the afternoon rest. I lay down on my bed, but the heat was so oppressive I could not sleep. Teresa had said there would be a storm before nightfall. I hoped it was true; rain would break the heat.

But when I arose after an hour or so, the sun still beat down out of a cloudless sky. My beautiful rooms oppressed me. I could not help contrasting their elegance with the mean, stifling houses in the village. I thought of the man who might even now be lying in some such foul cellar on a bed of verminous straw—feverish, perhaps dying. . . . The picture was too vivid, too painful; with a stifled exclamation I ran from the room, snatching up a straw hat as I went. I had not visited my friends in the village lately. It might distract me from my painful thoughts to see how they were getting on.

Piero was nowhere to be seen. One of the grooms, a nice-looking boy who could not have been more than sixteen, accompanied me.

The village looked like a city of the dead. Only a few starved dogs lay panting in the shade. The afternoon was wearing on, though; shortly the villagers would begin to emerge from their houses. I glanced up at the sun. No, I was not too early; and I was sure of a welcome at any time.

The groom had to pound on the door for some time before anyone answered. Finally the door opened a crack. I could see two eyes, wide with surprise or fear, then the door opened wide and I saw Alberto, Giovanni's older brother. He was one of my favorites—a frank, open-faced boy with a beautiful smile. He was not smiling now.

"Signorina?" he said slowly.

"May I come in?" I held up the basket filled with food.

Instead of moving back, Alberto came out onto the doorstep and closed the door. He spoke urgently, waving his hands. I caught only a few words, but his gestures made his meaning plain. He was telling me to go back to the castle.

I stared at him, offended and hurt. He had gestured toward the horizon, and there, it was true, I could see storm clouds beginning to darken the sky. But the storm was a long way off. There was no hurry.

Suddenly there was a stifled exclamation from my groom. I turned and saw that another man had joined him. They spoke together, and the groom's swarthy faced turned a queer gray shade.

"Signorina," he said urgently. "*Subito—al castello, per piacere—*"

"What is happening?" I demanded. "What—no!" For he

had dared to lay hands on me and was pulling me toward my horse. I resisted, more indignant than frightened.

"*Momento!*" Alberto ran down the steps and caught the groom's arm. Another conference ensued; and then the stranger turned to me.

"Signorina—will you come with me?"

I started. He spoke not the local dialect but pure, elegant Tuscan. Even his appearance had undergone a subtle change. His dark face had a stubble of beard which, with his rough clothing, gave him a villainous appearance; but now I realized that his long, thin nose and fine-boned face were not those of a peasant. I hesitated. And then, some distance away, perhaps on the far side of the village, I heard sounds. Voices were raised, some in alarm, others in command.

"*Sì, soldati,*" said the stranger. "The soldiers who search for the Falcon. Will you come, signorina?"

I picked up my skirts, lifted them high.

"Where?" I asked.

"This way." I followed him into a street so narrow my hoops brushed the fronts of the houses. Then he stopped before a door half hidden in a deep archway, and knocked—a strange combination of knocks, with pauses in between. The door opened.

It was the dark, evil-smelling cellar of my worst imaginings. A single candle smoked and sputtered, giving off barely enough light to enable me to see shapes. I saw two people—men. There might have been others in the shadows, but I did not look farther; my eyes went straight to the man who was lying, as I had pictured him, on a bed of straw in the corner. The candle had been placed so that its dim light would fall on his body. His shirt was open, and rough bandages covered his breast. His head also seemed to be swathed in bandages, but he was conscious; when he saw me, he let out a stream of hissing, vehement speech, and tried to sit up. The effort was too much. He fell back, his head striking against the earthen floor.

His remarks ended a low-voiced but vigorous debate between my guide and one of the other men. I did not doubt that it concerned me, and the propriety of bringing me here, but I cared nothing for that. Pulling away from the hands that would have held me, I ran across the room and dropped to my knees beside the wounded man. As I did so, one of the guards struck out the candle.

"*Stupido,*" I said angrily. "How can I see?"

A voice spoke close to my elbow. It was that of my guide.

"Signorina, our leader has lived thus far only because few of us know who he is. Not even your family could save you if the enemy thought you could identify him."

The reasoning was doubly convincing in its appeal to my fears for myself and for the wounded man. There was only one flaw in the argument. I already knew the Falcon's real identity. His head was covered by a close-fitting hood that concealed even his hair, with slits for eyes, nose and mouth; but before the light was extinguished I had seen a mark on his bared chest— the same mark I had seen once before on the chest of my cousin Andrea.

Not for an instant was I tempted to mention this. There were traitors everywhere. Besides, there was no time for anything but the vital question.

"Does De Merode know he is here?" I spoke in French. It was necessary to communicate quickly and accurately now, and my assumption proved to be correct. My guide answered in the same language, and in the accents of a cultured man.

"Perhaps not. This town is known to be his base. It would be logical—"

I cut him short. "It doesn't matter. What matters is that the town will be searched, down to the last kennel. We must get him out of here."

"But where? No place in the village is safe now."

"The castle. I will hide him in my rooms."

"Impossible, mademoiselle! Some of the servants are with us, others are not. You could not get him to your rooms without being seen. Besides, the castle is probably being searched by now. A troop of men, headed by De Merode himself, was seen riding in that direction less than half an hour ago."

This news shook me to the core. Was De Merode already suspicious of Andrea? Several of his remarks, meaningless at the time, now took on a new and terrible significance. But Andrea's absence would prove nothing; only the capture of the Falcon would do that, and that I must prevent at any cost.

"He can be hidden somewhere in the hills," I said, urgency

quickening my voice. "I'll think of something. But first we must get him out of town. If he could ride——"

"I can ride, signorina. Or run, if I must."

I had thought him unconscious. My hand was touching his breast, and at the sound of his voice I must have pressed down harder than I meant, for he gave a muffled grunt of pain. His voice was clearly disguised, a soft, hissing whisper. He spoke the local patois, but clearly and distinctly. He went on, "Where is your groom? Your horses?"

His men were well trained. With a minimum of speech and the utmost speed, the plan the Falcon had hinted at was carried out. I did not inquire whether my groom's cooperation was forced or voluntary. While the Falcon struggled into the jacket and plumed cap that was the Tarconti livery, I stood biting my nails with nervous excitement. We did not leave through the door by which I had entered, but followed a passageway into a tiny piazza nearby, where the horses were waiting.

The storm clouds had come nearer. The sky was a queer sullen gray. The dim light was a godsend, but we would need more help than that from heaven. My companion was a grotesque sight, for the jacket was far too small for him, and his masked face was hardly inconspicuous. The disguise, if it could be called that, would pass muster only at a distance; but that was all it was designed to do. Any soldier who caught a glimpse of us would assume I was accompanied by the same servant who had come to the village with me. He would not dare stop me. If he tried to——well, we would have to face that if and when it happened.

My erstwhile guide, looking even more like a bandit, caught me in his arms and flung me into my saddle.

"Mademoiselle, I beg you, stay with him," he said urgently. "He will try to send you away; but he is too weak, he can't go far alone. If I can, I will meet you outside the town—he knows the place—but if I should be caught. . . . Promise you will not leave him!"

"I promise." I turned the horse's head to follow my "groom," who was already disappearing into a roofed passageway.

Though it was past the hour when the town usually awakened to life after its siesta, there was not a soul to be seen. Even the dogs had disappeared. We went at a slow walk, the horses' hooves scarcely audible in the dust that carpeted the back streets. He led, I followed; never were the *vincoli* wide enough to allow two horses to go side by side. It would have been a wonderful place for children to play hide and seek—winding, narrow, with culs-de-sac and mysterious low archways leading into unknown darkness. We, too, were playing hide and seek, but the loser of this game would pay a bitter forfeit.

I had not known this part of the town existed. It must not have changed for five hundred years. I would have been lost within a few minutes, but the man ahead of me seemed to know every foot of the way. He took a winding, circuitous path—and not always by choice. Several times he turned suddenly away from a street when the muffled sounds of activity were heard there. Once I saw a flash of scarlet passing in the distance.

Finally we came out of the village onto a narrow plateau. The transition was almost as abrupt as if a wall had separated town from country, and indeed a few crumbling foundations showed that the ancient walls had once stood here. From the high point a narrow path had been beaten through the weeds that covered the hillside. We were halfway down the path, within a few yards of a grove of trees, when a shout behind us made me turn my head.

Thunder muttered overhead; the sky was curtained with low-hanging clouds. But the scarlet coats stood out against the sober gray stone of the houses on the hill. One of the soldiers raised an arm, as if in summons; or perhaps he was aiming a musket, I could not see distinctly. I turned and rode on at the same deliberate pace. If I had been alone I am sure I would have urged the horse into a gallop. My hands were wet with perspiration, and my shoulders hunched in anticipation of a bullet.

No shot came, of course. The soldiers must have known who I was, and they would not dare to fire. But they would report having seen me, and if De Merode learned that his quarry had escaped the trap of the village, he might put two and two together.

I dug my heels into my horse's sides and came up beside the other rider. We were on level ground now, and under the shelter of the trees. He turned his head away, and I thought, How foolish men are! He still doesn't know I have recognized him. I knew I must leave him to cherish that comforting delusion. He still thought of me as his "little cousin," too young and irresponsible to be trusted with his deadly secret. I would show him that a woman could keep a secret, and spare him the burden of fearing for my safety.

"Sir," I said primly.

His eyes flashed with an emotion that might have been amusement as he turned his head toward me, but he made no reply. I persisted.

"You must find a hiding place. If those men report to their officer—"

"*Sì*." I had spoken French. He replied in the hoarse Italian he had used before. Then he pointed. "You—" The extended finger stabbed emphatically. "You go, there. I—" And his hand swung around in a ninety-degree angle.

"No, I have no intention of leaving you."

His eyes flashed again, but not with amusement. He raised his hand threateningly. Since I knew he had no intention of striking me, I stood my ground, my chin raised. After a moment he shook his head, muttered something under his breath, and rode on.

We must have proceeded for ten minutes, although it seemed much longer. The sky steadily darkened; the leaves hung still in the hush of the imminent storm. The air was hot and close. I found it hard to breathe. The path, such as it was, had disappeared; we twisted through narrow ravines, between the trunks of towering pines, scratched and scraped by the brush.

If the Falcon hoped to discourage me, he did not succeed. My dress was ripped by thorns, stained by berries. Insects bit me, perspiration poured down my face, but I pressed doggedly onward. The straight, unyielding figure ahead of me showed no signs of faltering, but I had not forgotten the promise I had made to the strange man who looked like a bandit and spoke French like a courtier. I would have gone on even without that. I myself had seen the Falcon wounded; the bullet must have passed straight through his body; and he had been on the move ever since, with no time to rest. The approaching storm was a further complication. It would be a bad one; the longer it held off, the greater the ferocity of wind and rain would be. This I knew from my brief experience with Italian weather. The injured man must have shelter from the elements as well as from the ferocity of his foes. But I had no idea where it was to be found.

We were riding through a narrow canyon when a man darted out from behind a rock. He was middle-aged; his long hair was grizzled and his face was half concealed by a bushy beard. I don't know which of us was the more startled, I or my poor nervous Stella. She reared, and I went sliding off her back. The newcomer ran to help me to my feet. He was a stranger—a peasant, by the look of him—and badly frightened, to judge by his pale face and rolling eyes.

It is amazing what resources the mind can command when it is forced. I was very bad at the local dialect. Now I understood what the man was saying, thanks, in part, to his eloquent gestures, but mostly because of the urgent need to understand.

The soldiers were coming. They had not caught. . . . I did not recognize the name, but I knew who was meant—my former guide. He was still at liberty, but he was closely pursued; he dared not meet us for fear of leading the pursuit in our direction. The horses were now a danger, we must leave them. He would return them to the castle stables. We must proceed on foot.

"But where?" I did not expect an answer. But the answer came—from the Falcon.

"Le tombe," he said.

I looked around.

Straight ahead, where the ravine widened out, a rounded hill loomed up against the stormy sky. I had thought the terrain was beginning to look familiar. Now I knew where I was. The valley ahead was the valley of the Etruscan tombs. And one of those tombs had a door, whose secret was known only to the members of the family.

"Come," I said, holding out my hand to him. "Hurry."

For a long moment he did not move. Then he slid slowly off the horse's back and fell into a crumpled heap at my feet.

The peasant cried out. The sound seemed to echo in the still air—and I realized that it was not an echo at all. Behind us in the ravine a man had shouted.

"Help me," I gasped. *"Aiuto. . . ."* Stopping, I seized the fallen man roughly by one arm and tugged at him. He tried to help me, but it was not until the peasant added his strength to mine that we succeeded in raising the Falcon to his feet.

I had stopped thinking sensibly. All I cared about was reaching shelter with the man I was trying to save. I didn't care about the horses or the poor unfortunate peasant who was risking his life to save us. I had forgotten my terror of the tomb. Once we reached it, we would be saved.

I never knew the name of the man who helped me that day. He was only an illiterate, untrained peasant, but he was strong and he was loyal. With the wounded man between us, we stumbled on to the mouth of the valley of the tombs.

The sight of that desolate place would have daunted even a confirmed atheist. The livid, rolling clouds closed it in like the roof of Hades; in the eerie light the shapes of the great rounded monuments looked like a city of demons. As we stood there gasping for breath, with the weight of the half-conscious man dragging at us, there was a rustle of movement among the weeds. Something came out—something that shone with a pallid white light. . . .

I let out a sound that was half scream, half hysterical laugh. The spectral form was one of the big white rabbits. Unafraid, it sat up on its haunches, its paws folded demurely over its breast, and stared at us with great liquid eyes.

The sight was too much for my assistant. He had faced the dangers of the rope, the firing squad, without faltering; but this diabolical vision touched the deeper layer of superstitious terror that is stronger than courage. He let out a shriek and fled.

I flung both arms around the limp body of the man whose sole support I now was. His weight made my knees bend, but by a superhuman effort he managed to keep his feet and we staggered on until we reached the mound of the princess.

Here a new difficulty arose. I could not remember where in that vast stone circle the door was located. The mound was at least a hundred feet in circumference and the door was masked by shrubs. I felt as if my arms were about to break off. The Falcon had one arm around my shoulders; as we stood there, it weighed more and more heavily till it pressed me to the ground. He had fainted at last. I huddled there in the prickly grass, with my arms around him, and heard voices at the entrance to the valley.

I was reduced to the precise mental state of a fox, or any other hunted beast. Survival was the only idea in my mind, for myself and for the man whose head rested on my breast. His uneven breathing scorched my skin through the thin muslin of my dress. A jagged spear-length of lightning streaked across the sky. In its brief light, objects stood out with eerie distinctness. The unconscious man stirred, moaning. I thought I had reached the uttermost limits of terror, but that sound assured me I had some distance yet to go. With the strength born of panic, I pressed his face against my breast, stifling his groans. In the abnormal stillness the slightest sound would carry; our pursuers might have heard him, as I was able to hear what they were saying.

Perhaps because it was their common language, they spoke in English. I recognized one of the voices. I had heard it before, the day of my first meeting with De Merode.

"What a horrible place," he exclaimed. "Are those truly the graves of unbelievers, those great high mounds?"

He spoke loudly, as men will do to cover up their fear, and his companion replied in the same tone.

"So it is said. You are not afraid of the dead, are you, O'Shaughnessy?"

"And was it not my own ancestor, Brian O'Shaughnessy, who fought from midnight to dawn with a great skeleton shape to win the treasure of the kings of Tara? Yet," the Irishman added in a lower voice, "only a fool would challenge the infernal powers. Lie quiet, all you pagan souls; we'll not trouble you this night, 'tis a living man we seek. . . ."

His voice rose suddenly in a shriek, and his companion laughed—but somewhat shakily.

"It's only a hare, you fool of an Irishman."

"To be sure, to be sure. 'Tis only in England, that heretic island, that the spirit of a witch may take the shape of a harmless rabbit. Oh, devil take it, Williams, must we go into this place? No one but a fool would seek shelter here."

"Precisely why it would make an excellent hiding place," his companion said. "Come along, let's get it over with. It will rain any moment."

Dry branches crackled underfoot as they advanced. Another flash of lightning, brighter than the last, split the darkening sky apart. In its glare I saw a shape I knew.

The last five feet to sanctuary were almost the worst of the whole journey. More than once I cursed the inconvenience of female clothing; those dreadful hoops got in the way of every step I took. Only the fact that the soldiers were making as much noise as we kept them from hearing us. But finally my groping hands found the hidden catch and the door swung open. One last burst of strength tumbled the two of us over the threshold. I placed the wooden wedge as I had been shown, and pulled the door back into place.

CHAPTER 10

Time had no meaning in the stifling darkness. It might have been an hour later, or ten minutes, or a century, before I forced the slab open once again.

The worst of the storm had passed, but rain was still falling steadily. I waited for some time, listening, till I was sure the soldiers had gone. Then I crept out. I was careful to be sure the catch was wedged before I pushed the slab back into place, so that it could be opened from the inside—just in case.

I had not gone twenty feet before my soaked skirts were clinging to me, making every step an effort. I had removed my hoops before leaving the tomb. I wondered morbidly what excavators of a future generation would make of those peculiar objects, supposing that they found them centuries from now.

I knew the way back to the castello, but this was the first time I had traversed it on foot. I had not realized it was so far. Nor had I been fully cognizant of the difficulty of the terrain. Running water turned every slope into a stream of mud. My fragile slippers gave no traction; I slipped back two feet for every foot I gained, and my hands were soon scored and bleeding from the branches I grasped in order to pull myself up. It was a nightmare journey, and the need for haste made it seem even longer.

How long could an injured man survive in that dank, airless chamber, without food or medical aid? I had to leave him there, I had no choice. All my efforts to revive him had been in vain. I knew where the candles were, but I was afraid to light one. The slab seemed tight, but a slit of light might betray his presence to searchers. He was safe from capture there, but he needed help and I was the only one who could bring it. Blankets, I thought, inching my way up a brambly slope. Blankets and hot soup; fresh bandages, food. . . . How I would get these things to him I could not imagine, but I would have to do it somehow. I could trust no one—except Miss Perkins.

I believe her name was my last coherent thought. After that it was a delirium of rain and mud and thorny branches.

When I reached the lowest terrace of the gardens, the rain had stopped and a single star was visible through the rent clouds to the west. I stood there swaying with fatigue, and stared stupidly at the brilliant point of light. Then I saw that the castle was illuminated like a building on a festal day. Every window was ablaze.

So numbed was I by worry and physical discomfort that I might have failed to understand the significance of this unusual illumination. By a stroke of luck, the man in the shadow of the clipped yew moved so that I saw him before he saw me. The shape of his cap silhouetted against the sky told me all I needed to know. I dropped down behind a tree, my heart racing.

The castello had been invaded and occupied. All very suavely and courteously, no doubt; De Merode could not arouse Grandfather's open hostility. His excuse would be that he wanted to protect the inhabitants against the dangerous criminal still at large. How much did he know? I wondered. How much was only suspicion? And—more to the point—how many men were there hiding in the gardens? The Captain seemed to have an endless number of soldiers at his disposal; a ridiculous number to employ in the capture of a single local rebel. Of course De Merode was obsessed. His elusive adversary had become a personal threat. But he must have powerful connections in Rome to have acquired so many reinforcements.

Avoiding graveled paths and paved surfaces, I crawled on hands and knees through the wet grass. I had no plan in mind, only an instinctive need to avoid capture until I had time to decide what to do.

Below, and to my right, I saw the curious little towers of the garden house—Stefano's retreat. Stefano. . . . Surely he would help if he knew the seriousness of the situation. If I could reach him, I would sound him out, test him. . . . I suspected there was some antagonism in his feelings toward Andrea, but

family honor, if not affection, would surely dictate that he come
to his brother's aid. It was worth a try. It was the only scheme I
could think of.

I was shivering violently by then with terror and cold. The
night air was cool after the rain, and it chilled my drenched
body. My teeth began to chatter. I clapped my hand over my
mouth to stop the sound, but it was too late. A dark form leaped
over the wall and enveloped me in a crushing embrace.

"*Signorina!*" The whisper came just in time to stop me from
screaming. "*Signorina, sono io, sono Piero—non gridare, per
l'amore de Dio—i soldati. . . .*"

"Piero." I clung to him, gasping for breath. "I must see the
Count—take me to him."

He shook me till the coils of my wet hair smothered my
breath.

"*Dov'è lui?* Where is he? Quickly, signorina, tell me!"

"In the tomb," I whispered. "*La tomba della principessa.*"

The bruising hands left my shoulders and I dropped panting
to the ground. Piero was gone as silently as he had come.

He had not given me time to think; but if I had had time, I
still would not have known what to do. It was done now. Either I
had saved the Falcon or I had betrayed him, and only time would
tell which.

II

An hour later I was beginning to hope that I had done the right
thing after all. If Piero meant to betray Andrea, he would have
gone straight to the Captain; and obviously De Merode was still
waiting for news. I could hear him storming up and down
outside the door of my sitting room.

I had walked straight into the house after Piero left me. If I
had wanted to avoid the soldiers, I probably would have been
caught at once. As it was, I managed to reach the terrace before
anyone saw me. Then two of them converged on me with shouts
and brandished muskets. I let out a piercing shriek and sank to
the ground.

The pretended faint gave me time to think. Even after I had
been "restored to consciousness," I continued to babble and
sob hysterically. As a footman carried me upstairs, dripping

water all over his neat uniform, I heard Grandfather shouting at the soldiers, and their protestations. They had not touched me, they had not even recognized me at first. And no wonder. Miss Perkins let out a cry of horror when she saw me. As she told me later, she had never seen a more wretched-looking creature.

She and Teresa flew into action. Gallons of hot water, warm clothing, brandy, medicines internal and external. As soon as I was tucked into bed, Grandfather burst in and bent over me.

"My child! What happened? Can she speak?" he demanded, turning to Miss Perkins. "Is she. . . . Has she . . . ?"

I knew what he meant. Most girls know, although they are supposed to be ignorant of such things, and I had had one especially illuminating experience. The idea enraged me—not the idea of being ravished, but the fact that this was the foremost worry in Grandfather's mind. Men act as if we are pieces of property, I thought disgustedly. If the vase is cracked or the diamond flawed, it loses its value.

Miss Perkins tried to reassure the agitated old man, telling him that my injuries were superficial.

"But we—I must know what has happened to her!"

"No, no, she cannot speak, she is too badly hurt," said Miss Perkins, with magnificent inconsistency.

"I think I can talk a little," I mumbled, trying at the same time to look exhausted and to reassure Miss Perkins, by a meaningful look, that I knew what I was doing. "Is—is it the Captain I hear outside?"

"He cannot come in here," cried Miss Perkins. "You are in bed, in your nightgown."

She was right. I dared not face De Merode's cutting intelligence just then. But there was something I wanted to say; one last thing that might help.

"Tell him," I whispered. I held out a frail, trembling hand to Grandfather. "Tell him. . . ."

"Yes, my dear child." He pressed my hand. His eyes were wet.

"He captured me. . . . The Falcon. . . ."

Grandfather gritted his teeth.

"If he dared to lay hands upon you . . . !"

"Oh, for heaven's sake," I began angrily, and then remembered that I was supposed to be weak with shock. "No; no, he did not. . . . But he made me go with him—as a hostage. He released me near the quarry, on the road to Parezzo. It took me so long to get here, I was afraid, and it was raining. . . ."

I began to sob noisily. Grandfather squeezed my hand till I wanted to shriek with pain. Then he ran out. I heard him talking to someone in the outer room; both of them rushed out and the door slammed.

The place I had mentioned was as far to the north of the castle as the Etruscan cemetery was to the south. I had made my story as vague as possible, since I didn't know what my unfortunate groom had told the authorities; but if De Merode believed me he would send his men in the wrong direction, and Piero would have a chance to reach his leader.

There were too many imponderables in the plan, but it was the best I could do. I had flung my arm over my face to conceal the fact that my sobs were not accompanied by tears; I was far too anxious to cry just then. Now I peered out from under my sleeve and saw Galiana standing at the foot of the bed. I had not noticed her before, but it was not surprising that she should be there. She was attracted by excitement as a moth is by light.

"Get her out," I hissed at Miss Perkins. "I must talk to you."

Galiana was not anxious to leave, but Miss Perkins rose nobly to the occasion. As soon as we were alone, I started talking. Miss Perkins listened without interrupting; only an occasional sharp intake of breath betrayed the intensity of her interest.

"Did I do right to tell Piero?" I asked, finally. "I couldn't think, I was too upset. . . . If I have betrayed him . . ."

"No, no; an informer would have gone straight to the Captain. Furthermore, Francesca, logic suggests that Piero is one of the Falcon's supporters. We have all been worried about you, ever since you failed to return from the village. . . ."

"The groom," I interrupted. "The boy who went with me—"

"He has disappeared. Kidnapped? Or perhaps—"

"Another of the Falcon's supporters. It is possible. But never mind that. What were you saying about Piero?"

"I said that we were all alarmed about you, especially after De Merode arrived and told us the Falcon was in the area. He would not allow us to send men out to search for you, however.

None of our servants was permitted to leave the grounds. So—how did Piero know you had been with the Falcon? He must be in secret communication with the rebels. I have long suspected that the Falcon has allies in the castle—''

"His friend said as much," I agreed. "But Miss Perkins, if we are wrong. . . . He is injured and alone in that dreadful place."

Miss Perkins pressed me back against the pillow as I tried to rise.

"I hope you are not entertaining any notion of returning to the tomb," she exclaimed. "It would be madness to try, Francesca; you will be watched, be sure of that. The die is cast in any case. Either Piero has spoken, or he has found a way to relieve our friend. Try to sleep now. You have done all you could; you have done nobly."

"Sleep! How can I rest when I don't know what is happening? I am half mad with worry."

"I shall go down and join the others," Miss Perkins said. "I promise to come at once and tell you if there is any news. You must stay here, Francesca; you are supposed to be prostrate. You have displayed admirable courage so far. Don't fail now."

After she had gone I did try to rest, but it was impossible. Whenever I closed my eyes scenes of the past hours repeated themselves, flashing upon the blackness of my inner vision. Once again I saw the dirty cellar and the man who lay on the bed of straw; the shadowy valley and the eerie white rabbit; the mound of the princess's tomb, the gaping entrance hole. Again I held the unconscious man's head against my breast and felt his uneven breathing. . . .

I flung the covers back and swung my feet out onto the floor. It was impossible to rest. I had to move about or lose my mind.

The luxurious elegance of my sitting room was an irritant instead of a source of comfort. The warmth, the candlelight, the soft carpets reminded me too painfully of the damp hole in which I had left the Falcon. I began walking up and down the room. But I had not walked for long when a sound stopped me in my tracks. I stared dumbfounded as the door of the big painted armoire began to swing out—and was caught by four small white fingers.

The truth dawned on me before I had time to imagine worse

threats, and it roused me to tigerish action. In a single bound I reached the armoire and flung the door wide. Galiana had retreated behind a row of dresses, but I recognized her little black slippers and dragged her out with a ruthless hand.

"You are hurting me," she exclaimed indignantly. "Let me go, Francesca!"

"I am tempted to strangle you," I said, between clenched teeth. "How long have you been there? What did you hear?"

Her chin began to quiver. I relaxed my hold; but not because I was moved to pity. Quite the contrary.

"Sit down," I said, pushing her into an armchair. "Galiana, you frightened me half to death. What a silly thing to do!"

She gave me a sidelong look and began rubbing her arms where my fingers had held her.

"Not so silly as what you did," she muttered. "I was not in the armoire all the time, Francesca. I was listening at the door. I knew all along you were lying; I knew there was something you hadn't told. And I was right!"

"You couldn't have heard anything. We were whispering."

"Yes, you talked too softly," grumbled Galiana. "But—" Again came that sly sidelong look.—"But Miss Perkins has quite a loud voice when she is excited. She was most excited, wasn't she, when you proposed going back to the tomb?"

My heart sank. Miss Perkins *had* spoken vehemently then, and that single speech would have told a listener all she needed to know.

Galiana was not the most intelligent of women, but she was quick at intrigue. She was watching me closely, and she must have seen the consternation in my face—a tacit admission of the truth.

"You see, I do know," she said triumphantly. "I suppose it was wrong to eavesdrop; but you are wrong, Francesca, to keep secrets from me when you know how interested I am. How long were you with him? Do tell me who he really is. Just think, he might be someone I know!"

Again I was faced with a terrible decision. It was impossible to convince Galiana that she was mistaken. The circumstances were too damning. And once she got an idea into her head, neither logic nor threats could get it out. I had to persuade her to keep silent. But how?

The horror of the situation almost overcame me. Of all the people to discover my secret, Galiana was probably the most dangerous. She was an inveterate gossip, and too shallow to understand the seriousness of the situation. Stefano and Miss Rhoda would have kept silent; even the Prince would betray his principles before he would betray his son. But Galiana. . . . There was only one way I could think of, only one appeal that might control her tongue.

"Yes, he is someone you know," I said. And as she stared at me wide-eyed, I fell on my knees beside her chair and caught her plump little hands tightly in mine. "Galiana, it is Andrea. If De Merode finds out, Andrea will die; he will be hanged in the square at Parezzo, as Antonio almost was. And this time there will be no Falcon to rescue him. It is up to us—you and me—whether he lives or dies."

Galiana's eyes seemed to fill half her face. She had gone quite pale; there was no amusement on her soft mouth now.

"You are lying," she gasped. "It can't be."

"You needn't believe me," I said. "Tell De Merode, if you wish; I can't stop you. But if you do, Andrea's blood will be on your hands."

"No, no." Her hands twisted in mine. I held them fast.

"Will you swear?" I asked. "Swear to keep silent?"

"It is true?" Her eyes searched my face. "Yes, I see you are not lying now. I can't believe it. Francesca, do you think I would harm him? I would die rather than see him in danger! Is he hurt? Is he really in that horrible place? I must go to him, I must—"

"You must stay here and act a part, as you have never acted in your life! We must convince De Merode that we know nothing. Believe me, Andrea will be all right. Help has reached him by now. You can do nothing without endangering him; but you can save him by playing your part."

As I watched in breathless suspense, her lips tightened and she nodded.

"I understand," she said. "I promise. Francesca, you do trust me, don't you? You know how I feel about . . ."

"I trust you," I said, wishing I were as sure as I tried to sound. "We must begin acting now, Galiana. Go to bed and at least pretend to sleep. I know this has been a shock to you."

"Let me stay here with you," she pleaded. "You can say you were afraid to be alone. I need you, Francesca, I am so worried!"

"That is an excellent idea," I said. At least I could keep Galiana under my eye for the night, and by morning, if she changed her mind or lost her nerve, the Falcon would hopefully be beyond De Merode's reach.

So we went to sleep, side by side, in my big canopied bed. Galiana dropped off sooner than I expected. As I looked at her sleeping face, with traces of tears still on her lashes, I couldn't help thinking how ironic our situation was. Strange bedfellows indeed—the two women who loved Andrea Tarconti, and who shared his deadly secret.

III

Galiana was still asleep when I awoke next morning. I am sure I need not describe my feelings as consciousness returned to me; any reader of imagination will comprehend them, and will understand why the look I bent upon the sweetly sleeping girl was not entirely kind.

When Galiana woke up I had my hands full calming her. Her resolution was unchanged, but her nerves had weakened. I had to reiterate, over and over, the melodramatic phrases with which I had convinced her the night before. She was a creature of emotion—and God knows the situation was as incredible as the language I had used to describe it. We ate breakfast in my sitting room, and I was still encouraging her, when we received a summons to appear downstairs. I could only hope that my persuasion had been effective, because I feared that the crisis was upon us.

We found the rest of the family assembled in the library. When I saw De Merode standing by the fireplace, I knew my fears were justified.

The Contessa was seated in an armchair. She stretched out her hand to Galiana as soon as we entered, and the wretched girl ran to her and hid her face in the maternal lap.

I had read somewhere that the best defense is to attack, so I turned to De Merode and exclaimed angrily, "You see how you have affected us, Captain! We are all in a state of nervous excitement. Is this a courtroom, or a meeting of the famous Inquisition?''

"I don't know why you should say that, mademoiselle," De Merode said quietly. "I have not spoken to you as yet."

"You don't have to speak, you *look* threatening. Grandfather, what is going on? I am still shaken, and I think I have taken cold.''

I suppose my cough was not very convincing. Stefano was smiling thinly, but his smile was no more convincing than my cough. It was obvious that no one had slept well the night before. Stefano's eyelids were heavy and his eyes dull. Grandfather looked even worse. He was wearing riding clothes, and I wondered where he had been so early in the morning. Had the Captain forced him to accompany a searching party?

"Be calm, my child," he said heavily. "The Captain has assured us he will not take much of our time. He wishes to ask a few questions.''

"I told you everything I knew last night," I said.

"This is outrageous," Miss Rhoda added angrily. For once she was on my side. When I saw her shadowed eyes and the lines in her face, I wondered how much she knew.

De Merode ignored her, as he had ignored Grandfather.

"What you told us, mademoiselle, was somewhat misleading. My men scoured the area you described. They found no traces.''

"I don't suppose the man would stay there waiting for you to find him," I retorted.

"No, indeed. He must have moved very quickly, for we did find certain signs in quite the opposite direction. Bloodstains.''

"Bloodstains! But the rain—''

"They were in a sheltered spot. It struck me, you see, that this terrain contains a number of excellent hiding places, in the ancient tombs. And when I learned that one of those tombs has a heavy door, which cannot be moved unless one knows the secret. . . .''

"So you forced the Prince to show you," I said, with a calm I certainly was not feeling. "You are insulting, Captain. Only members of the family know the secret of that door.''

"But, mademoiselle, always you malign me. There is no such thing as a secret from the servants of a great household. These people know everything that goes on. Obviously one of them is in league with the Falcon, for we found the bloodstains within the tomb."

I had not been absolutely sure till then that Andrea had made good his escape. Miss Perkins' reasoning had been logical; but logic does not convince the heart. By a supreme effort I kept my face and voice under control. Out of the corner of my eye I saw that Galiana had raised a tear stained face from her mother's lap and was listening with parted lips. It was imperative that I hold the Captain's attention. I even managed, heaven knows how, to laugh.

"Human blood, of course," I said sarcastically. "How clever you are, Captain, to be sure it was not that of a poor wounded animal. Once again, I have told you all I know. I am not responsible for the workings of your imagination. So if you will excuse me—"

"One moment!" De Merode's nerves were beginning to show signs of wear too. His voice cracked like a whip. "You are quite right, mademoiselle, I have no proof of anything. I have only my suspicions, and my orders. Those orders are to capture this brigand at all costs." He turned to Grandfather, who had started to protest. "Your Excellency is no doubt aware that the political situation is increasingly grave. Garibaldi is on the mainland, and if he takes Naples, the Papal States will be next. Those serpents of Piedmont, Victor Emmanuel and Cavour, threaten our northern borders. If there should be uprisings in this area, they will need no further excuse to invade, on the pretext of restoring order. The aim of the Falcon, and men like him, is to promote such rebellions. I will stop at nothing— nothing!—to prevent this. The man must be found, and when he is, he will be shot, no matter who he is!"

His face was flushed with passion. As a soldier and a loyal subject, he had good reason for pursuing an enemy of the state; but it was clear to all of us that the mocking adversary who had humiliated and defeated him had become his personal enemy as well.

"A neat summary, Captain," Stefano drawled. "But I fail to

see why you are boring us with this information. Some of us know it already, and the ladies, I fear, are not interested in politics.''

"Ah, but this matter of politics may concern them closely," said De Merode. "Where is Count Andrea?"

Galiana cried out, and Miss Rhoda exclaimed, "What are you implying? Do you dare suggest—"

"Count Andrea is a known revolutionary," De Merode said. "He is strong enough and clever enough to play the role of the Falcon. He is a friend of Antonio—"

But now he had gone too far. Grandfather rose to his full height and spoke in a voice that quivered with suppressed fury.

"I too am acquainted with Antonio Cadorna, Captain. Do you accuse me of being the Falcon? I warn you, do not try me. I have cooperated to the full so far. Now I ask you to leave my house."

"I will go. But I will return, your Excellency, and if I find that any persons in this household are involved in any way with the Falcon, not even your influence can save them. If I must, I will shoot first and answer for the consequences."

He swung on his heel with a clash of spurs and strode out of the room.

Then Miss Rhoda—Miss Rhoda of all people—began to weep.

"Why did you irritate him, you wretched girl?" she sobbed, glaring at me. "He is dangerous, horribly dangerous. How could you be so stupid?"

Our alliance had not lasted long. I didn't entirely blame her. She needed some object for her fear and rage. I had been provocative, but I could hardly explain why.

"Be silent," Grandfather shouted. "She was right! Too long we have endured the insolence of this creature. This is how my loyalty, my assistance are rewarded! Francesca, my apologies. I should not have allowed him to speak to you as he did. And if Stefano were half a man—"

Shame stopped him before he completed this unworthy speech, but the damage had been done. Stefano's pale lips curled in the expression I knew so well.

"It is certainly a pity Andrea was not here instead of me," he agreed suavely. "He would have challenged De Merode and been neatly killed in the process. It must be such a comfort to the survivors of these gallant imbeciles to know that they died honorably, defending a maiden—even an arrogant outspoken maiden like Francesca. It would have served her right if De Merode had turned her over his knee."

Grandfather was quivering with rage. "I only regret now that I did not assist this man who calls himself the Falcon. At least he *is* a man, not a smooth-tongued coward!"

Clutching his gray hair in both hands, he went rushing out of the room. The others followed, Galiana leaning against her mother, Miss Rhoda with bowed head. Stefano remained seated, balancing his stick across his hands.

"He didn't mean it," I said. "He is frightened and angry, or he would never have said it."

"Thank you for explaining the Prince to me," said Stefano. "If you expect me to be equally noble—to say that I insulted you because I was distracted by worry—I am afraid you will be disappointed. I am not at all distracted, and I had excellent reasons for speaking as I did."

"Oh, you are impossible," I cried. "You have no heart, no feelings!"

Miss Perkins, who had been sitting quietly in a corner the whole time, rose and put out her hand, but I rushed past her. I was not going to give Stefano the satisfaction of seeing me cry.

It was a terrible day. We were like a household waiting for news from the battlefield. I tried to find Galiana, feeling that she was in need of all the verbal fortification I could render, but when I knocked at the door of the suite she and her mother occupied, Bianca would not let me in. She blocked the doorway like a black granite boulder. When I asked if she would at least tell Galiana I wanted to see her she shook her head and made the hoarse cawing sounds she used only when she was greatly agitated.

Miss Perkins was not to be found either. She and Galiana were the only ones I wanted to talk with, so I spent the rest of the day trying to find them and avoid the others. I took my meals in my room, sending word by Teresa that I was too unwell to come down. God knows I was unwell; I felt as if I were in a fever, alternately shaken by fits of shivering and by such restless impatience that I paced the floor of my room like a caged animal.

Miss Perkins finally came to me late that evening and insisted that I take a dose of laudanum to make me sleep. I agreed, on condition that she would do the same.

"You look terrible," I said. "What have you been doing all day?"

"Worrying. A futile exercise, I agree. There is still no news. That is hopeful, I think."

"I need more than hope, I need facts. What of Piero? I looked for him today, but could not find him. You don't suppose De Merode has arrested him?"

"Oh, no, Piero has been at his usual duties. I tried to question him, but he pretended he did not understand my Italian."

She looked so indignant I had to laugh feebly, and she went on, "He is a clever and loyal man; obviously he could admit nothing, he doesn't know whether I can be trusted. Besides, Francesca, we know all we need to know. De Merode searched the tomb and the Falcon was not there. You may be sure he has found a safe hiding place, or he would have been captured by now."

We went on reassuring one another in this way until the medicine began to take effect and I thought perhaps I could sleep. Miss Perkins stayed with me that night. I was in no mood to be alone.

IV

In any crisis one believes that life is unendurable; yet one can become accustomed to anything, even to constant uncertainty. Two days passed in the same way, and our nerves began to relax. They had to; it would have been impossible for them to remain at such a high pitch of tension.

I managed to catch up with Galiana, who swore she had not spoken. Of all of us she seemed the most affected. Her nerves were so strained she would jump at the slightest sound. Stefano stayed sulking in his house; Miss Rhoda reverted to her usual cold control; and Grandfather refused to discuss the subject.

He had enough to worry him in the political news, which continued bad—for him. Garibaldi was advancing on Naples, and the peasants in Calabria were welcoming him with open arms. At any time we expected to hear that the weak Bourbon king, Francis II, had fled the capital and that Garibaldi had entered in triumph. In our own area, rumors of rebellion were all about. De Merode's troops were arresting every stranger on suspicion of being a Piedmontese agent. One unfortunate merchant of Turin had been detained for three days in the fortress at Parezzo before he was able to prove his innocence. The incident created a stir, since the man's family was of some consequence, but it was evidence of De Merode's increasing mania.

In the midst of the furor Andrea came home.

We were sitting in the drawing room after dinner and I was at the pianoforte. Stefano had joined us for the first time in several days, but he had refused to play; so, in an effort to relieve the gloomy atmosphere, I had gone to the instrument myself. I was stumbling through a Verdi aria when the doors burst open and Andrea entered.

While the others stared, he came straight to me, scooped me up in his arms and kissed me soundly on both cheeks.

"I salute the heroine of the day! You look quite healthy and blooming, Cousin, for a young lady who has faced the mighty Falcon himself!"

It was all I could do not to throw my arms around his neck and return his kisses, I was so relieved to see him. He was blooming and healthy-looking too; apparently his injury had been less serious than I had supposed. Aware of the watching eyes of the others, I said primly, "Andrea, I think you had better put me down."

My smile and my sparkling eyes belied my words. I knew Andrea understood my real feelings—some of them, at any rate. Did he still believe me to be unwitting? If so, I was willing to continue the game; I would never initiate the subject, but would wait for him to drop the first hint. But oh, how I longed to tell him of my relief, my affection!

Andrea obeyed, with a smile and a wink. Then he went straight to Grandfather and kissed him, as is the endearing Italian custom. The Prince was too moved on this occasion to do anything but return the embrace heartily. He stood smiling and blinking while Andrea made the rounds, greeting the others. He would have embraced his brother too, but Stefano put him off with the point of his stick, and remarked calmly:

"Your exuberance is too much for an invalid like myself, Andrea. Welcome home. You missed the excitement, but I see you have heard of Francesca's adventure. Or should I call it a misadventure?"

"But the province is ringing with it," Andrea exclaimed. "Such wild stories! You must tell me how it really was, Cousin. Did you confront the Falcon with his own pistol until you could escape?"

He stood with his feet apart and his hands on hips, his blue eyes twinkling. It was almost impossible for me to reconcile this vision of manly health and vigor with the fallen hero whose helpless head had rested on my breast. . . . And at that thought I began to blush so furiously that Andrea burst out laughing.

"Ah, I have offended her modesty. Forgive me, Cousin. But you are famous; the report of your adventures has gone even to Florence."

"Then you were in Florence?" Stefano asked dryly.

Andrea's eyes shifted.

"And other places. . . . I have been very dull, I promise you. Tell me what you have all been doing."

"Andrea, I must talk to you," Grandfather said.

"I am listening, your Excellency."

"Come to the library. You too, Stefano. For once," Grandfather said irritably, "I would like to have a serious discussion without a pack of women interfering."

He stalked from the room. Andrea smiled and followed. Stefano pushed himself up out of his chair and limped after them.

"Well!" said Miss Rhoda indignantly.

V

I was unable to speak to Andrea alone next day, he was rushing around so, and in fact I felt flustered and embarrassed at the very idea. How could I speak freely when there was so much we had to conceal, even from each other? He had come to mean

so much to me, yet I did not know whether he shared my
feelings. He did not even owe me gratitude. After what he had
done for me, the least I could do was protect his identity. I
longed to be with him, and at the same time I was shy with him.

There was no need for me to warn him. Grandfather had told
him of De Merode's hints. According to Miss Perkins, who
knew everything that went on—perhaps because she unabashed-
ly gossiped with the servants—according to her, Andrea had
responded to this news with a shout of laughter and a statement
to the effect that De Merode did him too much honor. He only
wished he could claim the credit of being the Falcon. Unfortunately he could not.

So matters went for the next few days. I began to understand
the feelings of the peasants who live on the slopes of Vesuvius
and watch the ominous smoke plume rise into the sky. I felt as if
an explosion were imminent, but did not know how and when it
would occur. I had expected that De Merode would call on us
now that Andrea was back from . . . wherever he had been. But
the Captain was fully occupied elsewhere. The entire province
was seething like a volcano. Garibaldi had entered Naples in
triumph. King Francis had fled. Urbino had risen in rebellion,
the Piedmontese troops were massing on the frontier. The
Falcon had been seen in Parezzo. Andrea was home one
moment, gone the next. . . .

On the third evening after his return, we were again in the
Salone dei Tritone. The evening was cool; there was a fire in the
fireplace. I was at the piano. Grandfather was working in the
library, but the others were all there. Andrea and Galiana were
sitting together on a sofa in a shadowy corner. Painfully
conscious of them, I played even worse than usual. I was amazed
at how complaisant the Contessa had become over their spend-
ing so much time together. Surely it was from her mother that
Galiana had derived her ideas about marrying an elder son; yet
now the older woman smiled affectionately at the young pair as
Galiana flirted and Andrea gazed at her with the intent look of a
lover.

The Contessa's maid sat behind her, but by now I had
become as accustomed to Bianca as the others were. She was
almost part of the furnishings. Stefano was wandering aimlessly
around the room, something he seldom did. Finally he came to

me, where I sat idly fingering the keys, my short repertoire exhausted.

"Play something," I said. "Something loud. We are all too quiet."

"Francesca." Miss Perkins looked up from her embroidery. She did fancy work very badly, but in those days we all found it necessary to do something with our hands. "Francesca, don't bother the Count."

"It's all right, Miss Perkins." Stefano sat down as I vacated my seat. "Francesca is right, we are too quiet."

He played a Chopin ballade—the First. I have heard it many times since then, but never have I heard it played as Stefano played it that night. The poignant, passionate chords of the theme pulsed in the warm air. The music ended in a plunging arpeggio. For a moment Stefano sat still, his head bowed, breathing quickly. Then he rose.

"Andrea," he said, and made a beckoning gesture.

Andrea looked bewildered, but he obeyed the silent command, and the two brothers walked side by side across the room, toward the Contessa. They looked formidable as they came on, in silence, and the Contessa's eyes widened. Then Stefano stepped to one side.

"Hold her," he said, in Italian. "Quickly, Andrea, don't let her move."

His hand darted out and snatched something from the hands of Bianca—some small object she was holding under the folds of her skirt. The woman rose with one of her harsh, unearthly cries, and Andrea caught her arms as she snatched at the object Stefano had taken.

"Andrea, Stefano," the Contessa exclaimed. "What are you doing?"

After that first instinctive gesture, Bianca did not move. Andrea's eyes were wide as he contemplated the object Stefano was examining.

The rest of us converged on the group. At first I could not make out what Stefano had in his hand. His fingers were clasped tightly around the lower part of it. I saw only a rounded thing the size of a large marble, like a tiny doll's head. A lock of flaxen hair had been glued to it and it had painted features—crude and unrecognizable, but identifiable as eyes, nose and mouth. A sharp shining point protruded from its forehead.

Galiana was the first to speak.

"La strega," she gasped. *"Maladetta. . . ."*

"Good heavens," Miss Perkins exclaimed. "It is a moment! At least that is what they call it in my home in Lancastershire. Some of the foolish old grannies still believe they can harm an enemy that way, by abusing the doll. Stefano, what person is this image meant to represent? Let me see it."

"No." Deliberately Stefano squeezed the body of the doll until the waxen substance of which it was composed oozed out between his clenched fingers. There was something horrible about the gesture, as if he were mutilating living flesh. Bianca's eyes focused and she drew a long, quivering breath.

"You see," Stefano addressed her in Italian. "It does not work, Bianca. The one you meant to harm is still alive and well, although I have crushed the image." Turning, he flung the mangled thing straight into the heart of the fire. A white flame shot up and quickly died.

As it died, so did the life in Bianca's face. It went blank and flat, like the face of the crudely painted doll. A thin trickle of saliva came out of the corner of her slack mouth. Galiana shrieked. The Contessa put her hands up to hide her eyes.

"Take her away," she moaned. "I tried to teach her of Christ and the blessed Virgin; and behind my back she practices the arts of the Devil. Take her away, I beg."

Miss Rhoda rang the bell and one of the footmen came in. Bianca moved obediently as he put a gingerly hand on her arm and drew her away. Her chin was wet with the spittle from her mouth.

"Be gentle with her," the Contessa murmured. "She has sinned, but she did not know. . . ."

"I'll go with them," Andrea promised. "To be sure she is well treated. Contessa, don't be concerned, she will be cared for; a doctor, tomorrow. . . ."

Despite his reassurances, the Contessa began to weep piteously. Galiana and Miss Rhoda had to help her to her room. When they had gone Miss Perkins shook her head sadly.

"I fear a doctor cannot help her. The poor thing was always

weak-witted. This has destroyed her mind completely. Count Stefano, how did you know?''

''I thought there might be some basis for the servants' gossip,'' Stefano answered. ''You knew about it, Miss Perkins, but you are too rational to admit that such things exist. I know better. I couldn't believe the creature would actually carry her foul tricks into the drawing room, but when I saw her clutching something in her lap. . . .''

''Who was it?'' I asked. ''Why didn't you let us see it?''

''You are too inquisitive,'' Stefano snapped. ''What difference does it make? The image was too crude; I couldn't tell.''

''But I know.'' I began to twist my hands nervously together. ''Only three people have hair of that pale-blond shade. You and Andrea—and I. She has no reason to want to harm either of you—''

''She had no reason to want to harm anyone,'' Miss Perkins interrupted, in her most robust, common-sense tone. ''She is mad, Francesca; madness does not know reason.''

''There, I fear, you are mistaken,'' Stefano said. *''Sempre una ragione.* There is always a reason. The behavior of a madman is not irrational, it only seems so to us because it is governed by reasons we do not accept. Always there is an underlying motive, the *idée fixe.* Find that and you have the clue to the conduct of the insane. But in this case I have no idea what Bianca's motive was, or who her intended victim may have been. And we will probably never know, since she cannot speak or write.''

The incident cast a pall over the household. As if in keeping with our mood, the weather next day continued to be cool and windy. Rain threatened all forenoon. Andrea had left early in the morning to seek medical advice in Parezzo. At least that was his excuse.

''Was it wise for him to go?'' I asked Miss Perkins. ''If he encounters De Merode. . . .''

''He can't hide in the castle all his life,'' said Miss Perkins. ''Goodness, I wish it would rain. I am as nervous as a cat. Although I don't know why people say that; cats are usually very placid creatures.''

''You are right,'' I said, smiling. ''I think I'll go to the stable and visit my feline family. Perhaps it will give me something pleasant to think about. Will you join me?''

''No, this is the sort of day for a book in the library. I shall read Ovid. He is not calm, but he does distract one.''

So we separated—little dreaming under what circumstances we would meet again.

The mother cat still resisted my blandishments, but the kittens had become quite tame, thanks to the scraps of food I brought them. I played with my favorite—a bushy-tailed little tabby with ears so big he might have had rabbit ancestry—until he tired of chasing string and fell into the easy sleep of infancy. Then I went back to my rooms.

The note was waiting for me on the marble-topped table beside the chaise longue.

''Come to the tomb at once,'' it read. ''There is desperate danger. Tell no one. Burn this.'' It was signed, ''Il Falcone.''

Instinctively my fingers closed over the note, crumpling it. My heart was beating fast and hard. Something had happened. Had Andrea met the soldiers—had he been wounded again? I did not stop to think twice. I paused only long enough to burn the note and to snatch up a hat and shawl.

I could not ride. The grooms would have wanted to know where I was going, would probably have insisted on accompanying me. I had to go on foot, and fear made the path seem twice as long as it really was. I was panting and disheveled when I scrambled down the last slope and ran toward the tomb of the princess. Imagine my consternation when I saw that the door was open. I was sure he had fallen unconscious within, unable to close the stone. Gathering my skirts closely around me I descended the steps, calling his name. I had just reached the bottom when the door closed.

By some strange alchemy of thought the whole truth struck me in a single instant, and I believe my first emotion was not fear, but anger at my stupidity. Slowly I went back up the stairs and pushed at the door as hard as I could, but I was not surprised to discover that it did not yield a fraction of an inch. Once again I had been deliberately imprisoned.

My next move was to reach for the ledge on which Grandfather kept the candles. It was bare.

I sat down on the top step with my back against the stone slab that would be my tombstone. Oh, there was a faint chance that someone might look for me here, when my absence was noted; but the chance was not great. Stefano had come for me the first time because Miss Perkins had been suspicious of Grandfather. This time Grandfather was above suspicion. He was not the one who had sent that note. How could I have been so gullible? I had received a message from the Falcon once before. He had not signed his name then, he had used a little hieroglyphic as a signature. Miss Perkins had seen that message; therefore the writer of this note was not Miss Perkins. . . .

I would not have suspected her in any case. But I could no more suspect any of the others. Who could hate me so much? There was no doubt in my mind that I had been the victim of a series of attempts; the falling rock in this very valley, the bullet in the garden—perhaps even the rabid bat. But last night, when Bianca had been caught with her evil little doll, I had assumed it was she who was responsible for the other attempts. Why she hated me I did not know, unless in some twisted way she considered me a rival to Galiana's happiness. That made as much sense as any other theory I could think of.

I wanted to cling to the idea of Bianca as the culprit, but I realized that even if she had escaped from her prison room in the castle, she could not be responsible for this. She could neither read nor write. She could not have manufactured the false note.

The identity of the villain, the motive for wanting me out of the way . . . I had a feeling that if I knew one of the answers, I could probably deduce the other. But both were beyond me. I formed and discarded theory after theory, for none made any sense.

I daresay this description sounds as if I behaved in a cool, sensible manner. I was not sensible, I was simply paralyzed with the hopelessness of it all. There was no way I could get out by myself. All I could do was wait and pray that someone would think to look for me before I perished of exposure or lack of air. To sit quietly and use no more oxygen than necessary was the sensible procedure, but as the cold began to seep into my bones, I thought it would kill me before the air was exhausted. Thankful for my shawl, I huddled into it and tried to remain calm. Eventually I fell into a sort of stupor; it certainly was not sleep, and I do not like to think it was unconsciousness, but it had the same result. I was in danger of toppling down the stairs. So I crawled to the bottom and settled myself on the floor. My shawl was not much help. I was chilled to the bone.

I had to believe that rescue would arrive eventually. Without that hope, I could not have kept my sanity. I recited all the poems I had been forced to learn by my dear old teachers. Little did I think that the lines of Cowper and Pope would come back to me in such a setting. I did mathematical problems in my head, but that did not last long, for I had never been very good at mathematics. I repeated the capitals of the countries of Europe and the list of the kings of England from Alfred the Great to Queen Victoria. In a humiliatingly short time I had exhausted my entire stock of knowledge.

And I had solved the puzzle.

It was so simple, really. De Merode had told the household he suspected the Falcon had been hiding in the tomb, but only two people knew that I had been there with him, and that any mention of the place would fetch me as neatly as a tantalizing bait catches a fish. Miss Perkins I scorned to suspect. The other person was Galiana.

Once I thought of her and half accepted her guilt, other facts fit only too well. Bianca might have carried out the other acts of violence, but the poor simple-witted creature could not have planned them. She was only the hands; someone else was the brain. And how had she learned to hate me so? From Galiana, of course; Galiana, who loved Andrea and feared my influence with him. I knew her callousness, her indifference to suffering; I knew her ancestry. Was not Italy the home of the feud? Perhaps the girl hated me for her father's sake. And I had thought she was fond of me, in her shallow fashion.

Purgatory will be no novelty to me, if I ever arrive there. The timelessness must be the worst of it; time without measure, no way of reckoning its passage, no knowledge of when it will end. When a slit of light appeared at the head of the stairs I could only stare, thinking that my mind had given way altogether. Then I staggered to my feet with a cry. They had found me after all.

Incredulously I realized that it was still daylight—a blustery gray light, but daylight all the same. I had thought I had been in the tomb for hours. The sharp wind felt like heaven after those

airless depths. It fluttered the long veil of the woman who stood
on the stairs.

Yes, she wore a veil, a black veil. She also carried a dagger in
her right hand. It glittered faintly in the dusky light.

Not rescue, then, but another threat. Why had she come
back, hiding her face with one of her mother's veils? Perversely
that circumstance gave me a moment of hope. If she troubled to
conceal her identity, perhaps she did not mean to murder me
after all.

· The veiled figure leaned forward and gave its head an
impatient shake. It could not see into the darkness of the tomb
with the muffling folds dimming its vision. With a sudden
movement it flung the veil back.

A coronet of silvery hair gleamed dully like a tarnished
nimbus. Slowly but nimbly, her slim figure undistorted by the
hoops which would have impeded her movements, the woman
descended the stairs. I retreated. My mind, fixed in its
preconceptions, still refused to accept reality. The Contessa
must have learned of her daughter's crime, and had rushed to
release me.

I was not allowed to cherish the illusion for long. With a
sudden lunge she came at me. Backed against the wall, I threw
out my hands against the threat of the dagger, and felt a rope
drop over my wrists. The Contessa jumped back; the noose
tightened. I tugged at it, not believing what was happening.

"Stand still," she said sharply. "Don't try to escape. I need
you alive. I was in error. I acted too soon. But I thought he
would take my word—the word of a Fosilini, and that arrogant
young fool dares to doubt! He wants evidence. So you must tell
me how you knew. You didn't tell Galiana the truth. You are the
only one who knows—the only one who can identify the
Falcon."

CHAPTER 11

She had been speaking Italian, of course. I ought to have answered her in the same language, but I was scarcely capable of speech of any kind, I could only stutter, in English.

"What? What are you saying?"

She shook her head in a very natural little movement of mild exasperation.

"Stupid girl," she said gently. "How stupid they are, these English. She can't even speak a civilized tongue."

As some philosopher has said, there is nothing that concentrates a man's mind so much as knowing he is to be hanged. At that moment I knew, as clearly as if a celestial voice had announced it from heaven, that I must be cleverer, quicker, stronger than I had ever been in my life, or I would die.

The Contessa tugged impatiently at the rope. I pulled back. The noose around my wrists tightened. A slip knot—of course that was what it was. I could free myself of the rope easily enough. But she was between me and the stairs.

Then I seemed to hear, silently repeated, words I had heard before:

"Madness has its own kind of reason . . . Always there is an underlying motive, an *idée fixe*. Find that and you have the key to the conduct of the insane."

"Come," she insisted. "*Avanti*. The Captain is waiting."

"No, wait," I said. "I will tell you. But first you must tell me why you are doing this. *Sempre una ragione*. . . ."

A blast of air, funneled down the stairwell, lifted her veil around her like great black wings. She made no attempt to straighten it, but stared at me thoughtfully. I could see her features clearly now, and what I saw made me grow cold with terror. But the fear was not only for myself.

"*Una ragione,*" she repeated softly. "Yes, yes, there is a reason. But you are so dull! You should have seen it long ago. He must die, you understand. The other times he escaped somehow. It was the protection of Satan, whom he serves, perhaps. But this time—"

"The other times? They were not accidents, then. But I thought I was the one they were aimed at."

Her exquisite old face was distorted, not by anger, but by a furious contempt.

"You? I would not soil my hands on you. In a sense you are to blame for his death; if he had not come to love you, I would not have to destroy him. But he will not marry my darling girl now. So he must die. He deserves death. He is a traitor to God and his own class, but I would have spared him if Galiana. . . . It is better this way, she will be the Principessa Tarconti; too low a rank for her beauty, but the best I can do. My darling little girl. . . ."

Her voice trailed off in a crooning travesty of maternal love, all the more horrible because of the beauty of the emotion that prompted it. Her speech was confused; even at her best she did not make much sense, but I had heard enough to confirm my worst fears—and they were not for myself. She knew about Andrea and she meant to betray him. The knowledge that I must overcome her for his sake as well as for my own gave me additional strength and cunning. I spoke sharply, hoping to capture her wandering wits for a few more minutes.

"If you don't care about me, why did you trap me here to die?"

"Well, but why not?" She spoke with a chilling indifference. "The opportunity arose. It was too good to miss. There was no danger to me, the old man will be blamed. He is mad, you know. Quite mad. Oh, yes, it was safe, and I will shut you in again when you have told me. My darling will marry Andrea, he loves her, he always has."

And her voice trailed off into soft murmurs, in which the name of her daughter was blasphemously mingled with fragments of prayer.

There was no point in talking to her any longer. I understood the obsession, underlying her madness, but she was wandering farther and farther from sense every moment. She couldn't even remember the name of the man she wanted for her daughter.

I caught the rope and pulled sharply. She had not been expecting that move. Off balance, she stumbled toward me. One hard jerk freed my hands, and I struck at her arm with my clenched fist. The knife fell clattering to the floor.

I thought I had won then, but I had not reckoned with the horrible strength of the insane. In an instant the frail old woman was transformed into a raging beast who used teeth and claws as an animal might. I turned my head just in time to protect my eyes from her gouging nails; they raked my cheek instead, and the pain made me cry out.

I had planned to render her helpless, then bind her with the rope she had used on me. I knew I could never do it. My only hope was to run.

I reached the stairs before her, but only because she stopped to pick up the knife. I heard her grunting and scraping along the floor as I scrambled on hands and knees up the steep slippery steps. When I reached the top, the full force of the wind hit me. It was blowing hard; leaves and twigs struck my face and the gusts blew my skirts about. Immediately I threw myself against the door. But she was mad on only one subject; she had had sense enough to prop the door with a stone. My frantic push jammed it. I was tugging ineffectually at its weight when I heard her on the stairs.

I ran, stumbling over rocks and thorny bushes, holding my flying skirts out of the way of my feet. The worst thing about that crazy flight was not the brambles that raked my face and clothing nor the agonized speed that soon made every breath a piercing stab in my breast. It was the fact that I did not dare look back. I had to watch each step for fear of falling, so uneven was the terrain; and at each instant I expected to feel her hot breath on my neck, or experience the stab of a knife in my back. The darkening sky, boiling with rain clouds, was a fitting backdrop for that nightmarish flight.

Yet I reached the gardens of the castle without being caught, and there, in the shadow of the pines that fringed the lily pond, I dared to pause for an instant, my hands clasped over my aching ribs. No time, no time! She was there, some distance behind me but coming on—a lean, dark figure against the gray landscape. It had been clever of her to remove her hoops and veil her face. If she was seen, she might not be recognized. Stefano was right, the mad were not without powers of reasoning.

His name reminded me that I was not far from his house. The castle was still some distance away, across the whole length of the gardens and up a steep slope, but the little house would be inhabited, by servants if not by Stefano himself. Stumbling, I circled the pool and ran along the wall of the enclosed garden till I reached the gate. My goal was the library, whose French doors opened onto the garden.

I burst through them and then my strength failed me. I clung to one of the bookcases, panting for breath. Stefano jumped up from behind his desk. He was in his shirt sleeves, his coat hung over the back of his chair. Then Miss Perkins, who had been pacing agitatedly around the room, turned and saw me. She let out a shriek. I realized that my appearance must be alarming— my face white and scratched, my skirt hanging in shreds. I put up my hand to smooth my tangled hair and tried to catch my breath.

"Francesca!" Miss Perkins exclaimed. "Good heavens, child, what has happened to you? The soldiers are here again; they are searching for the Falcon, and they seem to think—"

"I know," I interrupted. "And so does the Contessa. She knows that Andrea is the Falcon. She has gone mad, I think; she tried to kill me—"

My breath gave out, but there was no need for me to continue. Through the open window burst the stark black figure of the madwoman.

She had eyes for no one but me. Without pausing, she rushed forward, knife held high.

My strength had deserted me. I couldn't move. Miss Perkins ran toward us, but it was Stefano who came between.

The confrontation seemed ludicrous—a frail old woman against a man who was, despite his infirmity, tall and broad-shouldered and half her age. But Stefano was handicapped by his inability to comprehend that he was not facing the gentle lady he had learned to respect, but a creature without remorse or fear. She struck him with the full weight of her body, and he went staggering back, trying only to hold her off; whereas she

was intent on murder. Their bodies hit the wall with such
violence that a picture fell with a crash of glass. Then Miss
Perkins picked up a bookend from the desk and hit the Contessa
on the back of the head. No sooner had she fallen than Miss
Perkins pounced on her.

"Your belt, Francesca," she exclaimed, tugging at her own.
"Seconds count now; she must not be found by the soldiers.
Hurry, hurry, we must render her helpless and hide her before
they take it into their heads to search this place."

While she bound the Contessa's hands, I fastened her ankles
together with my belt, and then Miss Perkins gagged her with a
strip of petticoat. I felt contemptible as I held the fragile limbs
in my hand; unconscious, the Contessa looked as gentle as she
was before madness had twisted her mind. But Miss Perkins'
hands were steady and her face was hard. When we had finished
she lifted the Contessa in her arms, quite easily, and carried her
into another room. Where she meant to hide her I didn't know,
but she seemed to have some place in mind.

It struck me then that Stefano had given us no help in this
unpleasant business. I turned. He was still standing against the
wall, where the Contessa's rush had driven him, and I thought at
first that the knife must have struck him after all. His face was as
white as his shirt, his eyes were closed; his hands, pressing hard
against the gilded panels, were all that kept him on his feet. As I
stared, thunderstruck, his bright head fell forward and he slid to
the floor. I reached him and was kneeling at his side before I
realized that he could not have been wounded in the brief
struggle. I had watched the dagger with the intense concentra-
tion of fear. Never once had it come near his body.

I knew then, even before I saw the first crimson drops stain
his white shirt. It was the first time I had seen him without a
mask—the muffling folds of a disguise or the equally concealing mask of conscious playacting. Without its mocking smile,
his face was dignified and gentle. I opened his shirt and saw
what I expected to see—folds of bandaging, reddened by the
reopened wound, and the birthmark—the sign of his race he
and his brother shared.

I was still staring, frozen with shock, when Miss Perkins
returned. She dropped heavily to her knees.

"Stefano," I said numbly. "It was not Andrea. It was—"

"Of course it was Stefano," Miss Perkins snapped. "How could you have thought Andrea was the Falcon? He is a charming, handsome, quick-tempered fool. It is this boy who has risked his life and fortune for his dream of freedom, and if we don't act quickly, he will be made to pay the full price. There is brandy in that cabinet. Fetch it—run!"

As she spoke, her stubby, efficient fingers were working at the bandages.

When I returned with the brandy, Stefano's eyes were open and he was trying to sit up.

"Not yet," Miss Perkins said. "Brandy is a poor substitute for blood, but it will help. Francesca, support his head while I—"

"Francesca will do nothing of the kind," Stefano said. "Get her away, Miss P. Hide her—you know the secret room—"

"The Contessa is already occupying that hiding place," Miss Perkins said calmly. "Francesca, do as you are told."

So I sat down on the floor and lifted Stefano's head onto my lap. I got no thanks from him, only a wicked glance from his blue eyes. As my hands touched his disheveled fair curls I wondered how I could have been so deceived, even with an actor of Stefano's skill deliberately misleading me. I had never been able to reconcile Andrea with the man I had held in my arms. If I had ever touched Stefano, even his hand. . . . There was no mistaking that sort of recognition, the instinctive knowledge of the flesh. He had been careful to avoid physical contact in recent days, but heaven knows he had good reason to shrink from even the gentlest touch. That morning in the library it must have cost him dearly to sit upright, much less converse so coolly.

Stefano started to speak again. Miss Perkins cut him short by pushing the glass of spirits against his mouth. He had to drink it or choke.

"Don't waste your strength arguing," she said. "If De Merode comes here, you must be on your feet and seemingly uninjured. He already suspects you. The slightest sign of weakness—"

"Nonsense," Stefano interrupted. "He suspects Andrea."

"He is not such a fool. We haven't fathomed his real intentions yet, I feel sure. The time is critical. You know that better than I do."

"The crisis is closer than you think. I have had to move the time forward; I got word from Turin this morning. Parezzo must rise tomorrow at dawn, and I must be there."

"You aren't fit to go," Miss Perkins said.

"I am perfectly fit. That damned woman only jarred me." Stefano rolled his eyes up so that he was glaring straight into my face. "I forget myself. Forgive my language, ladies—and leave me! Francesca, if you aren't out of this room in thirty seconds. . . ."

"Where is she supposed to go?" Miss Perkins demanded. "You are most unfair to her, Count. If she hasn't earned your trust by now. . . . You aren't deceiving me, you know," she added cryptically.

A wave of color flooded into Stefano's pale cheeks. I did not understand its meaning, but I was fascinated by this new display of emotion from a man I had considered without feelings.

"You are the most frightful busybody," Stefano said with a resigned air. "Help me up, Francesca, if you please. I assure you, I am not as weak as you think. That infernal woman pushed me into the wall, and the frame of the picture struck the wound. It hurt abominably, but no real damage was done."

As he spoke he was struggling to his feet. He leaned without reserve on my shoulder, and this demonstration of confidence pleased me more than I can say. I helped him to his chair, and noticed that he walked without any trace of a limp.

"So that was pretense too," I said. "Was it after your accident that you got the idea of using a counterfeit infirmity to conceal the identity of the Falcon?"

"I will tell you my life history another time," Stefano said. "At the present moment we have a more immediate problem. Can't you do something about her appearance, Miss P.? If De Merode sees her so bedraggled, he will assume she has had another tête-à-tête with the Falcon, and he may drag her off to prison."

So I made use of the basin and ewer in the adjoining bedchamber and straightened my hair, while I listened to the conversation going on in the next room. Though the situation was fraught with peril, I was filled with an emotion that was close to happiness. This new discovery was so right; it was like finding the proper fit for a dress that has pinched in an uncomfortable place. I returned to the next room in time to hear Miss Perkins say, "What are we to do with the Contessa?"

"There is no need to do anything with her," Stefano replied. "Don't you understand? In the next twenty-four hours the issue will be resolved. The uprising in Parezzo has been planned to coincide with risings in other cities—Urbino, Perugia, others. The papal mercenaries will fight, naturally; but there are not enough troops to handle a dozen different rebellions at once. That is why it is imperative that all the uprisings take place on schedule. Cavour will demand that the Pope dismiss his hired mercenaries. Pio Nono will refuse, and the Piedmontese will have the excuse they need to invade. Louis Napoleon has already agreed, secretly, not to interfere. Our people will be fighting on the side of Piedmont. At the very latest the Bersaglieri should be here within five days. But we need not wait so long to be safe. By tomorrow morning De Merode will be riding hell-for-leather toward Parezzo, and thereafter he won't have the time or energy to worry about you here."

Miss Perkins nodded. Her eyes were bright with excitement and admiration. Indeed, the daring, the skillful preparation of the plan was the cleverest thing I had ever heard.

"Wonderful," I said. "But, Stefano, there is still tonight. I share Miss Perkins' worries about the Captain. I have felt for a long time that we are underestimating him somehow. Can't you get your men in Parezzo to strike at once?"

"Impossible. The plot depends on a dozen different people. I couldn't reach them in time. In fact, I myself must start before midnight if I am to be there in time to lead the fighting."

"You can't go! You aren't fit to ride, much less fight."

"I must be there." His lips set in a stubborn line.

"He is right," Miss Perkins said reluctantly. "They rely on him and on his reputation. His presence will rally the peasants. And they need all the help they can get; De Merode's men are the best trained, the best led in the province. Only Schmidt, in Perugia, has a greater reputation for ferocity."

"Stefano!" A sudden thought struck me and turned me cold. "Are you sure De Merode does not know about the uprising in Parezzo?"

"I have arranged for him to receive a message from an

'informer' early in the morning,'' Stefano replied. ''I want him away from the castle as soon as possible. I share your distrust of him. But if he reaches Parezzo before the barricades are in place and the fortress is taken, our people will be in trouble.''

''What if a real informer has already told him?'' I leaned across the desk and looked straight into his eyes. ''What would happen to the rebellion if word got out that the Falcon had been arrested and shot?''

Miss Perkins struck the desk with her big fist.

''She is right! That is why De Merode is here today. He knows, I tell you; at least he has a strong suspicion. He means to trap you. But how did he find out?''

''The Contessa,'' I said. ''Oh, heavens, and it is all my fault! I told Galiana that Andrea was the Falcon. I had to tell her to keep her quiet; she knew where I had been that night. She swore she wouldn't tell, but I suppose she would not think that oath included her mother. . . . But the Contessa was not deceived. I don't know how she learned the truth. . . .''

''I think I do,'' Miss Perkins broke in. ''But there isn't time to explain now. You think the Contessa has been in touch with De Merode? Quite possible. But then he can't act without her testimony. Perhaps we are safe after all.''

Just as she arrived at this comforting conclusion, there were sounds of a disturbance outside. Stefano snatched up his coat and struggled into it as the door of the library burst open. One of the footmen came stumbling in; he tried to speak, but was stopped by a savage blow from the soldier who had followed him. Other soldiers crowded through the doorway. Their leader—the red-haired Irishman I had seen before—saluted.

''The Captain requires your presence, Count,'' he said. ''And that of the ladies.''

''Was it necessary to enforce your request so violently?'' Stefano inquired. It cost him an effort to speak coolly; his eyes flashed as he gazed at his servant, who was leaning against the door with his hands pressed to his face and blood trickling between his fingers.

''The man attempted to keep us out,'' said the Irishman insolently. ''He'll be none the worse for a lesson in manners.''

''From you?'' Stefano's tone and his raised eyebrows turned

the question into a subtle insult. He rose, leaning heavily on his cane. "Yes, I think I had better have a word with the Captain. But the ladies—"

"The Captain said everyone."

The soldiers escorted us to the library, where two men stood guard with naked bayonets. The castle had been taken, like an enemy fortress. De Merode must be desperate, or very confident, to have given up all pretense at courtesy. That this was indeed the case I realized as soon as I saw Grandfather. His face was grayish white, with a strained, pinched look about the nostrils. He did not so much as glance at us when we entered. His eyes were fixed on his younger grandson.

Andrea stood between two soldiers who held him by the arms. His hands were bound behind his back, but he was the coolest person in the room; his head was high, his lips were curved in a smile. Never had he so closely resembled his brother.

Galiana ran to me. The tears were streaming down her cheeks.

"He knows," she cried. "Francesca, he knows; but I did not speak, I swear—"

I put my arms around her. "Hush," I murmured, hardly knowing what I said. "Hush, Galiana."

De Merode turned to face us. His burning eyes passed over me and Miss Perkins as if we had been invisible. He looked directly at Stefano.

"This is a most distressing situation, Count," he said. "I assumed you would wish to bid your brother farewell before we take him away."

"Where are you taking him?" Stefano asked.

"To Parezzo."

"I thought that was where he was," Stefano said mildly. "You confuse me, Captain. My brother started out this morning in search of a doctor—"

"That is what you were told," De Merode said. "I fear he deceived you, Count, as he deceived his honored grandfather and a good many other people. The city of Parezzo is supposed to rise in rebellion tonight, and Count Andrea is the leader of the revolt. How it grieves me to be the one to inform you of this blot on an otherwise stainless family name! Count Andrea—"

"He thinks I am the Falcon," Andrea interrupted.

"How very naïve of him," Stefano said.

"I don't mind." Andrea's voice was quite calm. "Let the Captain concentrate his attentions on me; it will give the Falcon his chance to act. I am honored to serve, even in so small a role as this."

"Andrea, you must learn not to be so theatrical," Stefano said. "You are giving Captain De Merode the wrong impression. Captain, you are making a mistake."

"Am I?"

For a moment no one spoke. Then Stefano shrugged.

"Very well, Captain. Take my brother to prison—"

"He is not going to prison," De Merode interrupted. "I have changed my mind. The Falcon deserves death. O'Shaughnessy, take the Count into the courtyard and select a firing squad."

The guards led Andrea out. It was a strangely quiet moment. Galiana's tears had stopped. She and Andrea exchanged a long look as he passed us. Then Grandfather rose to his feet.

"I wish to be with my grandson when he dies."

De Merode nodded. "Escort the Prince," he said to the soldier who stood by Grandfather's chair.

Miss Rhoda, who had been crumpled in her seat, sat up. "I, too."

Grandfather stopped. His elbow bent, he offered his old enemy his arm. She took it. The two walked slowly toward the door, allies at last, and very touching in their grief and dignity. As they were about to pass out of the room, De Merode said, "The firing squad will await my orders, your Excellency."

Grandfather glanced at him. "You know, of course, Captain, that I will spend my last *soldi* and my last ounce of strength to make sure you pay for this."

De Merode bowed. Grandfather went on. The door closed. Then De Merode turned to Stefano. The moment had come, the moment for which all the rest had only been preliminary maneuvering.

"Well, Count? The choice is yours. Your life or that of your brother. Will you let the innocent suffer for you?"

Galiana lifted her tear-stained face from my shoulder.

"What does he mean? Stefano, can you save him?"

"Oh, yes," De Merode said. "If Count Stefano chooses, his

brother can be freed at once—to return to your arms, mademoiselle. Ask him now what he has done with your mother.''

''My mother?'' Galiana repeated.

''She is nowhere in the castle. I have searched. Ask him, mademoiselle; ask him if he will sacrifice your mother and your lover—his own brother—to his insane ambition. You can help me, if you will.''

Then I saw what the ancient noble house of Fosilini was made of. Poor Galiana, driven almost mad by suspense and fear, drew herself up to her full height.

''I don't understand,'' she said simply. ''But I trust Stefano and Francesca, and I do not trust you, Captain. You are a cruel man. I know nothing, but if I did, I would not tell you.''

De Merode shrugged. He had not expected anything from this quarter; he was merely testing all the possibilities and, in the process, giving another twist to the knife. This interview, the threat to Andrea and the anguish of his family, was part of De Merode's revenge for the humiliation he had endured at the hands of his foe. The choice he was giving Stefano was no choice. The Falcon would die in any case. If Stefano remained silent and let the execution proceed, De Merode would kill him too. But he wanted a confession, not only to justify his acts to the board of inquiry which Grandfather's influence would certainly demand, but to publish in Parezzo. The rebels must know that their leader was unable to lead them.

''Well, Count?'' he repeated.

Stefano had been leaning on his cane. Now he straightened up.

''You leave me no choice,'' he said, and began to remove his coat.

''Stefano,'' I cried, trying to free myself of Galiana's clinging arms.

''Stand back,'' De Merode exclaimed, pulling his sword from the scabbard.

Stefano laughed. ''What, are you afraid of an unarmed man and a pack of women?''

''Of these women, yes,'' De Merode said grimly. He pointed his sword at Miss Perkins. ''Did you think I would not investigate your Englishwomen? The old one is a member of an *emigré* secret society in London. The young one has been a thorn in my side ever since she came. Spies——''

He broke off with a hiss of satisfaction, his eyes riveted on the breast of Stefano's shirt, as Stefano tossed his coat onto a chair. The wound had stopped bleeding, but the bloodstains were damningly conspicuous against the white linen.

"So I was right," he breathed. "That bullet wound will be all the evidence I need when I take your body to Rome—after I have displayed it in Parezzo and crushed the revolt."

"Aren't you afraid your firing squad will obliterate the evidence?" Stefano asked mildly. Passing his cane from hand to hand, he seemed to be concerned with straightening his cuffs and smoothing his shirt sleeves.

"Do you think I am such a fool as to let you leave this room? You have too many tricks, Count."

Without warning he lunged forward, the point of his sword directed at Stefano's breast.

Stefano had been expecting the move, if the rest of us had not. He took one great leap backwards, landing on his toes with his knees bent, as the Captain's blade ripped harmlessly through his shirt front. He tugged at his cane. It came apart, displaying a length of shining steel.

De Merode swore aloud. "A sword-stick! I should have known. It won't save you, though."

I let go of Galiana, who dropped to the floor. Miss Perkins caught my arm as I moved forward.

"Stay out of the way, Francesca. You can only distract him. Lock the door."

I did so, just in time. Shouts from the men outside were soon followed by blows against the door. The heavy panels would hold . . . long enough. My back against the door, as if to brace it, I turned to watch the life-and-death struggle.

If Stefano had been in good physical condition, I would not have feared for him. But wounded as he was, with a weapon that was surely inferior to the Captain's heavy sword. . . . I felt suffocated as I watched Stefano slowly retreat, his fragile blade bending under the violent strokes of his adversary. Her advice forgotten, Miss Perkins circled the fighters like an old mastiff, watching for an opportunity to rush in.

In actual time the duel lasted only a few minutes. De Merode defeated himself. His rage was so extreme he forgot caution and, as Stefano said later, this was no time for chivalry. When the Captain stumbled over one of Grandfather's prized Persian rugs, Stefano ran him through.

The struggle had been short but violent. Stefano was gasping for breath when he turned toward the French windows and flung them open. "This way," he panted, as the library doors shuddered under the blows of the soldiers. "Quickly!"

Supporting Galiana, Miss Perkins and I obeyed. As I passed the fallen body I had a last glimpse of De Merode's face—the dark eyes glazed, and the white lips still set in a snarl of rage.

II

When we returned to the library an hour later, De Merode's body had been removed. The castle was in our hands. Stefano had signaled his supporters, who included most of the able-bodied servants in the castle, led by Piero. Demoralized by the death of their leader, the soldiers were easily disarmed.

I will never forget the moment when Andrea, freed of his bonds, came striding into the library where Stefano was giving orders to Piero. He went straight to his brother and flung his arms around him.

"Why did you not tell me?" he demanded, his eyes dimmed by tears. "Couldn't you trust me, Stefano?"

"You know it was not lack of trust," Stefano replied, trying to free himself of his brother's impetuous embrace. "Andrea, I am touched by your emotion, but if you aren't careful, you will finish the job De Merode began. My ribs. . . ."

Then silence fell, as Grandfather came into the room.

Italians are considered by the English to be overemotional. All I can say is that I have become quite accustomed to their outbursts of sentiment, and for my part I find them quite beautiful. There are times, though, when the emotional climate becomes almost unendurable; and this was one such moment, when the stately old man tried to kneel to ask the forgiveness of the man he had misjudged. As Stefano bent to prevent this, I realized how hard it had been for him to appear as a weakling in the eyes of the old man he loved.

There was little time for prolonged emotion, or for explanations. Time was passing, and Stefano was not the man to be distracted from what he considered his duty. A few hours later we stood on the terrace and watched the little band ride away to Parezzo and battle. We were all very brave. Grandfather stood straight as a soldier, his eyes shining with pride, and we women smiled till our jaws ached. Andrea, riding beside his brother, turned and waved the torch he was carrying in a flamboyant gesture of farewell. But Stefano did not turn, and as his tall, erect figure melted in the darkness of the long avenue, I knew I might have seen him for the last time.

Everyone knows what happened after that. On September 11 the Bersaglieri of Piedmont crossed the frontier, and within a month Umbria and the Marches were part of the new kingdom of Italy. Only a small strip of territory around Rome itself was left to the rule of Pius the Ninth. It was ten years later before Rome succumbed, and the ancient capital became the capital of the new Italy, ending a struggle for freedom that had taken almost half a century and cost the lives of many gallant men.

I fear we were less concerned, in the next weeks, with the epic struggle taking place elsewhere than we were with our own selfish concerns. Galiana was lucky; Andrea was slightly wounded in the fighting at Parezzo and was forced to stay at home after that, alternately cursing his bad fortune and basking in Galiana's adoring care. I was not so fortunate. After the papal garrison at Parezzo surrendered, Stefano joined one of the Piedmontese regiments as a liaison officer and followed the troops of Victor Emmanuel throughout the entire campaign. From time to time we would receive messages, or word of him; he was fighting with the gallantry we expected, and surviving; that was all we knew for weeks. The suspense was well-nigh unendurable, particularly because I had no assurance that Stefano ever devoted a moment's thought to me, while I thought of nothing else. By the time a week had passed, I was convinced he cared nothing for me. He had never demonstrated any affection; quite the contrary; he had done nothing but sneer and joke at me since I came.

The only consolation I had during those weeks was the love of those around me. Galiana and Andrea, who were awaiting only the return of Stefano to make plans for their marriage, could not do enough for me. Andrea's love comforted Galiana during her mother's illness. The Contessa's mind had given way altogether. She recognized no one except her daughter, whom she persisted in addressing as the Princess Tarconti. The doctors said she would not live long, but while she lived she would have the constant care and supervision her state required. It was she who had corrupted the mind of poor Bianca; everything the woman had done had been at the orders of the Contessa. Bianca was not mad, she was only weakminded and susceptible.

The object of her attacks had always been Stefano. Miss Perkins explained this to me during the hours we spent together. We talked over the whole affair, and the first thing I did was take her to task for deceiving me.

"After all our talk of spies, you were an English spy," I said, half jokingly.

"I thought surely you would wonder how Count Andrea found me so easily," Miss Perkins said, not at all abashed. "He told you the truth when he said Count Stefano had planned the entire business. He sent Andrea to certain parties in London, sympathizers with the Italian cause, who recommended me. I fear I did lie to you when I told you the Count had hired me through an employment bureau. But I assure you, Francesca, that I was not in Count Stefano's confidence, not until the very end."

"But you suspected him, not Andrea. I can't see how."

"The Contessa did, too. We older women, unlike you young girls, were not misled by dashing adventures and brave speeches. When you told me—and the Contessa, through Galiana—that you had identified the Falcon as your cousin, it was obvious that you based this on some physical characteristic. But Stefano and Andrea are twins, though most of us tended to forget this. It was equally obvious that Andrea was too heedless to maintain a disguise so long and plan his campaign so carefully. Stefano, on the other hand, was a perfect candidate— his habit of seclusion, his cool intelligence, his general character. The only thing against it was his physical disability, and you had hints enough, my dear, that that was put on. When he rescued you from the tomb, for instance. He acted without thinking then, and had to do some fast talking to cover up. I began to suspect quite early on, but it was not until after you had helped him escape from the village that I was sure. I watched Stefano after that, and it was obvious to me that he was in considerable physical distress. I taxed him with it and demanded to be allowed to help.''

''But the Contessa attacked him long before that,'' I expostulated. ''I turn hot with embarrassment, Miss Perkins, when I remember that I believed myself to be the endangered heroine!''

''You read too many bad novels at that school of yours, I expect,'' Miss Perkins replied with a smile. ''You ought to have read Miss Austen's *Northanger Abbey*, in which she shows another young lady being led astray by sensational fiction.''

''I still don't understand why the Contessa wanted to kill Stefano,'' I said, blushing.

''It was logical, in a mad way,'' Miss Perkins said, shaking her head. ''The Contessa was determined to see her daughter Princess Tarconti. Until you came, she was in a fair way of bringing it off. She had the poor child under her influence; Galiana would have married Stefano if she could have. After a time the Contessa realized that Stefano would never marry her daughter. But if Stefano were dead. . . .''

''His brother would be Prince Tarconti in time,'' I said. ''Yes, I see. She told me that, in her ravings, but I thought her mind was confused.''

''It was confused,'' said Miss Perkins dryly. ''You must admit that her methods were somewhat unorthodox. Yet they probably would have succeeded. Andrea has always loved Galiana, he would have married her in a moment. The Contessa told Bianca what she wanted, and the unfortunate woman proceeded to act whenever the opportunity arose. It was Stefano at whom the rock fall and the bullet were aimed. You happened to be with him on both occasions, but that was because he was seldom out of his house, and vulnerable, unless he was in your company. When he was within his own walls, with his loyal servants around him, it was almost impossible for an assassin to get at him.''

''But the bat,'' I began.

''Pure accident. You didn't seriously think that anyone could capture and control a creature like that? If the incident of the bat had occurred alone, without the other cases, you would never have dreamed it was anything but bad luck."

"Is there ever any such thing as luck, I wonder," I said thoughtfully. "I begin to think that life is one great complex pattern of interwoven acts and counteracts."

"I am a believer in free will," said Miss Perkins firmly. "Yet you are right, in the sense that every act has unimaginable and far-reaching consequences. One of the most astounding results of De Merode's plotting is the conversion of his Excellency. I do believe he is a firmer supporter of the cause of liberation than either of his sons, and he was once its greatest enemy."

"That is because he found himself inconvenienced," I said. "People often take up a cause when it suits their selfish motives."

"I do not like to see a girl of your age so cynical," said Miss Perkins reproachfully.

Suddenly, to my shame, I felt my eyes flooding with tears.

"I'm sorry," I muttered, turning aside. "But it has been so long since he left, and he never said. . . ."

"Jumping to conclusions is another fault of yours," said Miss Perkins unsympathetically. "You have been wrong fairly consistently, Francesca; but if you still think that young man is cold and unemotional. . . ."

Well, I knew he was not unemotional. What I did not know was whether he had any emotional attachment to *me*.

The last of the papal fortresses, Ancona, fell on September 24, after a gallant defense. We received the good news a few days later; but it was not until the end of the month that Stefano came home.

I was in the rose garden, and I did not know of his arrival until I looked up from my book and saw him coming down the path. He wore the dark-blue uniform of a Piedmontese officer. He had lost weight. His sunbleached hair formed a striking contrast to his tanned face, which was burned as brown as that of any peasant. I wondered how I could ever have thought Andrea was handsomer than he, and how I could have taken another man for him, even for an instant.

His long free stride faltered when he saw me, and he came on more slowly.

Any woman will understand why I acted as I did. For weeks I had been in agony over him; since the hard fighting at Ancona I had been convinced that he must have been killed, since we had heard nothing from him. Now I saw him safe—and in the reaction of relief I was absolutely furious with him. So when he stood before me, hat in hand, I said casually, "How nice to see you, Stefano. I do hope you enjoyed yourself."

It was the first time I had ever seen him at a loss for words. The dark blood rushed into his cheeks. I found myself, perversely, enjoying the situation.

"Men do enjoy fighting," I went on. "Don't they? I suspect that is behind the heroism and the gallantry we poor women ignorantly applaud. You don't fight from a sense of duty; you love it! While we sit at home and worry ourselves—"

Stefano put an end to this tirade, which was developing rather nicely, I thought, by picking me up off the bench and lifting me till my eyes were on a level with his. My feet dangled helplessly, a good ten inches off the ground.

"Just like a man," I said, somewhat breathlessly, because his hands were squeezing my ribs. "When you are losing an argument, you resort to physical violence!"

"Oh, no," Stefano said. "The physical violence is only a preliminary. This is how I counter arguments such as yours."

He kissed me. I felt as if my bones were melting.

It took me some time to recover. We were sitting on the bench, with his arm around me and my head on his shoulder, before I could speak sensibly again.

"It was very presumptuous of you to do that," I murmured. "What made you suppose that I would tolerate it?"

"I wouldn't have dared if I hadn't happened to meet Miss Perkins in the hall," Stefano said frankly. "She told me to do it."

"Miss Perkins? Oh, come now!"

"Well, perhaps not in so many words. But she implied in her tactful fashion that you might not be violently opposed to the idea."

"She was kinder to you than to me," I said. "For days and days I have been trying to get her—or anyone—to reassure me as to how you felt about me."

"If you did not know, you were one of the few who didn't.

Andrea taxed me with it weeks ago. Miss Perkins read my thoughts as if my head were made of glass. Even the Contessa knew. Why do you suppose she abandoned her schemes for me to marry Galiana?"

"So that is what Miss Perkins meant," I exclaimed. "I didn't understand her then. But how could I have known? You were horrid to me."

"As you were to me."

"I have been in love with you for a long time. I can't imagine why you didn't notice."

"With me—or with that poor mountebank the Falcon?" Stefano turned me in the circle of his arm and looked straight into my eyes. "I hope you did not fall in love with a myth, Francesca, for that person never really existed. I cannot tell you how glad I am to be done with him at last."

"I don't believe you," I said, half in jest, half in earnest. "The role you played here was the hard one. You had a wonderful time being the Falcon; don't tell me you didn't. He is a part of you, just as the sober scholar is a part. Don't cast him off altogether."

Stefano's eyes took on a reminiscent sparkle as I spoke; but he shook his head.

"I am really a very dull fellow, my darling. And you are so young. God willing, you may have me on your hands for forty or fifty years. Do you think you can endure it?"

"I don't know how I can convince you," I said helplessly.

He put his arms around me and drew me close.

"Try," he said.

SEARCH THE SHADOWS

New From the Author of the *New York Times* Bestseller, *Shattered Silk*

BARBARA MICHAELS

"*Barbara Michaels at her best!*"
—Mary Higgins Clark

"*Penetrating...Eerie, haunting and unusual. I loved it!*"
—Phyllis A. Whitney, bestselling author of *Silver Sword*

"*Intriguing!...The suspense lingers until the final pages.*"
—*Booklist*